M000020176

TIMES LIKE THESE

A BLUE IS THE COLOR NOVEL

JULIA WOLF

Julia Wolf ♡

Copyright © 2019 by Julia Wolf

All rights reserved.

No part of this book may be reproduced in any form or by any electronic or mechanical means, including information storage and retrieval systems, without written permission from the author, except for the use of brief quotations in a book review.

Cover by: Amy Queau

Editing by: Monica Black

Formatting by: Cora Cade

To music, which inspires me endlessly.

ONE

NICK

TONIGHT WAS GOING to be a complete and total shit show. I felt it in my bones.

Walking down the black painted hallway to our dressing room, a cup of tea in my hand, a sense of dread nearly overwhelmed me. The same dread had been bubbling in my gut for a couple months, but tonight, it had gone into overdrive.

One of us was going to fuck up.

The boys were sprawled out on the faux leather couches, Ian tapping an endless beat on his thighs with his sticks, David holding his guitar on his belly, strumming it lazily, and Jasper—fucking Jasper—staring off into space.

David sat up when I came back into the room. "Got your tea, lass?"

I took a sip, making sure to hold my pinky up like the refined gentleman I wasn't. "I didn't get this gorgeous voice by drinking Jameson."

Ian paused his tapping. "I hear them out there. They're foaming for us."

This was our hometown crowd. We hadn't played Baltimore in a while. Maybe a year. We were on the road seventy-five percent of the time, hitting city after city, country after country, but this would never stop being my favorite place to play. The energy was more honest here. We had to work harder to impress them. We were all products of this city, just like most of the people out there waiting for us, and no matter how far we traveled or how high we climbed, for better or worse, we were theirs and they were ours.

"They're either going to be really easy on us because they're excited, or brutal because they're pissed we haven't come around lately," I said.

David grinned wickedly. "They fucking love us and you know it."

My stomach said it was going to be the latter, though. I'd played bad shows before, where the audience booed and threw things—and hell, I'd probably deserved it. You don't get on stage and forget the words to your music—music you wrote—and not expect there to be repercussions from the people who'd spent their entire paychecks to be there. It took a shoe to the head to knock some fucking sense into me.

So, now I drank tea—advice received from an old British vocal coach—before shows instead of my previous ministrations of whiskey and weed.

But we weren't going to play a bad show. No way. Our music was on point. We'd rehearsed until we bled. We'd spent the last month doing shows at intimate clubs, just like this one. We could play our music in our sleep—though, we wouldn't; we cared too much not to give it our all. (I wasn't the only one who'd gotten a shoe to the head a time or two.)

I wasn't worried about the music. That wasn't where the dread came from.

It was something else. My eyes drifted over to Jasper again. He'd looked like shit for months now—with good reason—but he looked a hell of a lot shittier than usual.

All of us did. They said when it rained, it poured, and we'd been stuck in a deluge of shitty, shitty days. *I can really use some fucking sunshine right about now.*

A roadie stuck his head in. "Five minutes!"

My stomach gurgled as I took another sip of tea—not what I wanted happening five minutes before I hit the stage to sing for an hour.

I picked up a random Us Weekly magazine to try to take my mind off fucking everything. Thumbing through the pages, the first picture I landed on was a pop star I'd taken to the Grammy's last year. Her people had wanted to edge her up, and apparently being seen with a rocker was their definition of "edgy." I agreed to it because she had nice tits and I thought it might ease some of the incessant boredom I couldn't seem to shake. Turned out, I should've just stared at a blank wall instead. She'd had as little interest in me as I had in her—and she wore a damn turtleneck to top it all off.

Tossing the magazine aside, I sat down next to Jas and waved a hand in front of his face. "What's the word?"

It took a second for the fog to clear, but when it did, Jasper smiled. "Fuck."

I clapped him on the shoulder. "Good word. One of my favorites." Lowering my voice, I asked, "You ready?"

"I'm good, Nicky. When the show's over, I'm going home to sleep in my own bed for the first time in six weeks. Not much is better than that. Think I might sleep the entire week we're off."

"Think I might do the same." I studied his face. His sweaty, ashen face. "You feel okay?"

He wiped his forehead with the back of his hand. "Yep. Tired, but who isn't?"

I was. But I'd been tired for so long, I barely noticed it. I wasn't exactly sleep deprived. It was more of a bone weariness creeping in. If I didn't keep moving, keep making music, keep performing, it just might take over.

The roadie came back, letting us know it was time to go on. There was a lot I should've been asking Jasper. A lot I should've said. More than just asking if he felt okay.

It was showtime, though.

Like we'd done hundreds, maybe even thousands of times before, the four of us took our places on the dark stage.

Dread was still coiled low in my stomach, but adrenaline was taking its place. I heard them out there. Our audience. Our fans. The people who'd been with us since we were young, idiot punks with more heart than sense.

And then the spotlight shined on me.

"Baltimore." I shook my head, like I couldn't believe the word. Like I couldn't believe where I was. And in some ways, I couldn't. "Your boys are back."

They ate it up, like they always did. The venue was intimate, around a thousand people. I could almost hear their individual voices.

I signaled for them to quiet down. "Now, now children. Don't get too excited. I'm gonna sing your favorite songs, but David had a stipulation put in his contract that he no longer has to play in the nude."

David flipped me off, then thrashed on his guitar for a few beats, sending out a clashing, dissonant sound. The crowd booed and cheered, exactly what they did in every city we played.

Cupping the mic in my hands, I looked out over the sea of people, and spoke so softly, even the rowdiest person in the crowd held their breath to hear me. "You know who we are. You know what you came for. Hard and rough, then slow and easy. And you're gonna take it all. 'Cause we're Blue is the Color— and you fucking love us!"

TWO

DALIA

IF I WOULD HAVE KNOWN how my night would end, I probably wouldn't have gotten out of bed.

Scratch that. I wouldn't have agreed to see some shitty old has-been band with my sister.

(Has-been *might* have been a slight exaggeration, but I was cranky.)

But Melly had a way of talking me into things I never would have done otherwise. She batted her owl-like eyes and promised to love me forever, and I was putty in her hands.

I drew the line at matching Blue is the Color T-shirts, though. She'd even bedazzled mine, but a girl's got to put her foot down at some point, right? I mean, damn, a glittery, sequined shirt of a band I didn't even like? So much no.

And yet, here I was, standing in line outside a club in Baltimore, wearing matching shirts with my sister while she snapped selfies of us.

My new line was duck face. I refused to do duck face, no matter how many times Melly batted her eyes at me.

I tapped the spot on my wrist where a watch would have

been if I ever wore one. "It's getting late. How long will this show be?"

I knew how long the show would be, but since she'd forced me here, I felt it was my sisterly duty to give her a hard time.

She rolled her eyes, slipping her phone inside her bra. "It's not late, you're just prematurely old."

"Some of us have jobs we have to be one hundred percent at in the morning."

"Oh please, Dal. Have you ever given more than fifty percent at that job?"

She had me there. "I give at least sixty-five percent when Ronald makes an appearance." Ronald was my boss at the coffee shop where I worked full time, and skeevy as hell. He'd never done anything inappropriate per se, but he was one of those guys I held my breath around. If I drew too much attention, I knew he was bound to get handsy.

We inched forward in line, and I gave Melly's shoulder a good nudge. "How do you even like this band, anyway? Aren't they all like forty? The only time I hear their music is when it's flashback Friday."

Since we were big enough to reach the dial on our parents' radio, we'd been arguing over whose musical taste reigned supreme. Melly always won those arguments, because I'd been a sucker for her from day one. Thank Steve Jobs for the invention of the iPod. I saved every penny I found and babysat every child on my block to buy one so I was actually able to listen to something besides hard rock.

She nudged me back. "They're not that old, dummy! They just released a new album last year, which is played on constant rotation on the radio. You just don't like their type of music."

I nodded vigorously. "Exactly. So, can I go now?"

"You'd leave your little sister alone, at night, with all these big bad men around?"

I laughed. "You're such a little manipulator. How did you get so good at that?"

She shrugged. "Wasn't disciplined enough as a child, I guess."

"You're right. Let's start now and see if it helps." I smacked her ass. Hard.

She wiggled her bum at me. "Do it again, I like it!"

"Oh, gross! How are we related?"

She threw her arm around me, and I laid my head on her shoulder. "You're just as weird as me, but in a different, equally delightful way."

That was probably true. We'd been raised by parents who also found us delightful, and rarely felt the need to instill basic social conventions and niceties. They wanted us to live our truths as untamed birds, flying free, or some shit like that. That left two girls—now young women—who regularly said things they shouldn't and were left perplexed when they offended others.

Melly and I were also as close as two sisters could be, and even though our parents had major faults, there was no doubt they'd fostered our tight sibling bond. They never let us see each other as competition; instead, we were a team. Her success was mine, and vice versa.

Neither of us had done much to boast about yet, but we were on the cusp. I had a semester left of college and she had another year. Once we had our diplomas in hand, watch out world, the Brenner sisters would be making our mark. Knowing us, our mark would be made with graffiti and inappropriate language, but still...

"I've thought of how you can repay me for being your escort tonight," I said.

"How?"

"I just decided I'm going to watch *Riverdale*. You can't watch the new season until I catch up."

Her mouth fell open. "Are you seriously trying to kill me? If you binged shows like a normal person, then it would be no big deal. But no, you defy the entire point of Netflix by watching one show a week!"

I tapped her nose, grinning. "I'm a big fan of delayed gratification. But for you, I'll watch *two* episodes a week."

She looked like I was murdering her. "I thought you loved me."

"Fine, *three*, but that's my limit! This has to be a sacrifice for you, or it's not worth it."

Melly pursed her lips, giving me the evilest eye. Then she nodded once. "I accept."

We handed the bouncer our IDs, and as he was checking them, I whispered, "Okay, five." I talked a big game, but the idea of torturing Melly was a lot more fun than the execution.

When we finally made it inside, the venue was standing room only, so once we grabbed a beer from the bar, Melly and I nudged and elbowed our way close to the front. The opening act was already playing, and they weren't half bad...surprisingly. They had more of the folksy style I vibed with, so I gave them my attention and swayed to the music while Melly chattered away with the couple next to us.

When the lights went dark, she gripped my forearm. "They're coming! I can't believe I'm finally seeing Blue is the Color in person!" She squealed and jumped up and down, almost knocking my second beer out of my hand.

She had me laughing. It took a lot to get Melly this excited, but I guess finally getting to see the band she'd loved since middle school was the magic ticket.

"Calm, girl. They're just people."

She may have responded, but I didn't hear her. A spotlight

shone down on the center of the stage, and standing there, illuminated, was a god. *How had I never seen the leader singer before?* He wasn't my type, but my heart wasn't getting the memo. It was lodged in my throat, attempting to escape my body and leap onto the stage just to grovel at his feet. I didn't even know his name, but he was doing things to me. My jaw had probably come unhinged, but I couldn't move my arms to check.

He had the kind of hips that probably moved like Jagger, only he was towering, and even from my vantage point, I could appreciate the strain his muscles were putting on his fitted T-shirt. I couldn't quite make out the color of his eyes, but he scanned the crowd intensely under a heavy, knitted brow. *Maybe I could learn to love their music if he stared into my eyes with the same intensity.*

And then he started to talk. He sounded like he'd swallowed gravel. His voice was the human embodiment of staying up all night, smoking, drinking, and laughing with friends. It made me wonder where he'd been all my life.

Then I really heard the words he was saying. The well-rehearsed banter between band members. The faux arrogance... or maybe it was real arrogance. Whatever it was, it was obnoxious.

"I don't like him," I said into Melly's ear.

She rolled her eyes at me for the thousandth time that night. "Shut the fuck up, Dalia. I want to hear what he's saying."

We'd managed to push our way to the front, right below the bassist. Once the band started playing, I barely heard the music; my eyes stayed glued on the bass player. He didn't look good. In fact, he looked wasted.

"He's not playing the right notes," I mumbled.

Melly elbowed me. "Just listen!"

I was getting pissed. Melly had spent more than she could afford on these tickets, and she was owed an excellent show.

From the shit the bassist was putting out, and the lead singer was desperately trying to cover, she wasn't going to get it.

Taking out my phone, I pulled up the camera and hit record. If they were going to put on a shitty show, I was going to put them on blast on social media.

Right when I started recording, the bassist started swaying. Then his eyes closed, his hands fell from his bass, and he tumbled...right off the stage, crashing in front of us, on the other side of the barrier. Music immediately stopped, and security blocked our view of what was happening. Within minutes, we were ushered from the building into the hot night.

Show's over.

I WAS FUMING on the way home. "Can you believe he got so loaded he couldn't even make it through two songs? What bullshit."

"Maybe they'll do another show," she said shakily.

Melly was practically in tears—which never happened. She was as even keeled as they came. I wanted to rip Blue is the Color to shreds for doing this to her, just like I did to Peter Scampanelli when he lifted her dress on the bus her first day of school. Stepping on his toes with my eight-year-old feet so hard he'd cried had been worth the two days of detention, especially when he never messed with Melly again.

When we got back to the apartment we shared, she went to her room and quietly shut the door.

I should have just gone to bed, but I was never the type of girl who let things go. If there'd been some toes to stomp, I would have. Instead, I uploaded the video I recorded to Twitter, and wrote, "I wore a bedazzled shirt to a Blue is the Color concert and all I got was to see Jasper Antonio too drunk off his ass to stand upright. @BlueIsTheColor #hasbeens #BlueIs-TheSuck."

My French bulldog, Flamingo, gave me the side-eye from his spot on my lap, but he licked his own ass, so who was he to judge?

I sighed and looked into his big black eyes. "I know I'm not being very mature, but this dumb band made your Aunt Melly sad. You still love me, right?"

He licked my nose, which I took as a yes.

THREE

DALIA

WAKING up the next morning to find I'd been called a cunt on social media? Eh, it happens. Waking up to find my video had been retweeted thousands of times, including by the lead singer of the band in question, along with the simple words, "You're a fucking cunt"? That was new.

I wasn't sure I liked it.

Scratch that. I knew I didn't like it. And I definitely didn't like the c-word, especially when it was directed at me. But I didn't know what to do about it. Plus, I had to get to work, so there wasn't much time to dwell.

I was opening the shop—succinctly called Beans—and when I arrived, my co-worker, Mira, was waiting for me.

"Hey, girl." She yawned so wide, I heard her jaw crack.

I laughed, letting out a yawn of my own. "Same."

I was going to be dragging today, no doubt about it, but getting the shop ready for our first customers hardly took any brain power. I unlocked the door—Ronald have given me the keys and responsibilities of a manager without the title or pay raise—and let us inside.

As much as I liked being able to say I didn't work for a big corporation, sometimes I wished I did, solely for the bennies. No health insurance from mom and pop. I was out on my own in the big, wide marketplace, and let's face it, I had student loans and city rent to pay for. Health Insurance was my last priority. Yes, last winter I did buy fish antibiotics online when I had a cough that wouldn't quit, but that was neither here nor there. Plus, it totally worked, and I didn't grow gills or scales or anything.

But Beans was actually pretty adorable, and not the worst place to wile away my days. It was in a converted rowhome, with old, creaky wood floors, huge windows, and kitsch-filled shelves mounted on brick walls.

I'd interviewed for another job a couple weeks ago—an actual paid internship at a bank—and I'd thought I'd done a damn good job, but I never heard back, so I was stuck with Ronald, his twitchy hands, and fish antibiotics for the time being.

As she wiped down the espresso machine, Mira asked, "How was the show?"

"You don't want to know. It was as shitty as expected. Actually, shittier. They didn't even make it through two songs."

I whipped out my phone to show her the video and she gasped when Jasper took a header.

"Holy crap! Poor guy. I hope he's okay!"

And see, this was why I knew I was a terrible person. My first reaction was anger, whereas sweet Mira's reaction was concern.

"I'm sure he's fine. He probably just had to sleep it off somewhere."

She frowned. "I don't know. He looked like he fainted, not passed out. But you were there, you'd know."

Our first customer came in, so I put my phone away and didn't have a chance to check it again until the morning rush was over a couple hours later. We had one customer sipping a cafe latte, but other than that, the shop had emptied out.

"I'm going to take a break outside, if you're good here." Mira nodded, and I grabbed my phone. "Be back in ten, but let me know if you need me before then."

We had a few iron tables and chairs lining the sidewalk, so I sat down in one. I set my iced coffee and phone on the table and just took a breath. This job wasn't forever. One more semester of college—I was what the university lovingly referred to as a non-traditional student, meaning my ass was an old lady sitting next to twenty-year-olds—then I'd be out in the professional world, hoofing it to work every day in my business suits and sneakers while Dolly Parton sang about workin' nine to five...except probably not that last part. But I would have a "real" job. Hopefully.

Taking a chance, I checked Twitter...and then immediately exited. My mentions had blown up. I guessed I wasn't the only one who noticed the lead singer of Blue is the Color calling me the c-word. Shitballs.

Nothing like this had ever happened to me, and I wasn't quite sure how to respond.

A man approached my little table. I looked up at him, prepared to flay him with my ire, but then he asked, "Aren't you Dalia Brenner?"

I gave him a long, slow once-over. He looked fairly non-threatening in a middle-age, receding-hairline, dad-bod kind of way. "Maybe. Who are you?"

He handed me a business card. Or he tried to, but I wouldn't take it, so he laid it on the table by my phone. "I'm Roberto Fox with Buzzfeed. I wanted to ask you about your video."

I stood up, my metal chair making a loud scraping sound on the sidewalk. "I don't know what you're talking about."

"You're Dalia Brenner, right? Your picture's on your Twitter account. You're pretty distinctive looking."

I narrowed my eyes at him. "You're creeping me out, Roberto."

He held his hands up. "Didn't mean to. I wanted to ask how it feels to be called a—"

"Don't say it! I hate that word!"

"Can I quote you on that?"

"What? No! I don't want to be quoted. I just want to go to work, then go back home and take a nap. See how none of my future plans involve talking to you?"

He tapped his card on the table. "All right. But if you find you *do* want to answer a couple harmless, easy questions—"

"I won't."

"—you can call or email me anytime."

I picked up his card, my phone, and my coffee I never got to drink, and went back inside without another word.

What the hell had I gotten myself into?

Roberto Fox wasn't the last reporter to make an appearance at Beans. By mid-day, several more had stopped by, and even more had called. And they weren't the only ones asking questions. Word of where I worked had gotten out, so customers kept coming in and asking me about the show and the tweet. A couple douchebags had the nerve to call me a cunt to my face. It took every ounce of my self-control not to douse them with scalding hot espresso.

Because my life was a series of mishaps, today also happened to be one of the days Ronald stopped by. And when I said "happened to," I meant he deliberately came in to fire me. Wouldn't you know it? Blue is the Color was his favorite band, although his official reason for firing me was because my presence was causing an unsafe work environment.

There was no ceremony. No preamble. He walked in,

pulled me into the back, and told me I was done. I handed over my keys, told him to shove my last paycheck up his hairy asshole —okay, I didn't say that, because, hello, poor—and walked out of Beans with my head held high.

Actually, no. My pride was shot. I'd never been fired in my life, and I was...embarrassed? Also seething. Fiery with rage at a band I'd never be able to take it out on.

Luckily, this time, I knew better than to tweet my anger. Instead, I went home with my tail between my legs, snuggled my dog, and ate a lot of ice cream—ice cream I now wouldn't be able to afford because I no longer had a job.

Twitter was still crazy, but I scrolled through my direct messages anyway, just for the hell of it. Right there, in the middle of my DMs, was one with a little blue checkmark next to the name. Someone from the official Blue is the Color Twitter handle had sent me a message.

Hey, this is Jasper. Can you call me?
410-555-5309

Holy shit. I tapped out a reply before I could really think about it, which was the exact opposite of my normal decision making process.

Hey, Jasper. If I call you, are you going to call me a c-word too?
If the answer is no, then feel free to call me. 443-555-8783.

I shoved a spoonful of ice cream in my mouth. There was probably no chance I'd ever hear from him, and that was fine. What would I even say to him? *Sorry I put you on blast on Twitter? How's the hangover?* Not a conversation I was interested in having anyway.

But then my phone rang.

So I answered it.

"Hello?"

"Dalia?"

"Yeah?"

"This is Jasper Antonio. We sort of met last night."

"Oh."

He let out a chuckle that turned into a coughing fit.

"Are you okay? I think I just heard one of your lungs hit the floor." I had just enough empathy to be concerned for the stranger whose actions led me to my current situation— unemployed and soon-to-be ice-cream-less. Maybe because I wasn't completely innocent in this scenario.

He cleared his throat and rasped, "I'll live." He cleared his throat again, and it sounded like he was pounding on his chest. "Turns out, I'm pretty sick. It's a respiratory thing. I'm not looking for pity, just wanted to explain my performance last night. I shouldn't have been on that stage."

I slumped back on the couch, feeling like every bit of the c-word I'd been dubbed. Before I could offer up my first born as penance, Jasper went on.

"I read what Nicky tweeted to you and saw how it blew up. You didn't deserve that."

He sounded completely sincere. Was he actually *that* nice? I wouldn't have been, had the roles been reversed. "I'm really fucking sorry, Jasper. I just assumed you were wasted and...I'm sorry."

"No worries, honestly. It's my asshole friend who owes *you* an apology," he said.

I laughed softly. "My Twitter account will never be the same."

"Shit, are you being harassed? Tell me how I can help." His voice was so full of concern, yet so weak, my heart clenched. Even though my life was in shambles at the moment, he had me wanting to reassure *him* everything would be okay.

"Don't worry about it. It's not anything I can't handle."

He sighed, then coughed some more.

"Are you a big fan of Blue?" he asked.

I thought about lying, but decided against it. "Not really. I was just there to keep my sister company."

"Are you close? With your sister?"

This entire conversation was surreal, but I went with it. "The closest. She's actually the reason I got so pissed off about the show getting canceled."

He listened as I told him about Melly. He laughed when I brought up Peter Scampanelli's maimed toes. He told me he didn't have siblings, but he considered his bandmates his brothers. It was easy to forget Jasper Antonio was a pretty big deal. I would've said he reminded me of the guys I knew, but I didn't know anyone as nice as him.

"Listen, I'm staying with Nicky so he can watch me like a hawk and make sure I don't die in my sleep or whatever. Would you be willing to come over, so we can meet face to face? For my peace of mind."

It was on the tip of my tongue to say no, but I didn't. I accepted his offer, because after this phone call, I kind of wanted to meet him too, and I *really* wouldn't mind making some trouble for the man who was responsible for the implosion of my entire day.

"Give me the address."

FOUR

NICK

"I'M NOT GOING TO APOLOGIZE."

Tali just stared at me, unblinking.

"I swear, I thought it was a dude!"

Same blank stare.

"I deleted the tweet. Isn't that enough?" I shoved a hand through my hair, the dread in my stomach still churning, even though shit had already gone down. The shoe had dropped. Jasper had passed out in the middle of our show from an upper respiratory infection and exhaustion. It couldn't really get worse than that.

He'd gone to the hospital where they'd dosed him up with meds and he slept for twelve hours. Now he was at my place, resting in the guest room, and I was being trampled on by the band's manager, Tali.

"You know the answer. You can't publicly call a woman a cunt—whether you believed the Twitter account belonged to 'a dude' or not—and not face repercussions. And let's be real, don't you feel the tiniest bit shitty?"

I crossed my arms over my chest. "Nope."

She threw her hands up. "Well, you should! What were you thinking, Nick?"

"I was thinking my best friend was basically on death's door and this chick is making a fucking joke of it—making a joke of the band."

I'd been blind with rage when I'd read that tweet while sitting next to Jas's hospital bed. I pictured some keyboard warrior, a tough guy down in his mom's basement, thinking he was so special getting one over on us. I figured the video had been pilfered from an actual fan and I didn't hesitate to let my fingers fly.

"Look at me," Tali ordered.

I did. In the five years she'd been with the band, I'd never seen her angrier. It was a terrifying anger too. She got really quiet, and I could almost see the flames burning behind her eyes.

"*You* made a joke of the band, Nick. You have little girls who adore you. You have women who've listened to your music since they were in middle school. Boys who look up to you and watch your every step. And you chose to use your platform to spout off misogynistic vitriol. You sent your rabid fans after a girl who had maybe a hundred followers. Don't even try to tell me you didn't know what you were doing. I know you, and I know your mean streak. I've tolerated it because I care about this band, but if you want me to continue being your manager, you will *never* use that word to refer to a woman again. And you *will* apologize."

Dread choked me. It traveled from my gut to my throat and lodged there until I couldn't breathe. Tali was right. She was always right, but in this case, she was more right than ever. I didn't regret the word, but I regretted the platform. Using social media that way, to get back at someone, a woman, was a breach of trust with our fans, and now I'd have to earn it back.

"Okay. Tell me what I have to do," I said.

She took a breath to speak, but Jasper emerged at the same time. He still looked like shit, but a little less like death.

Tali hopped up from her seat. "Jas, you shouldn't be up."

He waved her off and shuffled into the living room. "I know. I'll go back to bed in a minute after I take a piss. I just wanted to let Nick know he's expecting a visitor."

I frowned at him. "You're not having a chick over to *my* house when you have a fucking infection, Jas."

He leaned against the dining room table, sounding out of breath. "I wouldn't do that."

Raking at my hair again, I sighed. "I know. Sorry. I'm on edge. Who's coming over?"

He grinned. "A foul-mouthed little birdie named Dalia Brenner."

Tali's eyes widened like she knew who he was talking about, but I drew a blank. The name sounded familiar, but I couldn't place it.

"Nooo. How?" asked Tali.

Jasper shrugged. "I called her."

I looked back and forth between them. "Who?"

He smirked. "Oh, you'll see."

If he was smirking, he had to be feeling better. I knew he'd barely slept in the last two months, so the twelve hours he got in the hospital had probably made the biggest difference. At this point, I didn't even care if he was laughing at me, so long as he was laughing. I wasn't too proud to admit last night had scared the shit out of me, and if I never saw another hospital again for as long as I lived, it would be too soon.

My doorbell rang, followed by a vigorous pound and quite possibly a fucking kick.

"Who's kicking my door?"

"Why don't you answer it and find out?" Jas looked like the Mona Lisa with dreadlocks. Stupid secret smile.

I didn't know what I expected when I opened the door, but it wasn't a grown-up version of little orphan Annie. Only, instead of Mary Janes and a red dress, this version had on combat boots and torn jeans. Same hair and freckles, though.

I raised an eyebrow. "Yes?"

"Where's Jasper?"

She raised up on her toes and tried to peer around me, but I blocked the doorway. "How did you get up here?"

She stepped back, huffing a curl off her forehead. "The doorman let me up, obviously."

"Hmmm. Really? Then I guess he's going to be fired, because I didn't approve you."

She mimed biting her fingernails. "Oooh, you're so big and bad and scary. You like having power over people you deem beneath you?"

"Who the fuck are you and what are you doing in my doorway?" I spit out.

She tilted her pointy little chin up and met my eyes. Hers were brown, and just a fraction too big for her face. "I'm Dalia fucking Brenner, and I'm here to see Jasper."

From behind me, Tali laid a hand on my shoulder. "Hi, Dalia. I'm Tali, Blue is the Color's manager. Please come in." She kicked my heel and muttered for me to move it.

Next thing I knew, Tali was leading this...this stranger into *my* house. And all I could do was stand there and watch it happen.

Jasper was still at the dining room table, but he'd taken a seat. He looked like he was about ready to fall asleep again, so this little visit would be put to an end quickly.

"I would hug you, but I don't want to get you sick," Jasper said to Dalia.

She sat in the chair across from him. "How are you?"

"All right. You don't have any idea what not sleeping does to the body until it's been a solid week of only closing your eyes for twenty minutes at a time, you know?"

Dalia nodded. "Your body forced you to take a break."

He tapped the table in front of him. "Exactly." He met my eyes. "Nick, get your ass over here and meet my new friend, Dalia."

I was hovering in the entryway to the dining room, trying to figure out what the hell was going on, but I'd come up empty. Jasper and the intruder were acting like they were besties, but I'd never heard him mention her. I came closer to where they were sitting.

"We're really sorry about everything that's happened," Tali said to Dalia. "Tensions were so high last night and some of us..." she looked right at me, "were understandably overly emotional."

The intruder nodded. "I get that. But here's the thing. That word just doesn't slip out. Have you ever said it?" Both Jasper and Tali shook their heads while I remained completely lost.

"What word?"

Dalia turned her attention to me, giving me a sugary sweet smile. "Cunt." She waved like a beauty queen. "Hi, I'm the See You Next Tuesday."

Oh, fuck.

I slumped down in the chair next to Jasper. "How?"

She snorted, and it was cute. Everything about her was cute, which I'd come to realize in our five minutes of acquaintance, was actually a well-crafted disguise meant to disarm. I wasn't taking the bait. Jasper and Tali were head over heels, but she could take a long hike with her big brown eyes and Kewpie doll lips.

"How what?" she asked.

I turned to Jas. "How is she here?"

"I invited her."

Tali touched Dalia's arm. "What Nick means to say is we're glad you came because he'd planned to contact you to apologize. And that he's going to make a public apology as well. He won't use your name, if you're not comfortable with that."

"My name's out there, believe me. Your creepy fans were loitering at my job today."

I jerked my head back. "What the fuck?"

She lifted a shoulder. "The internet."

As if that was some type of explanation.

"Are you okay?" asked Jasper.

And yeah, I probably should have been the one asking that. When I rage-tweeted last night, I hadn't expected to become the villain within twenty-four hours, yet here I was. I just needed a twirly mustache and top hat to complete the look.

"I've had better days, but I'll be fine," she said.

Tali kicked me under the table. She didn't have combat boots on like Dalia, but her stilettos were no joke. It took me a minute to catch my breath after having her razor-sharp heel embedded in my shin.

"Dalia, I owe you a big apology," I said.

She leaned back in her chair, staring me down. "That's right, you do."

I stared her right the fuck back down. "I apologize for calling you that word."

She tilted her head. "Funny how you have trouble saying it in person."

"Tali threatened my life if I ever said it again, and funnily enough, I believe her," I said.

Dalia nodded at her. "I respect that."

Jasper slowly stood from the table. "This has been fun, but I need to get back to bed."

Tali rose, circling the table quickly to help him. "I'll be right back. Be nice."

"Why'd you look at me?" I asked innocently. She clicked her heel against the metal leg of my table, and I got the message: *be nice, or say goodbye to your balls.*

When they were gone, I turned back to look at the intruder. Dalia. What a silly, doll-like name for a silly, doll-like girl.

"Are we done?" I asked.

She leaned forward, her elbows on the table and little chin jutted out. "Are you always such a dick?"

"Not always. Must be you."

"Wow." The breath whooshed out of her. "I knew I shouldn't have gone last night. It was one of the worst things that ever happened to me." She stood up, gathering her obnoxiously large bag.

"Happened to you? Doll, anything that's happened since last night was *your* doing. *You* came to our concert. *You* went home and posted that video of Jasper. *You* made false accusations against him. I just fucking responded to *you.*"

"I can't be the only one who posted a goddamn video! There were a thousand people there."

"Yours is the one being retweeted thousands of times. Jesus, if it had been any of the other guys, if it had been *me*, I wouldn't give a fuck." I leaned my forehead on my hands, eyes squeezed shut. "But it's Jasper, literally the nicest human on the planet, who doesn't deserve his name being dragged through the fucking mud. You have no idea what he's been through. He's just another rock star to you."

She didn't respond, but I could hear her breathing. Panting. I opened my eyes and looked up at her. I didn't know what I expected. I guessed tears? A quivering chin? Instead, I got a quietly raging ball of redheaded fury.

"*You* have no idea what I've been through. You callously

threw your celebrity around, not giving one thought to the person on the receiving end. Hey, guess what? I got doxxed by creepers and fired from my job—the job I desperately need to be able to pay my bills and finish school. I've apologized to Jasper, but I will *not* apologize to you. Ever."

I blinked at her. Long, slow blinks. I couldn't quite believe what I was seeing and hearing. And I didn't really know what to say.

My genius response: "What's a doxx?"

She pulled her bag higher on her shoulder. "Forget it. I'll see myself out."

I wasn't planning on arguing. My little intruder would be forgotten as soon as she walked out that door.

Tali came back downstairs before she made it to the door. "Are you leaving?" She looked at me. "Were you mean?"

Dalia let out a half-hearted laugh. "He was pretty mean, but that's not why I'm leaving. I need to find a new job ASAP so I can actually pay rent this month."

"What happened to your job?" she asked.

"Fired. Apparently my boss didn't appreciate the calls and visits from reporters and customers calling me *that word*. So, like I said, I have to find something else."

Tali tapped her chin, appraising Dalia closely. I knew what she looked like when an idea had been sparked, and right now, she looked like she'd had the mother of ideas. It made me nervous.

"You should work for us," Tali said.

I sprung from my chair like I'd hit the eject button. "*What?* No. We're leaving in a week for the Swerve tour. We don't have a job for her here."

Dalia narrowed her eyes at me. "I'm available to travel." She turned to Tali. "What kind of job?"

At the same time I said, "No," again, Tali said, "How about

you be our Jill of all trades? Fill in where we need you. Could be selling merch, setting up dressing rooms, running errands. Kind of like a PA. We're going to be gone for two months on a festival tour. Lots of bands, non-stop travel. It'll be hot and sticky, and you'll be exhausted to your bones by the end of it."

Dalia shoved her hands in her pockets, pulling the waist-band of her baggy jeans lower and revealing a wide slash of skin that looked far too soft to belong to such a hard-ass woman.

"I need fifteen an hour, and I have to be back at the beginning of September for school."

Tali held out her hand for a shake. "We'll do twenty, and we'll have you back in August. We leave on Sunday. I'll email you all the details tonight."

They shook, and I just stood there like an idiot.

The little intruder waved at me. "Bye, Nick. See you Sunday!"

And then she was gone, but there was zero chance in hell I'd be forgetting her.

Tali held up her hand. "Nope. Don't say a word."

I didn't say a single thing. A word had brought this intruder into my life. My lips would be fucking zipped from here on out.

FIVE
DALIA

I SLAMMED my butt down on my suitcase, squishing two months of clothes, linens, and toiletries into a carry on. Flamingo growled at the suitcase, like he was helping me fight our mutual enemy. If he only knew what me packing signified, he'd probably be ripping my luggage to shreds. Mingo was a mama's boy.

"I'm sure you can bring a bigger bag," said Melly. She was laying on my bed, eating a Twizzler, watching me struggle.

"Tali was emphatic about how little storage space the bus has."

When I left Nick's condo a week ago, I hadn't let myself believe the job offer was legit. But by the time I got to my apartment, Tali had sent me an extremely detailed email, laying out my job description and the tour schedule. From the emails we'd exchanged over the last week, I got the feeling we were very different types of people, and I liked her a lot anyway.

I liked Jasper too. We'd checked in with each other a few times throughout the week. He was actually sleeping again—not quite the recommended eight hours, but his four to five was a whole hell of a lot better than what he had been getting.

I still felt guilty as hell for posting that video of him now that I somewhat knew him. He was the quintessential nice guy boy scout who'd never fuck his band over by getting wasted before a show. I didn't know guys like him existed anywhere, let alone in a pretty damn famous rock band.

Too bad nice guys automatically went into my friend column.

I was a chaos magnet. Show me a swirling, whirling, dervish of a man, and I'd throw myself into his path every time. I'd been sucked up, tossed around, and spit out more times than I could count, yet I always came back for more.

It was true I had issues, but who didn't?

"Tell me about him again. Don't leave out any details," Melly demanded.

I yanked the zipper shut on the suitcase, then grabbed my backpack to stow my electronics. Flamingo climbed atop the conquered suitcase and made himself comfortable, stretching his little white paws out in front of him.

I kissed him right between his big bat ears. "Who? Jasper? His dreadlocks are even more gorgeous up close."

She threw her Twizzler at me, and it bounced off my forehead. Instead of being offended, I picked it up and tore a piece off with my teeth.

"No, you dummy. I'm talking about Nick 'The Rock God' Fletcher. How did he smell? What was he wearing? Did you mention me?"

Sliding my laptop into my backpack, I grimaced. "He's an asshole, Mel. That's all you need to know."

She sat up and grabbed my hands, giving me those owl eyes I couldn't seem to resist. "Please, sissy? Indulge me, since you're basically living my fantasy."

Melly had been so damn supportive about this whole thing. When I first told her, I hadn't missed the flash of jealousy in her eyes, which I'd completely understood—she was such a massive fan and I...wasn't. But I also figured that was why I had been offered the job, because I wasn't some crazed fangirl.

I sighed, wrapping my charger cord around my hand. "I didn't smell him, so I can't tell you that. He *did* look freshly showered, so do with that information what you will."

She held out her arm. "I have goosebumps. How can you be so cool about this?"

"Because I met him. I was in his house." I sat down on the bed next to her, and Flamingo took his rightful place on my lap. "He's a real live human to me, not some teenage fantasy. Plus, he sucks."

She groaned dramatically. "He doesn't."

"Sorry, babe. He does. Anyway, to answer your question, he had on jeans and a T-shirt. No shoes. Really nice feet."

Nick Fletcher was probably used to women falling at his feet, and while I hadn't done that, I *had* taken note of his feet. They were tan, with long toes—not finger toes, just nice, elegantly long toes—and well-groomed toenails. I had a thing for nice man feet, and his were some of the nicest I'd seen.

"Who cares about his feet? What about his eyes?"

"He had two," I deadpanned.

She threw another Twizzler at me. "If I can listen to your soliloquies about his feet, you can tell me the exact shade of green of his eyes."

I laughed and threw the Twizzler back at her. I actually had put some thought into his eyes. It had been pretty hard not to. They were striking, despite the hardness behind them. Because make no mistake, Nick *wasn't* a nice guy.

"They were sea glass green. Like that big chunk we found at the beach when we were kids."

She clutched her chest. "I think Mom and Dad still have it.

I'm going to steal it and gaze upon it while pretending I'm staring into his eyes."

"I'll cut you."

"If it's with the sea glass, I'd gladly let you spill my blood."

Biting my lip, I scratched behind Flamingo's ears, making him flop onto his side in ecstasy. "Can we be real for just a sec?"

"Yep. Lay it on me."

"I'm nervous."

She flung her arm over my shoulders. "Thank god. I was beginning to think you were an android or something. You've been so blasé about the fact that you're going to be spending the next two months traveling all over the country with a pretty fucking famous band, on a tour with thirty other pretty damn famous bands. Not to mention, you've never been on a plane or left the east coast. You know. No biggie."

So, yeah. Today would be my first plane ride ever. Pretty crazy to reach the ripe old age of twenty-five having never flown the friendly skies. That was a big cause of my nerves. I'd YouTubed and Googled everything I could possibly want to know about the flying experience, but I still felt like I might vomit. Of course, from my research, I knew air sickness bags were provided in the seatbacks in front of me.

I *had* been disappointed to learn they no longer gave out wing pins to first time fliers. Apparently, my fantasies of what air travel was like were based on nineties airline commercials.

Was I nervous about all the other stuff? Yeah, kinda. Two months was a long time to spend in close quarters with strangers. And when at least one of those strangers hated me, there was a high possibility of extreme awkwardness and discomfort.

"Just pet my hair and tell me it'll be okay," I said.

Because Melly was the best, even though she was a brat, she

wrapped me in her arms and rocked me back and forth while she hummed, just like our mom always had.

"I'm going to miss you, sissy," she said.

"Same." My chest grew heavy as I looked at her, trying to imagine what it was going to be like not seeing her face every day.

We sat there for as long as we could, but then I had to face the music. Or, as the case may have been, the metal tube of death.

I gave Flamingo a thousand kisses, and he seemed to be getting suspicious. He was used to being adored and showered with affection, but this was overkill, even for him.

I held his little, flat, wrinkly face in my hands. "I love you, my sweet baby." He licked me from my chin to my nose to show me the feeling was mutual. "You be a good boy for Auntie Melly, okay? And don't grow too much while I'm gone. And don't let her be a bad influence on you."

He gave me a little *ruff ruff,* then meandered over to his bed, sprawling out like the king he was.

Melly drove me to the airport, and as each mile ticked by, her neurosis took over.

"You have your ID?"

"Yep. Two forms."

"Sunscreen? You know how easily you burn."

"I do."

"Tampons?"

"Check."

"Condoms?"

"Always. I'm a safety girl."

"All your chargers?"

"Present and accounted for."

"Do you know where you're going when you get there?"

"Tali emailed me all the deets. I'm good. California, here I come!"

She'd pulled up to the drop-off area, and we both stalled. Melly asked me a hundred other questions, and I answered each one. Then we hugged and hugged until a police officer yelled at her to move her car.

Once she helped me get my suitcase and backpack out of her trunk, she pulled me into another tight hug. "Call me as soon as you land. And send me a selfie on the west coast!"

"Will do. And *you* call *me* if you need anything. And take good care of my dog." I kissed her cheek. "Love you, babe."

"Love you, sissy."

I stalled a little more by standing on the curb, watching my little sister drive away. We'd never really been apart outside of the first three years of my life before she was born. I didn't even count those years since I'd spent most of them willing her into existence. A little time apart would do us some good.

After some research, I selected an aisle seat. I'd have easy access to the bathrooms—although I was hopeful I wouldn't need one—and I wanted to have a good view of the action.

My seatmates ended up being an older couple who eyed me warily as they sat down. Yes, I had a button nose and a freckled face, which tended to give the impression I was a sweet, nice girl, but I was also heavily tattooed, so that left people confused. *Did sweet, nice girls have tattoos,* they'd wonder. The answer was of course, yes, but I wasn't a sweet, nice girl.

I'd planned the flight out in my head. I had six hours to kill, so I'd spend at least an hour working on graphics for a website I was building for an indie bookstore. I'd also loaded my Kindle with books, so I'd spend another portion of the flight reading. And snacks. I brought so many snacks. And a bagel, because you never knew.

Fifteen minutes into the flight, it was clear none of those

things would be happening. With the first jostle, I actually let out a yelp.

I tried to cover my outburst with a smile. "It's my first flight," I explained to the woman next to me.

"There's nothing to worry about, honey." Her voice was soothing, and I wanted to believe her, but then the plane jounced again, and I was certain we were all doomed.

"I'm Bea, and this is my husband, Harold. We've been flying this route for fifty years."

"Dalia," I said.

"Your tattoos are pretty, honey. I'm glad they're flowers and not skulls," Bea said.

I gripped the arm rests. "Thank you. Skulls aren't really my style."

She leaned closer, studying my arm. "Couldn't you have stopped at just one or two?"

I told her no, that I liked being colorful. We had a friendly debate, then Harold showed me his faded tattoos from his time in the Navy. Bea scrunched her nose and said she'd never liked them.

Bea rubbed my arm any time we went through turbulence, and although I didn't really feel better, I thought she'd probably at least hold my hand when we went spiraling toward out fiery deaths.

When we landed at LAX, I had tears in my eyes and my fingers ached from gripping the arm rests for six hours straight. Bea and Harold walked with me to baggage claim. They'd sort of adopted me, and thank god, because I wasn't sure I would have survived the flight without them.

Before we parted ways, she handed me her phone number scribbled on a piece of paper and pink knitted socks.

"I knitted those for my granddaughter, Stephanie, but I

think you need them more." She patted my arm. "Call us if you need anything, honey."

Once I called Melly and relayed my near-death experience —the brat laughed—I found an Uber to take me to the stadium where the tour bus was parked.

My adventure had had an inauspicious beginning, but things had to go up, right?

SIX

NICK

THE INTRUDER'S arrival was loud and bothersome, which was exactly what I'd expected. God knew why I tried to nap in the middle of the day on a tour bus surrounded by sixty other buses. Maybe it had been too long since I'd been on one. Maybe I was just getting old. Twenty-three-year-old Nick wouldn't have believed he'd be napping on the Swerve tour a decade later. Back then, the only time I napped during the day was when I'd passed out from being wasted.

Now, I needed my fuckin' beauty rest so I could perform tomorrow.

But the thin sliding door dividing the bunks from the front lounge wasn't enough to drown out my entire band fawning over *her*. Rolling out of my top bunk, I scrubbed my hands down my face and went out to see what the fuss was about.

The first thing I saw when the door slid open was a round, full ass in tight jean shorts. Once I caught sight of her, curiosity got the better of me and I let my eyes travel down, stopping in surprise at the pink bows tattooed at the top of her thick, creamy thighs.

Jesus, fuck, fuck.

Dalia had been pretty covered up the one time I saw her, but now, in the California sun, her clothes had shrunk, and the amount of skin on display had multiplied. Even from the back, I could see her skin was lush and colorful.

Jasper hugged her, and I stepped farther into the space, but no one paid any attention to me. All eyes were on Dalia, except David, who winked at me and tipped his bottle of beer in her direction.

"Man, that sucks," Jasper said. "If I'd known, I would have flown with you."

She shook her head. "I made a friend on the plane, Bea. Didn't help." Her words sounded stilted, like she was having trouble getting them out.

Tali took her hand, leading her to the leather couch. "Sit, sit. We'll get you some water and food. You'll feel a lot better."

She glanced over her shoulder at me. "Nick, can you grab a bottle of water out of the fridge? Dalia's had a rough go of it."

I automatically followed Tali's orders. I was still trying to get back into her good graces after last week's fuck up. I did every interview, social media post, and kowtowing she'd demanded. I wasn't too dumb to realize she was essentially our backbone. She'd devoted her life to making *our* lives easier, and sometimes we could be real pricks. So, while I wouldn't rub her feet and call her Queen Tali, I could grab a bottle of water without complaint.

When I handed Dalia the water, the paleness of her face struck me. Not her normal porcelain doll pale, but pallid, like she was seconds away from either spewing or fainting.

"What's wrong with her?" I asked Jas.

"Bad flight," he answered.

"My ears still work," she reminded us.

I sat down on the couch across from her, next to David.

"Do you get motion sickness or something? Because, you

know, we're going to be doing a shit ton of driving over the next two months."

"Today was Dalia's first flight, Nicky boy," David said.

A laugh burst out of me. "No way."

Dalia stood up quickly, swayed, then immediately sat back down. "When my eyeballs stop bouncing around in my head, I'm going to tell you what a dick I think you are."

David slapped my back. "Damn, Nicky. Girl's already got your number."

Tali threw eye daggers at me. "Get her some of your stash."

"Not going to happen," I said.

"Nick." She did the quiet voice again. The one that made my balls run for cover inside my body and the hair on the back of my neck stand at attention.

I threw up a hand. "Okay. Damn, Tali. You don't have to use the voice."

Except she did, because she knew how I was about my stash. Everyone knew how I was. No one dared to touch it, even David—and he was the original dickhead button pusher. My stash was sacred and not to be shared. Need twenty bucks? Sure. Need a lift? I'd probably give you one. Want a piece of my chocolate? Turn the other way and pretend we've never met because that is the rudest question I've ever heard.

Handing over a Kit Kat to the intruder was physically painful. Watching her fucking bite into it like a troglodyte instead of snapping off each section like a civilized human had me balling my hands into fists just to stop myself from taking it back.

"Can't believe you gave the new girl your chocolate," muttered David.

"Don't plan on seeing it again. Where's Ian?"

"Chasing Malka around somewhere."

I shook my head. "Fuckin' Malka."

Ian and Malka had been on again, off, and off, and on, and off again for a couple years. She had her own band, and I liked her both as a musician and a friend, but she was toxic when it came to Ian. She turned him upside down and all around, sent him running, then pulled him back. He always went when she called, and now, she was on the road with us—well, on her own bus—for two months. I just hoped Ian survived it.

"Yep. Fuckin' Malka with the magic pussy."

Jasper threw a water bottle at him. "Come on, man. You don't talk about our friend like that."

David just laughed. "Hey, I like her. I'm just sayin', girl's gotta have something pretty damn special between her legs to keep Ian crawling over broken glass to get to her."

"Or maybe it's something between her ears," said Dalia.

Everyone looked at her. *I* looked at her. Her cheeks had pinkened, and her brown eyes were a lot less glassy. And I couldn't help that my eyes drifted lower. I'd like to say it was the art on her chest that drew my attention, but that'd be a lie. Curvy wasn't enough of a word to describe her. I'd have to go back in time and pluck a word from the fifties. Dalia was *stacked* in a Marilyn Monroe way. All soft, exaggerated curves. Her tongue was the only thing sharp about her.

"You got me. Girl's got charm," David conceded.

"Feel better?" asked Tali.

"Much. Thank you, Nick, for the chocolate. I hadn't eaten since I left my apartment and things were touch and go for a few minutes there. My sympathy for Jasper passing out on stage has been renewed. I really thought I was going to go down."

"Girl, we have to get you some real food," said Jas.

Dalia nodded. "I'm into real food. Super into it."

Tali hopped up. "Let's go to the catering tent. I'm telling you, this tour can be draining, but the food never lets me down. Luckily, I sweat buckets every day or I'd gain ten pounds."

Jasper went with them, promising to bring dinner back for David and me.

"So." David waggled his eyebrows.

"So what?"

"So, she's pretty as fuck. You didn't mention that in any of your rants about her."

I pulled out my guitar from under the opposite bench, not really into this line of conversation. There was no doubt Dalia was pretty, but so what? Pretty girls fell into my lap on the daily. Pretty was tiring. I'd had a record contract since I was twenty—there had been a lot of pretty. I didn't get stupid over it anymore.

"She is. She also doesn't belong here." I strummed my guitar. "Jam?"

"Always." David grabbed his guitar from the back of the bus and we jammed, rocking out to some Green Day and Red Hot Chilli Peppers. Music was our original bond. When I met David in third grade, we got into a fist fight over who was the better guitarist: Mike McCready from Pearl Jam or James Iha from The Smashing Pumpkins. I went home from school that day with a chipped tooth and a best friend.

The guy drove me to drink. He said and did shit that made me question his sanity, but he'd been a solid, have-your-back, fight-a-gator-for-you friend since day one.

"You ready for the next two months?" he asked.

"Not even a little. Man, I think we're getting too old for this. I saw some of the guys, the newbs, and they looked like they could be our children."

He tapped the top of his guitar. "Nah, we've got another couple years before they're my kid's age."

I laughed. "How's Emma? Is she coming to a show?"

"Hilarious. As if I'd want my fifteen-year-old daughter at

one of our shows. I'd be leaping off the stage the first time some douche looked at her."

I got up, stretching my back. "She's going to come to a show someday. I'm surprised she hasn't asked."

"Oh, she's asked. The answer is 'hell no, babydoll.' Anyway, she's not into our music. Maybe because I'm her dad, and dads are never cool."

"True."

David had Emma when he was eighteen, the product of a one-night stand. He'd never been in a relationship with her mom, but even back then, he'd always been in his daughter's life. And back then, before we started touring, Emma had been our little mascot, sitting on the floor with her blocks while we practiced. I could talk a lot of smack about shit he'd done, but his parenting was not one of them.

I went back to my bunk to read while the bus was quiet. These moments were rare on tour, so I always took advantage of them. At some point, I must've drifted off, because I woke to my book on my face and rustling sounds. I pushed back my privacy curtain just enough to check out the sound, and got another view of Dalia's ass, this time up close and personal. She was standing on the bottom bunk, leaning into the top bunk, which happened to be directly across from mine, spreading sheets on the thin mattress. Then she climbed into the bunk, on her hands and knees, reaching the far corners.

I'd seen bows tattooed on the back of a couple girls' legs before, but they were something else entirely on her. Her thighs looked like a soft place to land. Like they'd cradle my hips and never let me leave—not that I'd want to.

What the fuck? Why am I thinking about getting between Dalia fucking Brenner's thighs?

"Rainbows, huh?"

She startled, banging her head on the top of her bunk. Then

she turned around, her legs dangling. How our bunks ended up right across from each other was a mystery. We had eight on our bus, four sets of top and bottom. Dalia and I were both on top, with David below me and Tali below her.

"I like my sheets." She smoothed a hand over her colorful bedding. "What are yours? Black, like your soul?"

I turned on my side and opened the curtain wider. "Blue, like the band."

"Well..." She hopped down from her bunk, and I didn't fail to notice the way her tits bounced. "Since our beds are right across from each other, I hope you don't snore or masturbate too loudly."

Then she sauntered away, her ass swaying and jiggling as she walked back to the front of the bus.

Dalia fucking Brenner. The little intruder with the sweetest damn ass I ever did see. I should've probably gotten up and scrounged up some dinner, but I needed a couple minutes to collect myself, so I threw my book back over my face and tried not to think about every single one of her soft-as-sin curves.

SEVEN

DALIA

SLEEPING in a bunk on a tour bus was what I imagined sleeping in a coffin would be like. Sleeping across from Nick Fletcher was a test of my patience and fortitude.

He still hated me, so why couldn't I hate him? I wanted to. God knew I did. But being here, seeing him in his element, had made him all the more attractive.

Still, I couldn't help needling him. When he gave me one of his precious Kit Kats, I'd purposely taken a bite of it just to see his reaction. If I hadn't been so weak from hunger and exhaustion, I would have laughed at how white his knuckles had gotten.

And the masturbation comment. Well, I wouldn't have minded hearing him stroke his dick—so long as I could watch too.

Jesus, it had been too long since I'd gotten laid. No one had interested me lately. Every guy my age seemed to want to settle down—and I so wasn't there yet—or do the fuck buddy thing, which I didn't find too appealing either. A fun, loosely committed relationship was up my alley, but I hadn't taken the time to seek that out. If I wanted to get to the true root of my issue, my last asshole boyfriend, Bastian, had done a number on my opinion of men.

I got up early, grabbing a lightning fast shower in the microscopic stall at the back of the bus. A little product in my curls, fresh clothes, clean teeth, sunscreen—Melly would have been proud—and I was good to go. I was tiptoeing past the bunks, heading to the front lounge, when a hand shot out and grabbed my arm. I was not ashamed to say I squeaked.

"Mind making me a cuppa?" Nick's gravelly voice came from inside his bunk.

"Cuppa what?" I hissed.

He chuckled. "Tea, doll. Just plug in the electric kettle. I'll be out in a minute."

I didn't argue because I didn't want to wake everyone up. Tali had given me an extensive list of jobs to do, but making tea for Nick wasn't on it.

Still, it wasn't a huge deal to plug in a kettle while I made my own coffee in the Keurig. And actually, I thought it was cute that the big, bad rock star started his day with tea. *A cuppa.*

I was lounging with my feet up on the couch, sipping my coffee, when Nick came out of the back, sliding the door closed behind him. He made his tea, then sat on the couch across from me, carefully blowing on his mug before taking a sip.

We were quiet for a moment as I sipped my coffee and surreptitiously checked him out. He'd taken a shower too, so his sandy hair was darker and slicked back from his face. I almost shuddered when I got down to his feet. *Please, lord, let it never slip out in front of him that I find his feet sexy. Please, spare me my dignity just this once.*

"Have you forgotten what it's like not to have money?" I asked.

A deep line formed between his brows as he frowned at me. "No, Dalia, I haven't."

I turned to face him, pulling my knees under my chin. "I was just wondering. I did some reading on the band after I accepted this job, so I know you didn't grow up with a whole hell of a lot. Same as me. But when you heard yesterday was my first flight, you laughed. And that made me think you'd forgotten."

"How old are you?" he asked.

I tipped my chin up. "Twenty-five."

"By the time I was twenty-five, I'd traveled around the world three times. I owned a house and two cars. I'd put a lot of mental distance between my childhood and my new reality, but I'll never forget the feeling of going to bed hungry because the only meals I ate that day were at school, or walking through snow with holes in my shoes because my mom forgot her promise, once again, to take me to Goodwill to find a new pair. I guess, though, I do get wrapped up in this life, and things that are so commonplace for me, like air travel, are a luxury to someone else. I was a jackass to laugh."

I was surprised he'd admitted it, and it took me a moment to regain my ground. I'd thought he'd laugh again. Instead, he'd given me a sincere answer. A thoughtful one.

"Do you remember your first flight?" I asked.

He looked down at his tea for a beat, then nodded. "I do. We took a rickety prop plane to New York for a show. I looked like you when I got off, only greener, and I puked my guts out in the airport. So, all in all, you did a lot better."

"Yes...well, I try. My Uber driver kept checking on me, making sure I wasn't going to die in his car. I have to say, his driving did not help the situation."

He snorted. "You made it, though. What's Tali got you doing today?"

I had a list. Tali loved lists, as I'd come to realize. She had lists for the guys, lists for me, and the back lounge, which was mostly her domain, was plastered with lists. I had a feeling managing the band and touring with them was a lot of work, and she'd delegated some of the more menial tasks to me.

"My first task of the day is to hang up band posters around the venue. We're limited to twelve, but rumor is they're not really strict about it. We want people to know when you guys are going on tonight."

"Dalia..." He was smirking at me. I didn't like it.

"Yes, Nick?"

"You know we're one of the headliners on this tour, right? I mean, we're kind of a big deal. People know when we're going on."

Right. Of course that was true. But when he said it like that, smirking at me like I was a silly little girl, I wanted to kick him.

"You know, I don't even like your music."

I gasped when the words left my mouth, but surprisingly, Nick laughed.

"What the hell?" he asked through deep, rough chuckles.

"I don't know! Sometimes I just say things! I'm sure your music it great, but what I meant to say is I don't really know it. I could probably name one song. And even then, I couldn't sing it."

He smiled like I was the most amusing creature he'd ever encountered. "What song?"

"'Feels Like Fall.'"

Nick took a breath, then crooned in his gravel voice, "You're my fall, autumn in your eyes." He paused, raising a questioning eyebrow.

"Rings a bell. But you better keep going, because I'm not sure," I said.

"I don't want it all, I just don't wanna fight. Leaves on the ground, crunching under my boots. You don't come around. No, you don't come around, now that it's fall..." he trailed off, and I spontaneously orgasmed on a black leather couch, inside Blue is the Color's tour bus, in Los Angeles, California, right in front of Nick Fletcher. I now understood groupies. If he kept singing like that to me, I'd throw my panties at him. Hell, I'd go unpack my suitcase and throw all my clothes at him.

He'd been appealing before, with his pretty feet and sea glass eyes, but add on that smoky voice, and he was a god.

Then, he went and ruined it all. "Your cheeks are awfully pink. Did I make you wet, Dalia? I seem to have that effect."

I *had* been wet and panting. I wasn't immune to the rock star effect. I *was* immune to the asshole effect, though. I instantly became as dry as the Sahara.

"Not even the slightest. If my cheeks are pink, it's because I'm embarrassed for you. All you have in your bag of tricks is a decent voice and forgettable lyrics. If you think that impresses me, then please, think again." I looked down at my non-existent watch. "Gotta jet if I want to get any breakfast."

I ran off the bus as fast as my legs would carry me while attempting to also look cool, calm, and in control.

I wasn't. In control, that was. But still, I did have a busy day ahead of me, and as I walked by the rows and rows of tour buses filled with sleeping musicians, I realized the enormity of this tour.

The schedule ahead of us was punishing, and the sheer amount of coordination to get seven hundred people from one city to the next, ready to play for crowds of thousands in the sweltering sun, was mind boggling. But as I walked through the makeshift community full of buses, tents for porches, and asphalt for yards, I saw some of the cogs that powered the machinery at work. Roadies pushing speakers toward stages. Trucks emptying septic tanks on buses. Authoritative-looking people with clipboards and walkie talkies, scurrying from one point to the next.

I was a bit player in all this—an easily replaceable gear, without which the machine would keep on ticking. It was humbling to step back and acknowledge that.

I found the catering tent easily, and even though the clock hadn't hit eight yet, there was already a short line. Jasper and Tali had warned me they'd waited over an hour for food at times, but it was always worth it. And as I eyed the crispy bacon and waffles, I agreed.

Once I had my tray piled with food, I surveyed the quickly filling tables. Suddenly, I felt like the weird girl back in high school no one wanted to sit with. Everyone was paired off, their groups already established, no room for the redhaired girl who really had no business being there.

Just as I was about to sit in a corner and hide, muttering I wanted to be alone anyway, someone called my name.

When I found the source, I was confounded, but I walked to her table. *Her* being an ethereal beauty with cotton candy pink hair and tats from her knuckles to her neck. She waved at me cheerfully as I made my way over.

"Dalia, right?" she asked.

"Yeah. And I'm sorry, I should probably know who you are, but I'm blanking."

Her smile grew. "I'm terribly offended." She held her hand out, and I set my tray down in front of an empty seat to shake it. "Malka. I'm friends with the Blue boys. They described you to a T. Please, sit!"

Malka went around the table, introducing me to everyone. She had a soft German accent I could have listened to all day. The members of her band smiled politely, then went back to their conversations. Next to her was Ian, who barely acknowledged my presence. He hung on her every word, just like everyone else at the table. Malka was one of those people, the kind who made you feel like you were her best friend and the most important person to her. I was always drawn to those people, even though I knew they made everyone feel that way and it wasn't anything special about me.

"And the sweet boy next to you is Moses. He's the singer in a rad band, Unrequited. You have to hear them play at some point on the tour."

I turned to the guy next to me, getting my first good look at him. He looked my age, maybe a year or two younger, with dark eyes and full, thick lashes. Oh, he probably got into a lot of trouble with those lashes—*and* the dimple that appeared in his right cheek when he grinned at me.

"Hey, red. You can call me Mo," he murmured softly.

Oh yeah, this boy was trouble. The voice, the eyes, the dimple—it was a lot.

"I actually think I've seen you before. Didn't you just play a show in Baltimore?"

He chuckled. "I did. Can't believe you were there. What are the chances?"

He didn't need to know the reason I was here now was because of that show. Instead, I told him how much I liked his music. Aside from the beers I'd imbibed, it had been the only thing I'd enjoyed that night. His style was less thrashing and wailing, and more crooning, quiet, folksy beats. Melly liked to tell me I was born in the wrong era, that I should wear long skirts and flowers in my hair. I wasn't a hippie, and I sure as shit wasn't about to wear a skirt, but I liked what I liked.

"So, you're traveling with Blue is the Color? How's that going?" Mo asked.

I laughed. "Ask me in a few days. I'm only twelve hours into my tenure, so I'm reserving judgement."

"Oh. You're not in the business?"

"Nope. After the tour, I'll be back to my regular, broke

student life. I have one semester left on my web marketing and design degree, then I'll join the working masses."

Mo steepled his fingers under his chin. "Oh, cool. I should show you the band's website. It's atrocious. None of us know shit about web design, so we had a friend make it two years ago, and it hasn't been updated since."

Reaching into my back pocket, I slid out one of the business cards I'd started carrying with me a while ago. I didn't like the whole schmoozy, begging for business deal, but I *did* like money, so anytime web design came up, I slipped out one of my cards lickity split.

"Email me and I'll take a look. And you can check out my portfolio on *my* website. See if you see anything you like."

He picked up my card, flipping it over in his hand. "You're like a legit businesswoman. That's really cool. Seriously, I'm going to email you tonight."

"Looking forward to it."

Ian got up from the table at the same time I did, so it would have been awkward if we didn't walk back to the bus together. Although, the walk back was pretty awkward since he still seemed to have no interest in me.

"Do you like these tours?" I asked.

He shrugged. "Some days I do, some days I don't."

"How about today?"

"Eh."

"What's the city you're most looking forward to playing?" I asked.

"Fuck, I can't even remember half the places we're going. I don't know, I guess when we play at Merriweather in Maryland. Crowd's always on fire for their hometown boys."

"Any advice for me on surviving the next two months?"

We'd arrived back at the bus, and he paused before he stepped on, taking a good, long gander at me. I took a good long gander at him too. He wasn't really my type with his long-limbed lankiness, but he had his charms. At least appearance wise. His personality left something to be desired. But maybe when you've been in a fairly famous band most of your adult life, you don't really need to worry about having a decent personality. Maybe good personalities were just for us regular folk to cultivate.

"My advice: don't wear flip flops. People have been known to shit on the ground out there and no one wants shitty feet."

Well damn, good thing I packed my boots.

WE'D KILLED it in LA, and overnight, we'd been magically transported to San Diego, and the one thing I knew for sure was Dalia was an early riser. This morning, she'd managed to get showered and dressed, all without waking me. I was surprised to see her in the front lounge, sipping coffee and having a murmured phone conversation. I was even more surprised to see she'd turned the kettle on for me.

Her back was turned to me when I walked in, so I stood there, listening.

"Oh god, I met so many musicians yesterday you probably would have recognized, but I had no clue who they were. Oh, but I did meet the singer from Unrequited. You know, the band that opened for Blue. He was pretty cool."

I knew exactly who she was talking about. A little shithead named Mo. Couldn't have been older than twenty-three or twenty-four. Malka had gotten them the gig opening for us in Baltimore. I hadn't been impressed, but seemed like they *had* left an impression on the little intruder.

"No, no, I won't have the chance. I know, babe. I'll get to dip my toes in the Pacific one day, and so will you. We'll do it together. Love you too, Melly."

She quietly hung up the phone, and my chest tangled into knots. This girl did something to me...something I didn't like. My urge to take care of her was just as strong as my urge to fuck with her. Today, the first urge was winning out.

"I'll take you."

Dalia jumped out of her seat, holding her mug out in front of her so it didn't slosh on her clothes as she clutched her chest with her other hand. "Fuck, Nicky, you just shaved at least three years off my life."

Oh, sweet baby Jesus. The boys were the only ones who called me Nicky. I tolerated it from them, but I swear, hearing it from her pretty pink lips had me half hard in a second. Her tiny shorts and crisscross contraption of a tank top only had more blood rushing below my waist.

"I'll take you to the beach," I repeated.

Her hand fisted at her hip. "You like listening in on phone calls?"

"Kinda hard not to on this bus. Are you taking my offer?"

Her eyes narrowed. "Are you going to drown me?"

"Possibly."

She pursed her lips and hummed for a beat, then nodded. "Worth it."

With that decided, I set about making my tea, feeling her eyes on my back. I could almost hear the questions on the tip of her tongue.

"Ask," I said.

"How do you have time to take me to the beach?"

I bobbed my tea bag up and down in the hot water, breathing in the steam coming off the surface. "We don't go on until eight tonight. I can't sit around here all day." What I didn't say was I probably would have done exactly that, but yeah, the beach, with Dalia, was a hell of a lot more appealing.

"Okay, then why?"

I turned around to face her and found she'd moved to the end of the couch closest to the kitchen, so I took a seat directly across from her.

"Because what you said yesterday, about flying for the first time, got me thinking about firsts. And I don't think you came all this way not to have some firsts."

Her eyes widened just a fraction. Then they softened an inch. And then the corners of her lips tugged up, and the shutters behind her eyes went down.

"Sorry, babe, you're about ten years too late for my virginity. It's sweet that you care, though." Pulling her bottom lip into her mouth, she peered at me from beneath her eyelashes, twirling a ringlet around her finger.

I groaned and shoved a hand through my hair. Then Dalia let out a little sniffling laugh. Her shoulder were jumping around as she tried to hold it in, but I saw the way her eyes were dancing. Today, *she* was fucking with *me*.

"You are the actual worst," I said.

"I know, I totally am. When someone's kind to me for no reason, I never know how to take it, so I make jokes. It's my thing."

"Yeah...well, it's a bad thing."

She held a hand up. "Still learning and growing over here. And thank you. I can't believe we're going to the beach!"

The door to the bunks slid open, and Jasper stepped out. "We're going to the beach?"

Dalia clapped. "Hell yes! Nicky is making my dreams come true."

Jas met my eyes, and mouthed, "Nicky?" I just shrugged, knowing I'd hear shit about it later.

David stumbled out of the bunks. "What's this about the beach?"

Apparently, we were all fuckin' going to the beach.

Tali arranged for a limo bus to cart our asses to Pacific Beach. She'd stayed behind, saying she had far too much work to do to play in the sand, but she'd given the bus driver specific instructions to have us back by three, whether we came willingly or he had to hog tie us. Ian hadn't come either, staying to watch Malka's show and chase her around the festival with his dick in his hand. If I ever chased a woman like that, I hoped someone took me out back and put me out of my misery. A piece of ass was never gonna be worth losing my mind.

We were probably a sight to all the families on the beach, a bunch of tattooed motherfuckers dressed in all black descending upon their sandy haven. Buddy, our tour bus driver, was doubling as security, but when we arrived, he set up an umbrella and lounge chair, and went right the fuck to sleep.

Jasper and I set up a couple more umbrellas, while David plopped on the sand and lit a cigarette.

"Do people still smoke?" asked Dalia.

David laughed. "Nah. This is all an illusion. I'm actually eating kale right now."

"Good. I was concerned. Because, you know, smoking has been known to cause cancer and make you smell disgusting. Have you ever kissed someone who smokes? Lick an ashtray, it tastes better."

David had a temper, so I stopped what I was doing to watch.

"I'll remember that if I ever think of taking up smoking." He stubbed his smoke out in the sand, then pocketed the butt.

I shouldn't have been worried. The little intruder seemed to drive everyone to madness. If anyone else had said what she did to David, he'd have told them to fuck right off. Not her, though. She plopped down next to him, rubbing sunscreen all over her face, and informed David the ocean was just one big fish bathroom. The fucker howled this time, slapping his leg as he laughed.

"She's something, huh?" whispered Jas.

"Mmhmm. Something. Not sure what."

He elbowed me in the ribs. "What's up with you arranging a whole beach day for a girl you don't like?"

I elbowed him back. "Needed some vitamin D. Don't read into it."

"Sure, dude."

I scanned his face. He looked good. He'd rocked the fuck out of the show last night, playing better than he had in months.

"You feeling good still?" I asked.

His eyes turned to the horizon. "I kind of feel like I shouldn't, but I do. She'd be happy I came to the beach. She was always telling me I didn't slow down enough."

A huge fuckin' lump of sadness landed in my throat. I had to swallow a few times just to speak. "She'd also tell you not to feel guilty for being happy."

He nodded. "She would, you're absolutely right. Same goes for you, Nicky. She'd tell you to do what makes you happy, even if it's unexpected."

By pure coincidence, my gaze landed on the spot in the sand where Dalia and David had been a minute ago. The only thing there now was a pile of her clothes. I would have thought the rapture had happened and she'd ascended to a higher plane, leaving Jas and me behind, only I was pretty sure he'd make it to Heaven before any of the rest of us.

"What the hell is he doing?" Jasper muttered.

I followed his line of sight, spotting David charging into the ocean with a shrieking Dalia over his shoulder. That protective urge had me wanting to plow through sandcastles and leap over small children to save her. Then I realized her shrieking was out of pure joy and slowed my roll.

David tossed Dalia through the air like a sack of potatoes, and she landed with a splash in the waves. I shook my head when she surfaced and grabbed his shirt, pulling him down with her. I'd expect nothing less from her, but David didn't know who he was messing with.

"Ocean?" asked Jas.

"Yeah, man. Ocean." I ripped my T-shirt over my head and kicked off my shoes, then Jas and I made our way down to the water. David was ringing out his T-shirt and Dalia had her back turned to us, standing in knee-deep water.

Her strappy tank top contraption had been traded for a black polka dot bikini, and she was all pale, pale skin and soft, soft curves. Her bathing suit was almost more modest than the tiny shorts she'd been wearing the past couple days, but I was a sucker for that dip in a woman's waist, and Dalia's dip was exceptional.

The ocean lapping at my feet pulled me away from my slow perusal, and I hissed. "Fuck, that's colder than I expected."

Dalia smiled over her shoulder. "Now, imagine being thrown into it."

David chuckled from his spot in the wet sand. "You loved it."

"I kinda did." She headed back to the beach, a silly grin tugging up the corners of her mouth. "It would have been nice to apply the rest of my sunscreen first. I'm going to burn in about thirty seconds if I'm not doused in SPF 50."

David held up his sodden shirt. "Think you got your revenge, babydoll."

She kicked water at him. "You most definitely started it."

"Are we swimming or what?" Jasper asked.

Dalia wrinkled her nose. "Not much of an ocean swimmer.

But I do need a picture to send to my sister and parents. Hold that thought while I get my phone."

All three of us watched her walked back to where she'd left her clothes. There was no possible way the other two assholes next to me weren't just as mesmerized by the jiggle of Dalia's ass as she walked through sand. Then she bent over, and I groaned involuntarily.

"This is ridiculous," I said.

Jasper laughed. "What? That you've got a woman who's your physical ideal pretty much in your face twenty-four-seven for the next two months?"

"It's ridiculous that she looks like that, but she's got the personality of Satan and I don't trust her. She ended up on this tour by being an asshole," I said.

David whipped my shins with his wet shirt. "Think it was you who was the asshole, Nicky."

"But I'm always an asshole. This is the first time it's resulted in a little intruder," I said.

"Meh. I like 'er. She's entertaining." David hopped up. "Now, I'm at the ocean, I'm going swimming. You guys in for a race?"

Jasper started running through the waves before David even finished his sentence.

"You fucker!" David howled. "I hope you get eaten by a shark! And not a great white. A tiny shark that takes it's time consuming your body!"

He took off after Jasper, and I laughed at the two of them more than I had in a long time. We'd had a rough couple months, and laughter was still at a premium. But seeing the two of them just fucking enjoying life, trying to drown each other in the Pacific, brought me back to when we first started out. When we were a bunch of kids who'd never been anywhere and actually appreciated the places we went and the sheer beauty of the world. I hadn't even realized I'd gotten jaded until I was so jaded, I didn't care.

"You're not swimming?"

Dalia had come to stand next to me while I watched Jas and David. She'd pulled a baseball cap over her head and had on sunglasses so big, her lips and pointy little chin were almost the only parts of her face still visible. And when the wind blew just right, I caught a whiff of her scent. It was sunscreen, oranges, and sweetness.

"Not a big swimmer," I replied.

"Me neither. I never had lessons. I mean, I can doggy paddle with the best of them, but the ocean is pretty intimidating with my subpar skills. I would definitely be the one to be caught in a riptide and pulled to my watery grave the first time in the Pacific."

She handed me her phone. "Take a picture of me?"

"You don't want to do a selfie like every single other chick?"

"Oh, believe me, selfies will happen. But if I sent one to my parents, they'd say 'Dalia Brenner, we want to see the scenery, not just your ugly mug.' So make sure you get a lot of the ocean in the background. In fact, make it mostly ocean, just a little bit of me."

She whipped her hat off and threw it on the ground next to me, then walked into the water up to her knees. When she turned around, my tongue tried to loll out of my mouth like a thirsty dog. Dalia was a modern-day pin up. A tatted up, exquisitely titted wet dream.

This was one of those times when I saw how jaded I'd become. The boredom that had set in with it all—the women, the excess, the whole lifestyle I'd had for over a decade. It took someone like her—so brightly colored, she was flaming, and curves so exaggerated, they were almost unreal, for me to sit up and take notice.

"Take my picture, Nicky! I'm pruning out here."

Shaking myself out of the hypnotic state her tits had put me in, I held up her phone. "Smile for the birdie."

She put her hands on her hips and cocked one out, looking adorable as fuck. I snapped a couple pictures, then held her phone up. "That's it! That's the winner. Photoshoot complete."

I set her phone down in her hat and made my way back to the umbrellas, parking myself in one of the lounge chairs with a cold beer from the cooler. Jas and David were still swimming around in the waves, and Dalia had retrieved her hat and phone. She lifted it up, and I assumed snapped a picture of me, before turning back to the ocean.

Seeing my boys happy unleashed some of the dread that had made a home in my gut lately. Even last night's show, which went as smooth as ever, didn't help ease it. But this, today, experiencing the simple shit we'd been taking for granted for way too long, was the calmest I'd felt in a while. It felt like maybe everything would be okay. We'd never get back what we had, but we'd survive.

I couldn't silence the voice in the back of my head that reminded me the only reason we were even here was the stupidly pretty redhead I couldn't wait to be rid of.

NINE

DALIA

AFTER SAN DIEGO and frolicking on the beach, downtime became a distant memory. A memory I'd hold dear forever and ever, but still a memory.

We toured the length of California, our merry band of misfits setting up camp in fairgrounds and stadiums. I spent the majority of my time dealing with merch—sometimes manning the counter, but also folding, labeling, sorting, and keeping track of inventory. Tali also had me out hanging posters every morning and working the lines, even though the band truly didn't need help drawing crowds.

The days blended together. Weekends lost all meaning. When we weren't parked, setting up, and prepping for that day's stop, we were breaking it all down, packing up, and back on the road, heading to the next city.

We had a long bus ride to Oregon, and the guys were up front, watching a movie, while Tali and I occupied the back of the bus, both of us on our laptops. Despite having been on tour for over a week, she was still a mystery to me, beyond the fact that she ran a tight ship and the band worshipped the ground she walked on...or, at least, they did everything she said. And I'd found I kind of did too.

I'd gathered that she'd been around the block many, *many* times in the music business and had worked with bands whose music I *was* familiar with. And she knew everyone on this tour. We'd walked to lunch together one day, and every other person we passed either nodded at her or stopped to speak with her for a few minutes. When we finally got to catering, the line was a mile long and I had to get back to the merch tent. After that, I'd avoided her at meal times so I didn't end up dying from starvation.

Somehow, in the next couple days, I had to finish up the website I was developing for the indie bookstore. I hadn't had a lot of time to work on it, unsurprisingly.

David popped his head into our makeshift office. "Whatcha doin'?"

"Working," I said, only glancing up for a second.

"Get outta here, troublemaker," Tali added.

Because he was David, he plopped down between us, peering over my shoulder to look at my screen. "What's that?"

"What do you think it is?"

"Are you typing in Klingon?"

I smiled at my screen full of code. "No. It's JavaScript. Tells the computer what to do." I clicked on my tabs, opening a different one. "This might be easier to understand. This is the new logo I designed for this little bookstore in Baltimore."

"Cute. Be More Books. That's in Fell's Point, right?"

"Yep. It's the sweetest little store. Normally, I don't have the funds to buy paperbacks, but when I do, I always find something to buy there."

He nodded, his interest shifting to Tali. "And what's up with you?"

She never stopped typing as she spoke. "Answering non-stop emails for you people. Could you guys work on being less in-demand, please? I could use a break."

I nudged her leg with my toes. "If you need help, let me know."

Her hands paused for a moment, and she smiled. "You're the best. Did you know Dalia's the best, David?"

"Clearly, I knew this. The rest of 'em? Eh. What do they know?"

I nudged his leg too...only I nudged it much harder. One might have even referred to it as a kick. "Hey! I happen to know Jasper likes me just fine. And Ian is...indifferently fond of me."

He gave me a sardonic grin. "No mention of the other guy?"

Pressing my lips together, I shook my head. Nick had been decent to me so far, mostly by barely acknowledging my presence. We seemed to wake up at the same time in the morning, a couple hours before everyone else, so we often shared the front lounge. But he usually slipped in his earbuds and drank his tea quietly while I texted with Melly or my parents. Or, if we were already parked at the venue, I'd head out to hang up posters or grab a bite to eat. There was no early morning bonding. No striking up a friendship at dawn.

At least he hadn't called me the c-word again. Which, I had to admit, was a pretty low bar.

"How was your summer with Nick Fletcher?"

"Oh, really good! He only called me a cunt once."

"Not too sure about the other guy," I replied.

David slid a finger inside one of my ringlets. "I think he likes you. Who wouldn't like a girl who looks like Annie gone bad?"

I gave him the stink eye. "If good looks were all it took to like someone, then I'm madly in love with Nick Fletcher. And you, and Ian, and Jas. Tali too, for that matter."

He gave my hair a good tug. "No fucking doubt. Anyway, there was a purpose behind my visit."

"Besides being annoying?" Tali quipped.

"Yep. Annoying you was just a bonus. I came to get new girl for the talent show."

"Shut the fuck up, David. There's no talent show," she said.

"Yep. Everyone has a talent. I'm convinced new girl has many."

I saved what I'd been working on and closed my laptop. I needed to stretch my legs and my brain was just about fried for the moment. Plus, a talent show sounded intriguing.

"Will I be the only one performing?" I asked.

He tapped my nose. "You'll just have to wait and see. And does this mean you've got a talent to show?"

I tapped *his* nose. "You'll just have to wait and see."

"You don't have to do this," Tali said.

I stretched my arms over my head. "It's cool. I needed a break anyway."

I followed David out to the front lounge to find three men sprawled on the couches watching *Black Panther*. None of them looked like they were waiting for me to join them for a talent show.

"All right, young men. Dalia has asked if she can show us her talent," David announced.

Slowly, three heads turned our way, and I slugged David's bicep. "You're such a liar!"

"So, you're saying you're without talent? Cool, cool." David plopped down next to Ian, who'd already turned his attention back to the movie.

"I'm saying you lured me here under false pretenses."

"Come on, Dalia. You show us your talent, I'll show you mine," Jasper teased.

I stood there, looking at the three men who were looking at me, debating whether I was bored enough to be their entertainment. When I thought about all the work waiting for me on my computer, my decision was made.

"I need balls," I said.

David's hand shot up. "I volunteer as tribute!"

"Fine. But they need to not be attached to anything."

He covered his crotch with both hands. "You evil queen."

I opened the cabinets in the kitchenette, then remembered I'd bought navel oranges at my trip to the grocery store the other day. Opening the fridge, I was pleased to find there were still four left, so I grabbed them all.

Holding two oranges in each hand, I raised my brows. "Ready for something so spectacular, you might not believe your eyes?"

Nick's eyes were fastened to my chest, like he was willing the new Unrequited T-shirt Mo had given me in thanks for hanging up some of their posters to burst into flames from the heat of his glare. *Guess he's not a fan.*

"Let's see it," he challenged.

I took a deep breath, and then I...juggled. I was a boss juggler. My dad had gone through many careers in my lifetime. His stint as a party clown was the longest he'd stuck to, and he'd passed his skills onto me. Melly never caught on, but I was his protege. I had some fancy moves too. I went for a full minute or two, tossing, spinning, going under my legs, passing the oranges back and forth between my hands, pulling out all the stops.

I tried to ignore their reactions so I could concentrate, but it didn't get past me that even Ian had paused the movie to watch me.

"Fuck yeah!" David yelled.

"Go, Dalia!" cheered Jasper.

Finally, when I was breathless, I caught the oranges and took a bow. "Thank you, you've been a great audience! Goodnight!" Waving, I disappeared behind the sliding door leading to the sleep area.

Then I came back out and took another bow.

David shook his head. "Didn't know you had it in you, kid."

I wiggled my fingers. "So many hidden talents."

Nick scoffed under his breath. "Useful life skill."

That rankled. It shouldn't have, but it did. It felt like a direct insult to my dad. Of course, Nick didn't know that. He was just making fun of me. And I gave two shits about what he thought of me. But my family? I turned into Lady Hulk when anyone messed with them.

"What can you do besides sing songs no one's listened to in five years?" I challenged.

A chorus of "ooooooohs" sounded, but Nick remained completely unaffected. His feathers were so smooth, and all I wanted to do was ruffle the hell out of them. He just sat there, his long legs stretched out in front of him, crossed at the ankle, his hands clasped on his stomach, staring at me, the corners of his mouth quirking up.

He said nothing. I wanted to punch his smug face.

Jasper hopped up. "My turn."

I squeezed in between Ian and David instead of taking Jasper's spot next to Nick. Petty? Yes. Optimal position for shooting daggers at him? Indeed.

"Everyone lift your feet. Give me some room," Jasper ordered.

When the aisle was clear, he unwound a leather cord from his wrist and used it to tie his long dreadlocks away from his face. Then he lifted his arms, and before I could blink, he was in a handstand, walking down the aisle. When he reached the end, with the grace of a cat, he was back on his feet again.

I was surprised to see Nick actually clapping for him.

"I think I can do that!" I looked around to see who'd said that even though I knew it was me. I hadn't done a handstand since high school. And I'd never done one in a moving vehicle. Why I spoke up would probably forever remain a mystery.

David pushed my shoulder. "Well, come on, babydoll. Let's see it!"

I tucked the front of my T-shirt into my shorts so my tits didn't fall out while I was upside down—if I managed to get upside down, that was—and got into position.

"No laughing if I fall on my face," I said.

"I promise nothing," David said.

It started off okay. I had no trouble getting into handstand position. I even managed to take a few steps on my hands. But then the bus swerved. I thought I was a goner at that point, but somehow managed to get back on my feet. Then the bus swerved again, combined with a bump, and I went flying—right on top of Nick.

He caught me, luckily, so my landing was pretty soft. His hands circled my waist, probably from instinct rather than kindness, and the force of my fall pressed my back to his chest and my head next to his.

It was instant intimacy, and I paused there, with my cheek against his, regaining my equilibrium mostly, but also liking the feel of him more than I thought possible.

His hands squeezed my waist, his mouth sending warm breaths through my ear and down my spine. "Dalia..."

"Hmmm?"

"You really are a ridiculous person, aren't you?"

I shot off him like I'd been zapped with a thousand volts. I didn't look at him, though. There was no part of me that needed to see his beautiful, wicked face.

"Oh shit. You okay, babydoll?" David asked.

I brushed my hands over my legs. "Yep, I'm none the worse for wear. But I think my portion of the show's over."

He grabbed the hem of my T-shirt as I tried to sneak back to the back of the bus. "Stay. Let's make Ian doing something stupid. If you leave, it'll be boring again."

"Why don't *you* do something stupid?" I countered.

He rubbed his hands together. "Why doesn't Nick show us his talent?"

"I'll pass," Nick said.

Jas batted his eyes at him. "Please, Nicky. For me?"

"Fuck it. Give me a song."

"'Glycerine,'" Jas said.

Nick rolled his eyes. "Really? I thought this was supposed to be a challenge."

"No stalling," Jas said.

I had no idea what was going on, but suddenly, Nick started the chorus of a nineties Bush song. I hated him, I really did, but he had the voice of a rock god. There just wasn't any point in denying it.

"'Mr. Brightside,'" Ian said.

Nick belted out the chorus of a The Killers song, then David called out a One Republic song, and they went round and round, Nick never faltering. He knew every chorus to every song they threw at him.

"'Skinny Love,'" I said.

He arched a brow at me, and then sang one of my favorite Bon Iver songs. I had to hold back a moan when his raspy gravel took on the lyrics I'd sung along to countless times. And his eyes never left mine. He could see how he affected me, and he ate it right up. But I couldn't help myself. Those eyes, that voice— even the smirk drove me crazy.

I didn't like it.

And yet, I loved it.

He made me simultaneously want to punch him and curl right back up in his lap. I laughed to myself as he moved onto the next song, because that feeling could summarize the whole of my relationship with Nick Fletcher. A push and pull, a punch and a snuggle.

TEN

DALIA

THE NEXT FEW days were a blur of exhaustion and avoidance. I worked twelve-hour days, and anytime I was on the bus, I stayed away from Nick. The memory of his voice in my ear, telling me he thought I was a ridiculous person, was still too sharp. And when I had a moment to myself, the memory of him singing my favorite song was still too sweet.

We were in Las Vegas, and a lot of people were hitting the casinos once they'd played their sets, but I didn't have a whole lot of interest. I didn't really have the funds to gamble, and the idea of paying twenty bucks for a drink made me gag, especially when there was an endless supply of booze around the buses. I wouldn't have minded seeing the casinos, but when Malka grabbed me to tell me there was talk of s'mores, my decision was made.

The boys were getting ready for their set on our bus, so Malka let me use hers to get cleaned up. Once I'd showered the day's coating of sweat and dirt off me—I was thanking my lucky stars for Ian's warning about the shoe sitch, because by the end of each day, the ground was coated in pure filth—I threw on a long, baggy T-shirt and boxers, basically my PJs, and headed off to find the s'mores crowd.

Twenty or thirty people had congregated by Unrequited's bus, some standing by a small fire pit someone had scrounged up, some in folding chairs, already munching on s'mores. Malka was easy to find with her pink hair and boisterous laugh. I set my chair up next to hers and sat down beside her.

"Hey, girl!" She held out a joint between her fingers. "Want?"

"Want." I took a long, slow drag, filling my mouth, then lungs, with smoke. It was probably psychological, but I felt relaxed and happy by the time I exhaled again. I wasn't a big pot smoker, but I was in Vegas with a bunch of rock stars. It would be wrong if I *didn't* partake.

Malka laughed at my limp neck once I'd passed the J back to her. "Long first week, eh?"

I let my head fall back and stared up at the desert stars. "Not long. It breezed by, to be honest. It's just exhausting being out in the heat all day, then sleeping in a moving coffin at night, you know?"

"*Ja*, of course. You have to love the music more than having a normal life to do this long-term."

"And you love the music?"

She smiled at me. "It's my life. Even when I'm old and gray, I'm going to need to be up on a stage, singing about my dentures or some shit." She tipped her head back too. "It's so pretty up there, isn't it?"

"Mmhmm. No one ever told me the stars looked different out here."

"This is nothing. Wait until the bus is driving through the real desert with nothing around for miles. You've never seen so many stars. It makes you feel so small."

I shivered. "I hate thinking about how small we truly are.

We're just a blip. Our lives mean nothing in the grand scheme of things."

"Oh, girl. Don't tell me you're one of those people who gets all philosophical when they're high. I might have to move my chair," she said.

I started giggling. It started small, just a little bubble, but then it grew until my shoulders were shaking and my eyes blurred with tears.

"You're going to move your chair!" I said through laughter. I wasn't sure if Malka even understood me, but she started laughing too.

I realized I was high as hell, but that didn't stop the giggles. I only paused when Mo squatted down in front of us with two s'mores in his hands.

"Will you be able to stop laughing long enough to accept my s'more?" he deadpanned.

I pointed to my mouth. "Put it in, Mo."

Malka snorted, and a fresh wave of laughter overtook us.

"I guess that answers my question." He smiled and shook his head.

Eventually, we accepted our s'mores, and Mo pulled up a chair next to me. Since we met at breakfast that second day, we'd ran into each other at every stop, sometimes sharing a meal, other times just sharing a wave, but he *had* emailed me with a link to his band's website. Their shitty website.

We were laughing about something silly and probably not at all funny when the Blue boys walked by on the way to play their set.

I wolf whistled at them, and may have catcalled. I'd never tell. But if I did, it would have been something about how good their asses looked in their skinny jeans. Whatever I said, it got their attention, and all four came sauntering over.

Ian stared at Malka intensely without saying a word. He

just kind of...hovered in the background, and she acted completely oblivious to him.

"Havin' fun, babydoll?" David asked.

I held up my half-eaten s'more and half-full beer. "You guys don't know what you're missing. Why don't you play hooky and roast yourself some marshmallows?"

Jasper chuckled. "We kind of have a thing we have to do..."

"Tsk tsk. So responsible," I said.

"Are you going to come watch us play?" he asked.

"Not tonight."

"Ever?" Nick asked from the edge of the group.

I shrugged and tipped my head back. "Maybe one of these days. Right now, this chair and these stars are calling my name. Do you guys ever look up? There are stars *everywhere!*"

David laughed. "I'll try to remember that, babydoll. See you on the flipside."

Sitting up straight again, I waved at them. "Bye, boys. I hope you get lots of panties thrown at you tonight!"

Mo, Malka, and I watched them go. I had to admit, the four of them together were a sight to behold. Each of them full of swagger and so damn sexy in their own way. Of course, my eyes might have lingered a little too long on a certain lead singer. And I couldn't help it if I flashed back to our day at the beach. His golden skin and lickable abs and gorgeous tats.

And his feet, half buried in the sand...ungh.

I'd taken a picture of him that could have been a permanent rotation in my spank bank if I didn't know how uptight and annoying he was. Oh yeah, and if he hadn't called me the c-word. It was pretty hard to bounce back from that.

"*How* did you start touring with them, again?" Mo asked.

Malka giggled next to me. She knew the whole, sad tale from social media and I'd filled in whatever blanks she had over breakfast one day. So, I told Mo the story too. Of course, he knew Jas had passed out, since he'd opened that night, but he hadn't heard about everything that followed.

He shook his head. "I can't believe that guy. I've been a fan of their music since middle school, but I always kinda figured Nick Fletcher was an asshole."

Something inside me bristled at that. Like maybe I was already a little protective over *my* boys. Even Nick. And sure, I could call him an asshole, because he was a lot of the time, but I didn't really care to hear someone else say it.

"No, he's just protective of his band. I sort of get it now," I said.

"I need another s'more," Malka said. "But I can't get up right now. The stars are weighing me down."

I snorted. "You know, I was wondering what was going on with my shoulders. They're so heavy! But I didn't want to say anything because I didn't want you to think I was weird."

She stroked my cheek with her chocolatey fingers. "No, *mauschen*. I truly believe it's the stars. They're heavy tonight."

Mo slapped his thighs and hopped up. "I'll go get them. Two?"

Malka and I looked at each other and giggled. "Two each," I said.

When he headed toward the fire pit, Malka grabbed my hand. "I think someone has a crush."

"Me? No. I'm just doing my thang."

She threw my hand back in my lap. "No, dipshit. Mo! I think he has a thing for you."

I glanced over at him, and he caught me, giving me a dimpled grin. God, he was just so...sincere for a rock star.

"He's cute, but meh. Doesn't make my heart go pitter patter," I said.

"Who cares about your heart? The Swerve tour is not for getting your heart involved."

I lifted a brow. "Oh really? Then what about the drummer boy you have following you everywhere? Is your heart not involved with Ian?"

She sighed and fluffed her pink hair. "Ian is...well, he lets me be the star. I love being the star, Dalia. The thing with Ian isn't love. Maybe it could have been when we started a couple years ago, but now, whatever we have is such a bastardized version of a relationship, it's barely recognizable."

"Well, I once dated a guy I barely liked for an entire year because he was an awesome tattoo artist and I couldn't really leave when the shading on my sleeves wasn't finished. And he kept giving me ideas for more tattoos to get me to stick around longer." I lifted my shirt, showing her the outline of a rose on my ribs. "I couldn't take it anymore, though, and now I have a tattoo I can't afford to finish."

She let out a howling laugh. "Oh, girl. We're both messes, aren't we?"

"I don't know. I've got it going on in some areas of my life. Men and relationships just aren't one of them. I've got time, though, and right now, I'm not looking."

"Mmhmm. Like I said, no hearts on tour. But there's so very much dick. You could trip and fall on one. I've done that a time or two over the years."

I laughed. "That sounds dangerous for everyone involved."

She flicked her wrist lazily. "Or fun."

Mo eventually came back with the s'mores, and then a few people got out their guitars, and someone else screamed out, "'Freebird!'" And that was all it took for the singing to start. No one wanted to sing anything they could hear on tour. By unspoken agreement, the group only picked songs from decades ago—songs so woven into the human consciousness, it didn't matter that none of us were alive when they were popular. It was like we were raccoons, only instead of being born with the knowledge of how to dismantle the lid of a trash can to get to the good stuff, we'd been born with the lyrics and music of classic American rock emblazoned on our souls.

We were in the middle of an epic rendition of "American Pie" when someone sat in the chair Malka had vacated sometime between "Hotel California" and "Tiny Dancer." When I heard that familiar, gravelly voice join in the chorus, I froze.

Scratch that. I didn't freeze, but I stopped singing. I turned toward the voice, and almost moaned. Nick, all freshly showered and wet-haired, was watching me as he sang about drinking whiskey and rye.

"This song is *so* long," I whispered.

He reached out and rubbed his thumb over my cheek. "You had chocolate on your face."

I slapped my hand where his had just been. "I ate a lot of s'mores tonight. Things were bound to get messy."

"As long as you didn't get into my stash. One piece is all you get."

I checked my non-existent watch. "You're done with your show already?"

He chuckled. "Yes, Dalia. You've been sitting here for a couple hours. Well...I assume you've been sitting here."

I puffed a curl off my forehead. "I definitely haven't moved. Malka ditched me at some point, and Mo's over there with his band, so I've just been hanging, looking at the stars and singing along."

"That sounds like a pretty damn decent night."

I thought about it for a beat. "Yeah, it was. One of the best nights I've had in a while, actually. Makes me homesick."

"A good night makes you homesick?"

"Mmhmm. It does. If my sister were here, it would be perfect." I pulled my leg under me so I could turn in my chair to face him. "She likes your music. Actually, she *loves* your music."

He shook his head, giving me a bemused look. "Most people wouldn't tell me they don't like my music."

"There's a slim chance it could grow on me."

He reached out and touched my cheek again. "More chocolate."

I was still just a little bit high, but not so high I could use it as an excuse for leaning against his hand. It was only for a split second, then I regained my wits. But in that split second, ten thousand possibilities ran through my head. Like how his hands might have felt elsewhere. That I'd never hate fucked anyone before. Also, I didn't hate him as much as I had yesterday.

"I'm surprised you didn't eat it," I said.

He looked down at his thumb, then lifted it to his mouth, and sucked it between his lips. "Fucking delicious."

"Got a thing for chocolate, huh?"

"Yep." He slouched down in his chair, tapping in time to "Sweet Home Alabama" on his flat stomach with his fingertips. The sing-a-long had gotten smaller, but no less enthusiastic. Mo had even broken out the harmonica. "I usually go directly back to the bus on these tours."

"How many Swerve tours have you been on?"

He closed his eyes, still tapping. "I don't know, five or six maybe. Our first one was when we were just starting out. We didn't have a bus yet, so we slept on a lot of locker room floors at stadiums. If we got lucky, we'd have a friend in another band who'd let us crash on their bus. And then we had this rickety-ass minivan we drove from city to city." Chuckling to himself, he shook his head. "But it was the time of our lives. We did shit like this every night. Back then, the music was important, but the whole experience was just as important."

This was the most I'd heard him talk at once. And he wasn't angry or messing with me. He was being real, and I lapped it up.

"Why'd you stop wanting the experience?" I asked.

His eyes opened, and the corners of his mouth quirked up. "The experience changes when it's your name up there in big, bold letters and most of the other bands are listed in fine print. It's dark enough that no one's really noticed me sitting here. If they did...well, they'd either pretend they were too cool to acknowledge me or ask me a million music questions. Either way, I can't just sit here and sing to seventies classic rock."

I blinked at him, even though I could barely make him out in the moonlight. "That sounded incredibly egotistical."

"Yeah, maybe. But I can back it up with a dozen examples of it happening. And listen, I get it. If I were to run into Dave Grohl or something, I'd lose my shit."

I snorted. "Wow, your ego knows no bounds."

He gaped for a second. "What? No, I wasn't saying we're on the level of Foo Fighters."

"Really? 'Cause that's what it sounded like!"

The truth was, I was being obstinate, arguing for the sake of arguing, because they *were* on the same plane as a band like Foo Fighters. I just didn't want to admit it.

He threw his hands up. "I wasn't, but whatever. I'm pretty sure I can't win with you, anyway." He stood, stuffing his hands in the pockets of his jeans. "Want me to walk you back to the bus?"

"No, I'm good here."

He looked around at the rows and rows of buses, then back to me. "It's not really safe for you to walk alone. People are drunk and out of their minds."

I waved him off. "I'll get Mo to walk me back. It's cool."

He hesitated, like he really wasn't sure he should actually leave. I pushed his thigh with my bare foot. "Go! You did your duty! I'm good. I just need to sing a little Tom Petty before I crash."

I was tired, and I really should have gone back with him, but

I wasn't finished being stubborn. He knew it, I knew it, but that didn't stop me from keeping my ass firmly planted in my chair.

Finally, Nick turned on his heel, but instead of heading toward the bus, he went straight to where Mo stood, close to the fire. He paused, saying something to Mo, his head jerking in my direction, then he stared him down for a beat before he set off into the night.

I watched him go dreamily. Despite the size of his ego, he really was a gorgeous man. Maybe he could be spank bank material. In my fantasies, he didn't speak, except to tell me how witty and stunningly beautiful I was. He'd probably sing to me too, but only Bon Iver songs.

I closed my eyes, imagining "Holocene" coming from Nick's mouth, all gravelly and slow. Oh yes, that would be quite a thing...

I WAS FLOATING ON A WARM, delicious-smelling cloud. I snuggled into the cloud, feeling its Nick-like shape.

"You're not magnificent," I murmured to the cloud.

A rumble rolled through me from the cloud. Must've been thunder. "You've made that clear, little intruder."

"You're magnificent too," I added.

The cloud lifted me higher and higher, until I was on another cloud. This one wasn't nearly as warm, though. I rolled onto my side and felt a cool breeze on my feet before a blanket of comfort covered me.

"Goodnight," the cloud said.

I snuggled deeper into my new cloud. "Goodnight, old cloud."

ELEVEN

NICK

THE DICKHEAD LEFT her there sleeping.

I knew it would happen. No matter how sincere his emo-boy music sounded, no matter how harmless he looked with his fedoras and dimpled smiles, Mo was still a kid with a fresh-off-the-presses record contract on his first big tour. He wasn't gonna worry about some chick who was way out of his league and he stood no chance with when willing pussy abounded.

I knew because I *was* Mo ten years ago.

Still didn't change how pissed I was when I backtracked an hour after I'd left Dalia there, only to find her curled up in her chair, all alone except for a couple dudes lingering around the dying embers of the fire pit. If they were lingering for nefarious reasons—like making sure no one was around before they...actually, no. If I let the thought form, I'd have to track those fuckers down and have a nice talk with them. Only, I'd be speaking with my fists.

I wasn't a fighter, not really, but men who took advantage of women deserved violence.

Even after I laid her in her bunk, I couldn't sleep, so I went out to the lounge, scrolling aimlessly through my phone. The dread in my gut had become sentient, crawling through my bones and limbs, whispering messages. Shit I didn't want to hear. Shit about my arrogance, my career, the band, and the future of it all.

Riding around on a bus for months was getting old. Hell, *I* was getting old. This lifestyle had probably aged me ten years. It wasn't just dread in my bones. Exhaustion was there too. That weariness. The band, my boys...they'd been my whole life for a long ass time. Same for them. Ian was always attempting some kind of relationship, and he'd been stuck on Malka for far too long, but he'd never been able to make a real go of it with anyone. And David and Jasper? Nothing had ever stuck for them either. Same as me. I'd tried once, but there was too much jealousy on both ends to make it work. Plus, I barely saw my girlfriend when I had one, so it was hard to see the point of even trying.

And I didn't know if I'd ever want a wife and kids and a picket fence, but maybe I wanted a dog. *Yeah.* I *did* want a dog. Why the hell shouldn't I have a dog? That was like the bare minimum of requests.

Yet, from here, on a tour bus in Nevada, having a dog seemed a long way off. We had the rest of the Swerve tour to get through, then two months in Europe, and then we had to get crackin' on a new album.

I dreaded all of it.

But, as a band, we'd built our own tracks, and now there was no telling how to get off them. We'd been around long enough that we should have been able to slow down and enjoy some of the fruits of our labor, yet we hadn't.

We'd taken a couple months off touring when Jasper's mom, Reinece, got sick earlier in the year, but even then, I'd been writing and composing and recorded a duet with a pop star who was now playing non-stop on the radio.

I didn't know how to slack off. My entire adult life had been hard charging, working toward a goal, and then, once I got it, the goal post was moved farther down the field, and I had to keep running and running.

Something had to give.

The door to the bus opened, and David staggered in, looking about as rough as he normally did after a night out in Vegas.

He laughed when he saw me there. "What're you doing up, man? I thought you'd have passed out a long time ago." He dropped on the couch across from me, laying flat on his back.

"Brain won't stop churning," I said.

"Ah, one of those nights."

"How was *your* night?"

"How is any night in Vegas?" he asked. "Lost some bones at the poker table. Met a couple lady friends. Fucked said lady friends. And now I'm back."

"Did you drink?" I asked carefully.

"Nah. Didn't even want to."

David had been completely clean for a few years, except for the occasional joint, but that barely counted. I wasn't sure he'd be labeled an alcoholic, but he'd been a messy drunk. Just night after night of blackout drinking, getting belligerent with strangers, with his chicks, and with the band. Ian, Jas, and I had just shrugged it off in the beginning. *That's just David being David.* But it wasn't David. Our friend was disappearing inside this major league asshole every night, and eventually, we just didn't want to be around him after shows. Only...I'd worried about him, so I'd stuck around, watching him self-destruct.

I didn't know if there was any one thing that made him quit drinking. He'd just...stopped. One day, he was shitfaced. The next, he was turning in at ten p.m. after having a cup of tea with me. The tea didn't stick, but the teetotaling did.

I still worried, though. On nights like tonight, when he was surrounded by all the debauchery Vegas had to offer, I wondered if he'd finally partake. And then we'd be back on the endless cycle of hungover days and blackout nights. But now, we were a lot older, and maybe it wouldn't be so *cute* when he trashed a hotel room or called a doorman at a club a dirty whore and got his lights knocked the fuck out.

I never said a word to David about it. Not back then, and not now. He probably knew, with the way I mother-henned him. He wasn't the kind to let things slide, not if it was something he could pick at. So his lack of chiding at the way I checked in with him led me to believe he needed it just as much as I did.

"Good on you, man. While you were out getting fucked, I sang by a campfire."

He snorted. "What the fuck, man?"

As I was telling him about my night, Ian wandered in. He always looked just a little shell-shocked after he'd been with Malka. Some part of me wondered if she was a vampire, with the way she left him glassy-eyed and stumbling. Or maybe David was right, and she really did have a magic pussy.

"S'up?" Ian asked. He lifted David's feet and flopped down on the couch next to him. David just used Ian as a footrest, laying his feet on his lap.

"David had a three-way and I did some wholesome shit," I said.

Ian gave me a lazy smile. "Same ol', same ol'."

"Pretty much. You chasin' Malka?"

Ian nodded. "I live for the times I catch her."

"That's sad, man. She's cool, but not that cool," David said.

Ian ran a hand over his hair. "I know it's fucked up. But I'm never gonna do the thing you want me to. If I'm around her, I get sucked into her gravitational pull."

"I bet that's not all she's sucking," David said. He didn't bother muttering under his breath. David wasn't a mutterer.

"That too," Ian admitted.

The three of us sat there shooting the shit until the sun started to rise. We hadn't done that in years. Jas was sleeping—Malka had given him some herbal shit to help with his sleep cycles—so he missed it, but mostly, it felt like old times. These three men were my brothers. We were mostly the same age, but a big part of me felt responsible for them. *I'd* started the band. I'd pushed us to go harder and grow bigger. I wrote most of the music and set the tone. And so, if one of them got sucked into a black hole of toxic pussy, or had a sick mama, or let the bottle take over their life, I was gonna be there, holding their fucking hands, whether they wanted me to or not.

I kept my thoughts about slowing down to myself. The dog was a pipe dream. I didn't know the first thing about having a pet, and maybe a guy like me wasn't cut out for that life. Maybe this was it, my boys, my music, and my guitar.

When I slid into my bed, exhaustion overtaking the dread, I caught just a glimpse of a sleeping Dalia, and the possibility of there being more than this for me slipped into my conscious-ness. But like any whim, it was gone just as soon as it had appeared.

THE TOUR HIT Salt Lake City, then we spent the next day driving to Denver. Most of the time we drove overnight, but sometimes, the schedule didn't allow it. Long days on the bus sucked ass. There were only so many movies I could watch and naps I could take.

Finally, we stopped for lunch at a Panera, and Dalia went around taking orders from everyone.

"What'll it be?" she asked.

"I'm coming in with you. Gotta look at the menu."

She held out her phone. "Here's the menu, Mr. Rock Star. Don't want to send the little town into a tizzy when they spot a gen-u-wine famous person."

I stood, pushing her phone away. "I'm not that recognizable. I'm not Dave Grohl."

She smirked. "Very true. You're not."

"Oooh, burn," David called after me. I held my middle finger up in response and took my happy ass right off the bus and into Panera, tucked into a strip mall, in the middle of nowhere.

Dalia trailed after me with a mile-long list of orders. "People are staring," she said under her breath as she passed me.

It was true, a couple people were staring, but it was more out of confusion than recognition. I'd traveled enough over my years to know what kind of music people listened to based on their location. There were always outliers, sure, but this was a country music town if I'd ever seen one. And since I wasn't Garth Brooks—fuck, did people still listen to Garth Brooks?—I wasn't too worried about being mobbed.

I stood right behind her, feeling her heat, and smelling every last bit of her sweetness, and said low enough only she could hear, "I think they're staring at you. You've got all that pretty ink on display and wild, curly red hair. You're like an exotic bird that got lost in the 'burbs."

She acted like she didn't hear me, but I saw the way her shoulders tightened as she read down the order of food to the cashier. I tossed in my order for a salad at the end. I didn't know why it was so entertaining to try to get her to *react*. Probably the boredom of being cooped up on a bus all day.

People *were* looking at her, though. Guys in Wranglers and cowboy boots. Women in long jean shirts and blouses buttoned up to their throats. And in the middle of it all was Dalia, wearing one of her tank tops and tiny little shorts. She was hard *not* to look at.

When we went to the other end of the counter, she finally looked at me. "I don't really love being called a bird."

"You're not like a pigeon, though. You're...I don't know. A peacock?"

She rolled her eyes. "You know the colorful peacock is the male, right? Hence the name. Pea*cock?* Peahens are pretty plain. So, basically you just said I'm a male bird."

"Damn, I actually didn't know that. Those fuckers are fancy, you have to admit."

There was a pause where she stared at me, and I stared at her, eyebrows raised, waiting, then she laughed. I should've known she'd laugh. She did a lot of it. Not usually about things I said, though. She seemed to find David the most amusing, which was shocking, since most people found him to be an unbearable asshole. Not Dalia, though.

"They are fancy," she giggled. "That's true. But I'm not the least bit fancy, so can I be a penguin? They're goofy as hell, short, and some of them have some crazy hair on top of their head. Plus, I do an amazing penguin walk."

I crossed my arms, frowning. "I don't know. I think I'm going to have to see this penguin walk. Not sure I believe you."

"I feel like this is a trick, but I'm going to do it anyway."

She straightened her arms at her side, then proceeded to waddle in tight circles around me. She even threw a couple squawks in. If people weren't staring before, they were now. Someone even had out their phone, taking a video of the human-sized penguin who'd escaped captivity to frolic around a chain restaurant.

She did one last waddle, fluffed her curls with her fingers, and stared straight ahead at the order pick-up counter.

"Are we pretending that didn't just happen?" I asked.

"I think my performance spoke for itself."

"It did. I bow down to Dalia, the penguin queen."

She turned, looked me directly in the eye, and squawked.

"You're a strange bird," I said.

"A strange penguin."

"Right."

I carried two large paper bags full of food back to the bus, and Dalia passed everyone's orders out. Buddy, our driver, had gotten out to stretch his legs, so it was just the band, Tali, and Dalia, sitting around the front lounge, eating sandwiches and salads.

We'd had a couple weeks of rich food from catering, that while delicious, did nothing for my girlish figure. And fuck me if I wasn't craving a simple salad and a nice piece of salmon.

Growing up, we didn't have a lot of money, and my mom wasn't any kind of cook, so dinners mostly consisted of food prepared in the microwave. It was surprising I'd gotten so tall with my piss poor diet.

But that first Swerve tour, we were freshly signed, hadn't even made a record yet, and were lucky to get fifty people watching us at the piddly little stage the tour promoters put us on. When the four of us walked into the catering tent and saw they were serving steaks, I was convinced we were in the wrong place. Hell, I'd never even had a steak at that point, so I thought they weren't for the likes of me.

Funny how so much can change in a little over a decade. Here I was, snubbing my nose at the food I'd once thought was too good for me. Not that I didn't tear up catering's chicken and waffles any time it was on the menu. I was just more conscious about what I put in my body these days.

"So, I have to head to New York for a week," Tali said. "Think you can survive without me?"

"Before Arizona?" I asked.

Jas tensed, and Ian threw his arm around his shoulders.

Tali's eyebrows pinched. "Unfortunately, yes."

"Jesus, Tal. The timing couldn't be worse. Can't you work something out with the label?" I asked.

"You know I would if it was work. But it's my dad. He's having a stent put in his heart and I just strongly feel like I need to be there. I'm sorry, Jas, guys."

The dread grew ten sizes in my stomach. I pushed my salad away, unable to eat another bite. I worried for Tali, her dad, and Jas. This dread in my gut was bound to turn into an ulcer one of these days.

"I get it, Tali. You know I get it," Jas said.

She sighed, looking relieved, but still anxious. I didn't blame her. I didn't really have a relationship with my dad, but Tali came from a tight knit family. She was always calling to check in on them, or they were calling her. And the heart was not a thing to fuck around with.

"Thank you, Jasper. And look, you have only have one interview in Phoenix. A local station. I've dealt with them before, and they're cool. They won't ask any off the wall questions. You guys know what you're doing, you're pros."

She told us about the shows she'd be missing and what our schedule was going to look like. And then she assured us Dalia would be able to pick up some of the slack, as far as keeping track of where we needed to be and when. The whole time, Dalia remained quiet. She didn't ask *why* we were so jumpy about Arizona, especially Jasper. She just watched, her sandwich frozen midway from the paper plate in her lap and her mouth.

Thank Christ the girl who'd waddled like a penguin in a Panera in the middle of nowhere was also a woman who understood not all situations called for cracking jokes and needed to be treated delicately.

So, we'd be facing Arizona alone. It wasn't that her presence would make it any easier to deal, it was more that she always had everything under control and *not* having her with us in the place that had been the setting for so much chaos in Jasper's life added to the dread we all shared. We hadn't played there in a couple years. The last time, Jasper's dad showed up, high out of his head, asking for money. A lot of money. Tali had dealt with him, shielding Jas from the worst of it.

The last time we'd been there was two months ago. For Jasper's mom's funeral.

Arizona was going to blow for a lot of reasons, but when I looked at my friend, the literal nicest guy on the planet, slumped across from me with dead eyes, I knew there was no possible way we'd get out of there unscathed.

TWELVE

DALIA

I'D SEEN the Rocky Mountains with my own two eyes. I *never* thought I'd be able to say that. Sure, in my fantasies, I'd make it to the west coast one day, but the middle of the country was pretty much a blur. I'd never even let myself dream of those middle states and all the wonders they held.

Tali gave me the day off in Denver, since she was leaving after Blue's show and I wouldn't have much down time until she got back, so after Mo and Malka played their sets, we loaded up in a couple cars—whose they were, I had no idea—and drove out to Red Rocks.

It could only have been a dreamer who came up with the idea to build an amphitheater in the middle of...well, red rocks.

I'd watched the Mumford & Sons concert at Red Rocks on YouTube more times than I could count, but to be standing where it actually happened left me breathless.

"It's probably the elevation," Mo said when I told him about my breathlessness.

I nudged his ribs with my elbow. "Come on! You don't feel the magic in this place?" I broke out my jazz hands, and sang, "We're on the stage where it happens, stage where it happens..."

He chuckled, looking away from me. "Did you just bastardize *Hamilton*?"

I lifted a shoulder innocently. "It was an homage. But tell me the truth, can't you picture Unrequited up there someday?"

"Maybe? One day?" He didn't sound sure at all.

Meanwhile, Malka floated along the cement in front of the stage, holding her hands up.

"This is where I'm meant to be. These rocks are my color. Wouldn't I look beautiful up there?"

I laughed. "You would. And more importantly, your voice would be gorgeous bouncing off the rocks. I'd pay to see that."

She dropped her hands and walked over to where Mo and I stood. "Your name will *always* be on the list, Dalia."

"What about me?" Mo asked.

She waved a dismissive hand at him. "Oh, please. You'll be a rich and famous rock star soon. You can afford to pay for tickets."

The rest of the group wanted to climb to the top of the steps —according to the brochure I'd picked up, there were around three hundred and eighty of them—so we started the trek.

I was in decent shape. Back home, I walked Flamingo as many times as he demanded, which ranged from twice to ten times a day. But the elevation at Red Rocks really was no joke. I was huffing and puffing halfway up the stairs and feeling just a little nauseous.

"Guys, I'm going to sit down for a minute. You can go on without me," I said.

The others barely paused, but Mo stayed behind. Because he was forced to by Malka. Why she didn't stay with me, I had no idea. I thought maybe she was attempting to play cupid.

"Out of breath?" he asked.

I plopped down on the stadium seat and leaned back to give

my lungs room to expand. "What? No, why would you ask that? I always pant. It's my normal state."

He shook his head. "You're funny."

"Am I? Then why aren't you laughing?"

He let his head drop, but I could still see his dimpled smile. "Not funny, ha-ha, funny peculiar. You're unique."

"Everyone's unique." I hated compliments, and I was pretty sure young Mo was attempting to compliment me in a round-about way.

"True. But I just...never know what you're going to say. Or where I stand with you."

I pushed his knee with mine. "That's because *I* never know what I'm going to say. And you're my new friend, Mo. So long as you keep bringing me s'mores, you'll stay in good standing."

He laughed that time, slapping his knee as it rolled through him. "I think I can do that. Actually..."

I raised a brow. "What?"

"I wanted to talk to you about rebuilding our website."

I was pretty surprised he was asking. I'd sent him my own website, which had my prices listed, knowing the band couldn't really afford me since they hadn't even put a record out yet. But a contact was a contact, and even if they couldn't afford me now, maybe they'd think of me down the road. Or, at least, that had been my thought.

"Okay, talk," I said.

He glanced around, looking uncomfortable, and I just knew what was coming. I girded my loins, preparing to turn him down.

"We can't really afford your rates right now..." he started. And then he waited. Waited for me to say *oh, don't worry about it! For you, it's free.* Well...that wasn't going to happen. I knew my worth. I knew what kind of bills I had to pay.

"That sucks," I said simply.

If he was going to ask for a discount, I'd make him work for it.

"The guys really like your work. *I* like it. You've got a lot of talent. So, I was just wondering if there was a friends and family discount. Like a deep discount."

"How deep?"

"Uh…" He pulled at a thread in the ripped knees of his jeans. "We could afford five hundred. In installments. Like ten installments"

I sputtered, assuming he was kidding. Yet he looked completely serious and sincere.

"Mo, I like you, but that's insulting."

I got up, needing to walk, to get away from him, so I started the second half of the climb. And yes, I pretended not to notice the ridiculously in shape people jogging up and down the steps like they were nothing. They'd put me to shame in my normal elevation, never mind when I was six thousand feet up.

Mo caught up to me quickly. "I'm sorry, Dalia. Seriously. I'm just fuckin' broke, and I need this, my career in music, to succeed. I feel like the website and an expanded social media presence would go a long way." He wrapped his hand around my arm, pulling me to a stop. "We could pay you the rest in a few months, once we record our first album. It's a possibility I could get the record company to front us the money to pay you."

Fuck. I'm gonna do it. "Listen, if I agree to this, you're not going to get some big fancy website. It's going to be plain and simple, but pretty. And easy to navigate. And if you're seriously implying you want me to help you build your social media presence…damn, Mo. That's a big ask! That's more of my time—which I charge a hundred dollars an hour for, by the way—and I don't know. I'm already busy on the tour, doing my regular tasks."

He didn't hear anything I said. Apparently, he'd only heard

me agree to the website, because he lifted me right off my feet, giving me a big bear hug. "You're the fuckin' best! You know that? I'm telling all the bands on tour how rad you are. You're gonna get so much work."

He set me down, and I straightened my shirt. "That would be lovely, but let's not mention the discount, okay?"

"Deal."

"Get your lazy asses up here!" I looked up, and Malka was standing at the top of the steps, waving at us frantically.

Finally, we made it to the top. The sky seemed to be a different shade of blue up here, and the sun was definitely brighter. The rocks were beautiful in their ruggedness and the contrast of the orderly stone seats carved out in the middle was both jarring and sort of magical. I stood there for a long time, both catching my breath and taking in the view.

I was adding seeing a show at Red Rocks to my bucket list.

"Has Blue is the Color ever played here?" I asked Malka.

"*Ja*. I'm sure they have multiple times, but I was here with them a few years ago. Well, I was backstage. My ex-husband toured with them and did the sound tech, so I came to a lot of their shows to be with him. At this one, though, I pretended the crowd was here for me. And I got to go on stage during sound check." She gripped my hand. "One day, Dalia."

Malka *was* a very talented musician, but her band, Sadie, was holding her back. I'd been around enough to know talent didn't mean a band would take off. It took the proper connections and luck. A lot of luck.

"Can we just stand here and admire this shit?" I asked.

"Yes. Let's."

I stood shoulder to shoulder with my new pink-haired, tattooed, German, rock princess friend, just absorbing the energy and feelings and utter beauty of nature meets man. Life was really crazy sometimes. Who would have thought I'd be here? My heart ached at seeing all these things without Melly, but I knew in my bones she'd see some amazing things without me.

I've been gone two weeks and I'm already incredibly mature!

"Want to stop and get some edibles on the way back?" Malka asked.

"Oooh! Think they have gummies?"

THE BUS RIDE from Denver to Phoenix was long, but we did a good portion of it overnight, so when I woke up way too early as usual, we were only a couple hundred miles away from our destination.

Once I had my coffee made and a shot of it in my system, I FaceTimed Melly.

"Yo," she answered sleepily.

"Meeeelllllllyyyyy," I said quietly. "Why are you still in bed? Isn't it like nine in the morning?"

She let out a dry laugh. "Think you just answered your own question, sissy. I don't have to be at work until eleven."

Flamingo climbed up Melly's chest and thrust his gorgeous black face onto the screen. I cooed at him and told him what a good boy he was and how much his mommy missed him.

In response, he tried to lick the screen.

"No, Mingo, don't lick my phone!" cried Melly. "This dog is bad to the bone. So spoiled."

"He's the best boy, and I won't hear anything else!"

She sat up and scooped my dog into her arms, and he gave

her a nice, juicy lick on her cheek. "I think he's my dog now," she said.

I gasped. "Don't try it, Mel."

"Fine, we can have joint custody."

"We live together. We already have joint custody."

"Do we live together? Because your ass has been really far away for a long time."

"Miss me?" I teased.

She let out a long sigh. "I do, actually. I didn't realize how much I would when you left. But I do. And I kind of feel like we're at the end of an era."

"Babe, I'm only gone for two months."

"I know, but, Dalia, we can't live together forever. You're almost done with school, and I have one more year. What if you want to move, or if I want to? It's always been inevitable, but I guess it's just hitting me now."

I covered my face. "La-la-la, I can't hear you!"

She giggled. "Fine. Pretend life isn't changing at a rapid pace. Tell me about the rock stars."

I sunk down into my seat. "Is it weird that they don't even seem like rock stars anymore? Most of the time, I feel like I'm living in the middle of a traveling-circus-slash-frat-house."

"Even the guys of Blue?" she asked.

I thought about it. *Did my Blue boys seem like rock stars?* They certainly weren't like the guys I hung out with back home. For one, they were all in their thirties. Full-fledged adults while I still felt like I was clinging tight to the last vestiges of my youth. I was shocked when I walked in on David FaceTiming with his teenage daughter. If I'd been more of a fan of the band, I probably would have known about his kid. Then again, he seemed quite protective of her, barely letting me catch a glimpse of her on the screen.

And Nick...well, the jury was still out on him. Sometimes I

thought he could turn out to be a friend. Other times...well, he just seemed miserable. Like he was constantly on edge. Living on edge was no way to carry on. I was lucky to have had very few edgy moments in my life. If there was an edge, I usually dove head first and smoothed it out. I didn't carry my troubles around like a badge of honor like some people. *Look how miserable I am! I bet you can't possibly be this miserable!*

"The guys of Blue...hmmm. They've been around the block enough to be more subtle in their partying. And they rarely hang out with the younger bands. I'm still figuring them out, I guess."

She bounced giddily on the bed, and Flamingo looking rather put out by her movement. "I still can't believe you're just hanging out with one of my favorite bands. How did you get this life?"

I shook my head, smiling at her happiness. Because despite missing me, and maybe even a little jealousy, I could always count on Melly to be happy for me. Our parents were flaky and overly permissive, but they taught Melly and me how to love openly and with our whole hearts. Neither of us had ever found the right man to lump all the heaps of affection we both contained, but when we did, I just hoped they were prepared to be loved by a Brenner girl. Because when we went in, we went all in.

We talked for a little while longer about all the sights I had seen—she made me swear we'd see a concert at Red Rocks one day—then she put Flamingo in front of the phone again.

I did my crazy baby talk to him, and his little, stumpy tail started wagging enthusiastically. He might've loved Melly, but he knew who his Mama was—the one who bought his food and toys and took him for walks in three feet of snow.

"Dal," Melly whispered.

"What? I'm talking to my Mingo," I said.

"Dal, there's a shirtless Nick Fletcher behind you right now."

I whipped around, and I didn't have to wonder how long he'd been standing there, based on his pinched lips, red face, and shaking shoulders. He'd born witness to my crazy dog lady ways.

I turned back to Melly. "I'm invisible, right? No one can actually see or hear me, *right*?"

I felt him lean down behind me, and then his voice rumbled in my ear. "That your dog?"

"That's Flamingo. Say hi to the mean man, Mingo," I said.

Mingo eyed Nick suspiciously, then turned around completely, showing us his little white bum.

Nick cackled. "Yep. He's your dog."

"Uh, hello. Adorable woman here too," Melly said.

Nick laughed again. "And definitely your sister. Hello, adorable."

Melly died. I saw her spirit float to the ceiling, doing somersaults as it ascended.

"You've made her life," I said to him. "I'm never going to hear the end of this."

"I'm Melly, and I love your music. 'When It's Gone' speaks to my soul."

He bowed his head. "That's amazing, Melly. You don't know how much that means to me."

"Okay!" I waved my free hand around. "I'm putting an end to the lovefest!"

Once I hung up, Nick collapsed on the couch across from me, his eyes doing a slow perusal of me.

"I turned on the kettle," I said.

"Thank you." He kept looking at me, cocking his head, like he was trying to decipher what he was seeing.

"Want me to make your tea?" I asked.

"Nah, I'll do it. So, uh..."

My eyebrows raised. "Yeah?"

He nodded at my arm. "Did you name the dog after your tattoo, or did you get a tattoo for your dog?"

I looked down at my half sleeve—a pink flamingo surrounded in lush green leaves and purple and red tropical flowers.

I grinned. "Wouldn't it be a little weird to name my dog after my tattoo?"

He shrugged. "I've heard weirder."

I traced my fingers over the design. "I had an ex—"

His eyes rolled. "Isn't that the way all these stories start?"

"Which stories?"

"Stories women tell about their tattoos. Always about an ex."

I hopped up from my seat. "If the bus weren't moving, I'd storm off. Why do you have to be such an ass all the time? And if I'm being precise, a misogynistic ass."

He tilted his head back to meet my eyes. "Sit down, Dalia."

I contorted my face. "Why would I do that?"

"Because you can't go anywhere. There aren't any doors to kick or slam. Might as well be comfortable."

"I'm going to sit. But only because I want to."

He shook his head. "Sometimes I forget how young you are. And then—bam!—I remember."

I stared him down from across the narrow aisle. Normally, when the bus was parked, the front part expanded outward, so the couches were separated by several more feet. Right now, though, Nick was uncomfortably close to me. I had a clear view of the amusement flaring in his sea glass eyes. The tightness of his golden abs. The absolutely wonderment of hot, commando dick in grey sweatpants.

He was a gorgeous ass, but still an ass. One I worked for, so any treading was done carefully. I loved this job too much to be sent home packing. The days were endless and sweaty, but I got to dance in the ocean, eat s'mores with rock stars, and commune with nature at Red Rocks. It didn't get a whole lot better than that. I could deal with one asshole guy. I'd dealt with asshole guys since the dawn of time.

"I got Flamingo from my old neighbor," I said. Nick leaned forward, erasing vital inches of space. "And by old, I mean *old*. She'd gotten him, thinking he'd be a lap dog, but he was too much for her to handle. I took him for walks whenever she asked, and played with him, even when she didn't. So finally, she just gave him to me—her crazy neighbor whom she knew was half in love with her dog already. She'd already named him Flamingo, and I thought it really suited him in some weird way, so it stuck."

He steepled his hands under his chin. "And the part about the boyfriend?"

I waved a dismissive hand. "My ex was a tattoo artist. I had wanted a cute little flamingo on my shoulder or hip, but he convinced me to get bigger."

"And do you regret that?"

I held out both of my inked-up arms. "Not a bit. Well, that's not true. I wish I didn't have to think of him whenever I looked at my tattoos. He wasn't the greatest guy, despite his artistic abilities."

"Temperamental artist?" Nick asked knowingly.

I shook my head. "Nope. Just not nice."

"I can't picture you putting up with that."

"You may think I'm young now—which I fully admit to being right smack in the middle of growing and learning as a person—but I was *young* two years ago. I thought 'not nice' was okay if it was followed by an 'I love you.'"

He frowned. "Sucks."

I snorted. "Sucks is right."

"But you got the ink and the dog. You're doing all right."

"What about you?" I asked.

"No dog."

I smiled. "I meant your ink. Any good stories?"

He pressed his hand to the side of his neck where his most visible tattoo resided. It was a pocket watch attached to a chain.

"This was my first."

I leaned closer to get a better look, and he dropped his hand to let me. "Bold choice. No going back from a neck tattoo."

He nodded. "That was kind of the idea. I got it after we signed our first record deal. The hour hand is on an eight and the minute hand is on twenty-two—the date we signed, August twenty second. I told myself I was never working a corporate job. Music was it, and I had no other choice but to make it, because my ass would never get hired to push paper with a fuckin' watch on my neck."

"I don't know. Companies are getting more liberal these days. If this music thing doesn't work out, I bet you could still find an accounting job," I teased.

He shook his head, smiling down at his lap. "You're a little shit, you know that?"

"My dad likes to call me that."

"Are you saying I remind you of your dad?"

I shrugged innocently. "If the shoe fits..."

Nick laughed, then got up to make his tea, and we fell into a surprisingly companionable silence.

"What time is the interview?" he asked as he stirred his tea.

"Oh. I'll have to double check, but I think it's right after we arrive. So nine. Tali's told them they'll have a half-hour total with you guys, so it should be painless."

He blew on his tea, silent for a moment. "Will you stick around?"

"For the interview?"

"Mmhmm."

"Sure, if you need me to. You guys don't go on until eight-thirty tonight, so I don't have to get my work done right away."

He took his spot on the couch across from me and pulled out his ear buds from his pocket, pressing them into his ears and closing his eyes.

Well, okay then. I guess this conversation is over.

I stared out the window, watching the rough, mountainous terrain go by.

Phoenix, here we come.

BY THE TIME we pulled into the stadium parking lot in Phoenix, the air on the bus was thick with tension and the dread in my gut threatened to bubble over. Jasper paced the small lounge, while Ian stared into space, tapping his sticks harder than normal against his thighs, and David had retreated into Tali's office in the back.

The entire time, I watched Dalia while her big brown eyes darted between the rest of them. I waited for her to ask what was going on. To crack a joke, so I could pounce. I wanted an excuse to be angry. I wanted to lose my shit and find some sort of release, even if it wasn't the right one.

But she stayed quiet, unobtrusive. She was watchful and full of concern, but remained an observer of what was playing out in front of her instead of a participant.

There was a knock on the door, then Malka walked onto the bus, a tight smile on her lips. She'd been here with us two months ago. She knew what this day meant to Jas. To all of us.

I thought she'd go to Ian, but she surprised me by hugging Jasper with a fierceness I'd never seen from her. She was fun and games, a good time. I never really considered her loyal, like someone I'd share a secret with. But with the way Jas hugged her back, he disagreed. And the way Ian's sticks slammed down on his thighs, he was just as affected by the display.

They separated, then she came to sit next to Ian, kissing his cheek softly and stilling his tense hands with hers. The woman had half my band wrapped around her. Not just her finger, but her entirety. It was disconcerting.

"I saw the news people setting up outside," Malka said.

Dalia clapped her hands and stood. She'd foregone her normal tiny shorts for a short, floral dress—and those damn combat boots. Maybe she thought she looked more professional since she'd been left in charge. In reality, she looked like every one of my youthful fantasies. The good girl gone bad. The angel and devil all mixed as one.

"I'll head out and go over everything with them once again. I'll come back and get everyone when I'm done." She raised her brows and glanced around the bus. "Good?"

Ian grunted, Jas looked out the window, and I nodded. "I'll find David. Make sure he's actually dressed and not planning on showing his dick to all of Phoenix this morning."

Dalia startled, then let out a short laugh. "I hadn't realized that was a possibility." She mimed writing on her hand. "Note to self: check status of David's pants before TV interviews."

She hurried off the bus, and I turned to Jasper. "You gonna be okay?"

He heaved out a long sigh. "What's okay? I just want to get through today, you know? I can't stand this feeling. Can't stand this state."

"I know, man. There's not a lot of good here for you," I said.

Ian shifted across from me. "Hate this. *Hate* it."

I scrubbed my hands over my face. "If I could figure out a way to get us out of here, I'd do it. I'd fix it."

Jas stuffed his hands in his pockets. "It wouldn't matter.

We'd be in another state, but what's broken can't be fixed. Not this time."

What was broken was Jas's heart, and maybe his spirit. Definitely the spirit of the band. We'd all lost a mother when he'd lost his mom. We were in our thirties, pretty damn worldly, but none of us had known loss like that. We'd been lucky, and we hadn't even acknowledged it. Not too many people can get to thirty-three without losing someone who was a vital part of their soul.

I couldn't say my feelings really mattered, though. Reinece had been his *mom*. She'd been important to me, Ian, and David, but I couldn't comprehend his loss.

Dalia climbed back on the bus, nervously tucking her hair behind her ear. Because it was her hair, it bounced right back out. Even her hair was defiant to the bitter end.

"David, get your fine ass out here," she called. He appeared from the back a moment later, giving her a sly smile.

"S'up?"

"I'm glad to see you're wearing pants. There were rumors you might not be," she said.

He raised one devious eyebrow. "There's still a chance..."

"I'm positive there are many people who'd like to see your junk, but the FCC and I aren't on the list." She addressed the rest of us. "So, turns out the reporter you guys have interviewed with in the past just had a baby, so they sent someone else. Her name is Maria Valez, and she seems to know the drill, but she put out a weird vibe..."

I huffed. "Let's just get this over with. I'm sure it'll be fine."

David peeked out the window, eyeing the reporter. "Did Miss Maria Valez mention me specifically? Because she looks like she could be my next ex-wife."

Dalia rolled her eyes. "She actually said, and I quote, 'David who?'"

Jasper laughed, slapping David on the back. "Sounds like your biggest fan, man."

Ian threw his sticks down on the bench and shrugged off Malka's hand. "Shall we do this thing?"

All of us tromped off the bus, looking like we were going to face a firing squad. It kind of felt like that too.

That first blast of Arizona summer knocked me back a step. If I didn't have a thing about keeping the bus, our space, private, I'd have retreated inside and invited the crew on board. Instead, I sucked in a breath of dry, boiling air, my lungs sizzling and crispy, and came face to face with my doom.

The reporter was friendly enough, but I caught the same vibe Dalia had. There was an uncomfortable hunger behind Maria Valez's overly made-up eyes.

I glanced over at Dalia, standing off to the side with Malka, while the sound guy attached a mic to my shirt. "You're staying, right?"

Shit, I hated how needy I sounded. Usually we had Tali with us, looking out and making sure things were kosher, but I had a feeling Dalia took her temporary role just as seriously.

"I'm not going anywhere," she said.

They'd arranged us in a clump, with Maria facing us. Luckily, our piece was being pre-recorded to air in an hour, so we didn't have to deal with going live. That gave us a bit of room to breathe. But if any of us flubbed or fucked up, I highly doubted they'd edit it out of the kindness of their hearts. They were probably gagging for it, because otherwise, we were a pretty boring interview. *Moderately famous rock band who avoided controversy and tabloids at every turn.* Not gonna sell too many high dollar commercial slots for the news station.

Maria turned on her megawatt, shockingly white smile when the cameras started rolling, introducing us, and lobbing a few softballs. She asked about the tour, our next album, gushed over how much she loved "Feels Like Fall." Everyone loved "Feels Like Fall." It was the most commercial, radio-friendly song we'd ever recorded. Even Dalia knew it, and she hated our music. Which killed me more than I'd ever admit.

I almost relaxed. This interview was no different than the thousand others we'd done. Even Ian managed to mumble a few words.

"I understand it's been several years since you performed in Arizona. Any reason behind that?" Maria asked, that hunger in her eyes blazing.

"We don't schedule our tours," I said. "Just a coincidence."

She could have let it drop there, but I saw it. She wasn't going to. She was out for blood. Maybe to make a name for herself and move up at the station. Or go national. All I knew was she wouldn't be getting a goddamn drop of mine.

"I understand you grew up here, Jasper. Does it feel good to be home?" she asked.

Jas shifted to my left, his hands diving even deeper into his pockets. "Baltimore's been my home since I was thirteen. Arizona just feels like one of the many stops along the ride."

"Do you get back here to visit a lot? Don't you have family that lives here?" she pressed.

"No, I don't. No family. All the family I have is right here next to me."

I threw my arm around his shoulder. "This guy's been my brother since the day I let him use my bunsen burner in eighth grade science class."

Maria would not be deterred by charming childhood stories.

"Weren't you spotted in the Phoenix area two months ago? Was that business or pleasure?"

Jas's head dropped, and David stepped forward. Ian gripped his arm to stop him. And I...I froze. I should've stopped the interview two questions ago, but I just stood there, letting all of it happen.

"It was private," Jas answered.

"Were you here for your mother's funeral? Isn't she buried in Phoenix?" she asked, laying the practiced sympathy voice on thick.

"Okay! We're done here! Cut!" Dalia stormed in front of the camera, blocking us from its view. "You can take your crew right out of here. Go back to your station and explain to your manager why you'll never interview Blue is the Color again. In fact..." she pulled out her phone, "I have her number right here. Why don't I call her now?"

Dalia wasn't bluffing. She pressed the screen, then held her phone to her ear. Maria attempted to placate her, placate us, but Dalia wasn't having any of it. She threw her body in front of Maria, who was easily five or six inches taller in her stilettos, blocking her access from us.

"Bus. Now," she ordered.

"Man, this is some bullshit. I'm outta here," David responded. He wandered off, throwing a barbed look in Maria's direction as he passed.

Jas yanked at his dreadlocks. "I can't be here right now. I can't breathe. I can't..."

Malka hugged him, speaking in a low voice only he could hear. He nodded against her shoulder.

"We're going to disappear for a while. I'll have him back for your set tonight," she said.

They walked away together, her arm around his waist. Ian watched them go, then he walked off himself, in the other direction.

All of this played out while Dalia was on the phone with the news station, calmly telling them what a piece of shit their reporter was. Only, she used words like "unethical" and "cruel," "callous" and "mean-spirited." Maria had stopped trying to get a word in and had gotten busy packing up her bags.

And I was numb.

I should've been pissed. Worried. Frustrated.

I felt like a void. A flat nothingness.

Finally, Dalia touched my arm. "Let's get back on the bus. They're leaving. None of that will air."

I let her lead me inside onto a couch.

"Do you want some tea? I'll make tea." I watched her fumble around with the kettle, just plugging it in took her three tries. It made my chest ache, and in the back of my mind, I thought, *Well, at least I feel something.*

"I don't want tea, Dalia."

I leaned forward, covering my face with my hands. "I let them down," I mumbled.

The seat next to me sunk down, then her sweetness drifted my way. The hand she laid on my back was tentative, but it broke me. I squeezed my eyes shut, trying to block it all out, but the ache was too big.

"Nicky..." Her voice was so soft, so unlike her.

I started fucking sobbing. Big, shoulder shaking sobs. There was no disguising it or holding it back. I was conscious enough of the situation to feel deeply humiliated, but I couldn't control any of what was happening to me. My body said, *Now's the time we're going to cry, motherfucker.*

Dalia's arms circled my shoulders, and my hands curled around her waist, pulling her closer. She shushed me like I was a little baby, and I fucking clung to her. She was an island of soft in a sea of sharp.

"It's okay, Nicky. You're okay," she murmured. Her fingers threaded through my hair, and my tears wet her neck and shoulder. She didn't comment or make me feel like shit. She just held me while my body emptied itself of years of un-spilled tears.

"She was important to you too, wasn't she?" she asked.

I nodded, the words lost. Reinece had charged into my life at thirteen and loved me like I was hers. She saw I needed it, that I was floundering and a year or two away from getting into the kind of trouble there was no coming back from, and she had none of it.

I'd never had a friend's parent take an interest in me. But the second Jas and I cemented our friendship, Reinece was all up in my business. She wanted to know the kids her son was hanging around with. And while most people would have seen a young punk with an angry scowl and a chip bigger than his scrawny shoulder, she saw more than that.

My own mom sucked. She wasn't abusive or anything, mostly just apathetic. She could take me or leave me. I was an afterthought. She didn't even blink when I basically started living with Jas and Reinece in high school.

"I have this...this dread inside me," I choked out. "It's overwhelming and constant. Sometimes I feel sick with it."

"When did it start?"

My shoulder was unbearably heavy as I lifted it. "Don't know. A few months ago."

Dalia's hands were in my hair and on my neck, and somehow, pulling some of the hurt out of me. I needed her to keep touching me.

"I don't think that's dread, honey. I think that's grief. Have you cried since she died?"

I fucking hadn't. My well had run dry a long time ago. I'd sat there while she was dying, holding her hand, and the tears just wouldn't come. It was like they were stuck, or maybe I'd forgotten how.

Well, the dam had burst, baby, and this one was a gusher.

I shook my head against Dalia's neck, and sobbed every last tear left in my body. And she just fuckin' held me. She had absolutely no reason to care for me. I'd given her none. But here she was, letting me fall apart in her arms.

And it felt safe.

I hated it. But I couldn't stop it.

"You want to tell me about her? What she meant to you?" she asked.

"I do."

She sat with me while I spilled it all. I couldn't look at her while I talked, so I kept my face at her neck, my words, my stories of Reinece, bouncing off the walls of her throat. I told her how I loved Reinece more than I ever loved my own mother. That she called me her boy. I told her how she came to all our shows, even at the divest clubs. She'd sit there, a middle-aged black woman, in her scrubs, fresh from a twelve-hour nursing shift, tapping her toes to our very early, very shitty music. I confessed the song her sister liked so much, "When It's Gone," was about Reinece. I'd written it after she'd told me her experience of leaving Jas's dad.

"Jas and I wanted to buy her a house when we finally started making money," I said.

Dalia played with the hair behind my ear, her fingernail scratching gently. "She didn't let you?"

"Nope, no way. She said, 'I'm the mama. My boys aren't going to be the ones to support me.' It took us two records for her to finally give in and take some money from us. Not a lot, mind you."

"Do you talk about her with Jas?"

I exhaled slowly. "No."

"Why?"

"Because, as much as she meant to me, she wasn't my mother. And I have to let him grieve how he needs to. It isn't my place to insert myself into his grief."

"Nick, from everything you just said, she *was* your mother.

And *you* have to grieve how you need to. You can't walk around every day full of dread and absolutely miserable. You're allowed to feel this."

I let out a humorless laugh. "Oh, I'm feeling it."

"But it's just us. I have no connection to Reinece. Don't you think you should have this cry with Jas?"

"I think I'm having this cry with you *because* you don't have a connection. Shit, I can't burden him with my stupid feelings."

"Oh, Nicky. Feelings are never stupid."

I couldn't say why I did it. Maybe it was the way she called me Nicky. Maybe it was delirium. Could've been the long minutes of inhaling her sweet scent. Whatever it was that made me kiss her throat, I'd never know. But my lips traveled the length of her neck, up to her jaw, with the mindless intention of finding her mouth. She whimpered, and the hand in my hair tightened.

But when my mouth hovered over hers, she stiffened, and my soft island let me go. She backed away, dropping me right back into the sharp sea. Funny thing was, it hurt more the second time around. It would've been better never to have left in the first place.

"I'm sorry," she whispered. "That's not what either of us need right now."

I raised my head, meeting her eyes. "No, I'm sorry. I shouldn't have laid this at your feet."

She grabbed my hand. "No, you should've! I'm glad you did." She rubbed her lips together for a moment. "It's the other thing...I'm pretty sure you don't even like me. You've got this flood of emotions coming out of you, and maybe my lips seemed like a good place to park them, but I have no doubt you'd regret kissing me, and then we'd have to be in each other's faces for another six weeks."

"Would you regret kissing me?"

She reached out to touch me, but I jerked away. "Nick..."

"Nah, it's cool. Thanks for being a shoulder when I needed it. I'm good now."

I got up, and went to the kitchenette, and without much thought, set about making a cup of tea. I didn't really want it. Mostly, I wanted the entire morning to have never happened. If I could have rewound a couple weeks and never have met this girl, that would have been even better.

Liar.

I could almost hear Reinece's voice in my head, and it made me...not smile, but almost.

"I've got some work to do, so if you don't need me..." Dalia trailed off, sounding almost timid. Definitely unlike her normal, fiery self.

Keeping my focus on the tea bag steeping in my mug, I nodded. "No, I don't need you."

She left quietly, without another word.

And that voice came back again. *Liar.*

FIFTEEN
DALIA

LET'S BE REAL HERE, kissing Nick Fletcher would have been amazing, right up until three-point-two seconds after it ended and he looked at me like I was the biggest mistake he ever made.

I might have been horny as hell, and had never had a problem with casual hook-ups, but I did have a problem with taking on wounded animals—and Nick was critically wounded, leaving trails of blood in his wake.

Only he didn't know it. Or maybe he didn't care. I'd observed him over our weeks stuck together in tight confines, and even more closely over the last week since the almost-kiss. I saw the way he watched after the band, checking in with them. I saw his concern when Ian went off with Malka. I noticed him asking David if he'd had anything to drink—I'd gathered it had once been a problem. And I couldn't help but see his helplessness when he looked at Jas. Like he desperately wanted to take his pain away, but didn't know how.

Those men had no clue how he took care of them, the way he poured himself into their well-being while completely neglecting his own. They were probably just so used to him being there for them, they didn't think twice about accepting his protection without offering any in return.

Maybe he'd never needed it, so they couldn't see how much he needed it now.

I saw it, though, and it broke my heart.

He basically ignored me all through Texas. We'd hit Dallas, San Antonio, and Houston, and while I'd picked up some authentic cowboy boots, Nick had barely even spared me a glance.

I thought maybe he was embarrassed—mostly about the crying and less about the kiss that never happened.

I was avoiding him too. Because as much as I said I didn't want to take on a wounded bird, the feel of his lips on my skin wasn't something I'd forget anytime soon. He'd affected me in more than one way.

"We're here, boring."

An automatic smile formed on my face before I even looked up. "Thanks, ass."

"I thought you'd be more fun when I first saw you," David said.

"Sorry, chuck. Girl's gotta make a living." Once I shut down my laptop, I slipped it in my backpack and checked around the back lounge for anything else I'd left behind.

Since Tali had gone back home, I'd taken over her office space as my own. I'd been keeping in touch with her, so I knew her dad's surgery had ended up more complicated than the doctors had initially predicted and his recovery was going to take longer than expected. She had brothers, but they were married with kids, so as the only daughter in a pretty traditional Italian American family, she took on the role as her parent's caregiver. I completely understood the need to be there; if one of my parents were sick, I'd drop everything too.

Although...she'd be back with us in a few days, so I'd probably have to tidy up or get the boot.

"Thought you were done with that bookstore website," David said.

"I am. Now I'm building one for Unrequited."

He walked ahead of me through the bunks, and I stopped to grab my suitcase stuffed with dirty clothes. We were spending the night at a hotel in a small town in Arkansas, which meant it was laundry day. *Finally.* I was afraid my clothes were going to get up and walk away on their own they were so stiff with sweat and dirt. What I really wanted to do was dump them all in the trash and start over fresh. What I'd actually do was sit in a laundromat on one of my only days off watching my clothes spin round and round in a washing machine.

The band had a laundry service, of course, but I was a lowly assistant. No laundry service for me. I was washing every scrap of fabric I'd brought with me, even my sheets.

Although, tonight, I'd be starfishing in the middle of a queen-size bed, in my very own room where I could do anything I wanted in the bathroom: take long, luxurious showers, actually blow-dry my hair, I'd probably even walk around naked. It was going to be amazing.

Once I'd checked everyone in at the front desk, I went back to the bus to hand out key cards.

"We have the entire top floor to ourselves, and honestly, I don't think security will be a problem in this little podunk town, but you never know, so don't get into any fights at the local honky tonk, okay?" I winked at Ian, and he just stared at me stoney-faced. One day, I was going to get him to crack.

When I climbed off the bus, Nick was holding my bag, which I'd left outside on the curb.

"Uh, that's mine." I reached out for it. "I can carry it."

"I've got it."

"Why?"

He flipped sunglasses from the top of his head over his eyes. "Because I'm a fuckin' gentleman."

"Are you?"

"Yep. Where to, Dalia?"

"I'm headed to the laundry room in the basement. Which I can do by myself."

He started walking, and I stood there for a beat, stumped. *Why was the guy who'd ignored me for a week carrying my suitcase?* No answers came, so I followed him inside the hotel.

We stood side by side, waiting for the elevator.

"Where's your stuff?" I asked.

"Buddy's taking it to my room," he said.

"Why aren't you hanging out with him?"

I laughed at my own suggestion, thinking of Nick hanging out with Buddy, the bus driver, possibly the surliest man on the planet.

"I'm pretty sure he'd shank me if I tried," Nick said, grinning.

Oh god, it was good to see him smile. He didn't do nearly enough of it, and it was a beautiful sight. His green eyes lit up, like sea glass catching the sun. And he had these crinkles in the corners that told the story of a hundred nights of laughter once upon a time.

The laundry room was just a dreary as a basement laundry room sounded. But I'd known many a laundry room in my day, so I was undaunted.

"Can I have my suitcase yet?" I asked.

"Tell me where you want it."

"In my hand."

He ignored my outstretched arm and placed my bag on top of a dryer.

"You're a terrible listener," I said.

"I've heard that before."

I tossed my stank clothes in a washing machine, no sorting required. If anything was white to begin with, it was now a lovely shade of grey. I threw in a packet of detergent and inserted my quarters, and my clothes breathed a sigh of relief as the clean water began pouring over them.

"Oh shit! I forgot." I pulled my shirt over my head and shimmied out of my shorts, tossing them in with the rest of the laundry. The only semi-clean piece of clothing I still had was my bathing suit, so I'd put it on under my clothes this morning. Only, I hadn't really planned on stripping in front of Nick.

"Don't mind me," he said.

I turned around, finding him hovering a few feet away. "So, now I'm standing here in my bathing suit, and it's not awkward at all."

He looked me up and down. "And cowboy boots."

I glanced down at my mid-calf brown leather boots with pink roses on the sides. I'd spent a hefty sum on these babies, and they were going to get worn, whether they matched my outfit or not. And honestly, cowboy boots with a polka dot bikini had a classic feel.

"Don't mock the boots," I warned.

"I would never."

"I feel you would."

He bowed his head, grinning for the second time in five minutes. "Possibly. But not when you're wearing that bikini. That's quite a look."

I glanced down at myself again. My high-waisted bottoms and halter top did just the right things for my curves—although, said curves were sadly shrinking from all the running around and sweating I'd been doing lately. But as comfortable as I was with my body, I wasn't *rock star giving me the once over* comfortable. So, I deflected.

"Oh please. Don't you make music videos with bikini clad models washing your car and rubbing soap all over their luscious tits?"

The line between his brows became more pronounced than normal. "Do you...do you think Blue is the Color is an eighties hair band?"

I made the same face. "Are you...are you making a joke?"

He shrugged, leaning against a dryer all sexy casual. The guy gave good lean.

"I'm known to crack a joke on occasion."

"What's the occasion?" I asked.

He slowly shook his head, eyeing me from top to bottom again. "Dalia fucking Brenner in a bikini and cowboy boots. Should be a national holiday."

"Why are you being so friendly today?" I asked.

"It's hard to avoid you. Gets tiring."

I pulled my bottom lip between my teeth, then slowly released it. "Why would you want to avoid me?"

He pointed to my mouth. "That. You do shit like that more than you know. *That's* why I want to avoid you."

"Because you're attracted to me?"

"Yeah. And I sure as hell don't want to be."

That stung. Yeah, I was rough around the edges, but I hadn't realized liking me was torturous. I guess I'd assumed since we'd shared such an intimate moment, Nick might have come to have more regard for me.

But, apparently, I'd been in the right place, right time, nothing more. It could have been Buddy there when Nick broke down. Although, I doubted Buddy would have held him. He was more of a "buck up, buttercup" sort.

Maybe I needed to take my cues from Buddy.

"I have some work to do, actually. Stay if you want, but I'm not available for banter anymore," I said.

Hopping up on a table in the corner, I sat cross-legged and pulled my laptop out of my bag. I scrolled around aimlessly while Nick watched me. No work would actually be done with him standing there, looming, leaning, being stupidly handsome. But I could fake it with the best of them. I opened a Word document and began a list of all the reasons I hated him.

1. Annoying.
2. Too handsome. Who needs to be that handsome? It's a waste on one person.
3. Called me a cunt once. Has possibly thought it multiple times.
4. Thinks being attracted to me is Hell on Earth.
5. Won't stop staring at me.
6. Doesn't share his chocolate.
7. Bad music.
8. Okay, it's not bad, it's just not my thing.
9. Even though it's kind of growing on me.
10. Pants too tight. Can see glorious shape of his ass almost constantly.

I'd been so caught up in listing the reasons I hated him, I hadn't noticed him edging closer until he was already reading over my shoulder. I covered the screen with my hands, but from his low chuckle, it was too late.

"What is that?" he asked.

"Work."

"Really? Because it looks like a list about me. Who else doesn't share their chocolate?"

"Many horrible people, I'm sure."

He pointed to number three. "I haven't called you that again, even in my head."

I closed the screen and looked up at him. "I believe you."

"If our music is growing on you, why haven't you come to see us play?"

"How do you know I haven't?"

His lips curved up. "I'd know if you were there."

"Oh? Do you have some sixth sense when it comes to me?"

He fingered my hair lightly. "Nope. But I wouldn't miss this in a sea of thousands."

"I know you probably think that's some kind of compliment, but to a girl who's been called 'stop light head' more than once in her life, it isn't."

His brows shot up in amusement. "Stop light head?"

"What little kids lack in creativity, they make up in cruelness. Luckily, I'm mostly over it."

"Clearly, I'm a fan of your hair. Did you get it from your mom or dad?"

"Both. We're a family of redheads. Although, my dad went stark white at forty. We told him we'd have to kick him out of the family when he did."

He crossed his arms, frowning down at me. Not meanly, just contemplatively. "You know, it's funny. When you told me you grew up without money, I just assumed you'd had a shitty early life like I did. But no, you've got your people. You're tight."

I raised my hand. "Yep. Well-loved child here. Happy childhood, loving parents, closely bonded, and all that jazz. But look at you, rich and talented and famous. And look at me, still poor, not-so-talented, and never gonna be famous. It isn't always the roots, sometimes it's the sun."

"Fuck, that's a good line. Can I steal it?"

I laughed. "It's not stealing if you ask. And I'd be honored if you stole it."

He found a scrap of paper and scribbled down my words. "You're more talented than you think, Dal. I'm feeling inspired, just from words that popped off the top of your head."

"I expect to be credited as co-writer."

"Of fucking course. Mind if I write for a minute?"

"Yeah. There's a notebook in the top pocket of my suitcase. You're welcome to it."

And then, Nick Fletcher, singer of the famous rock band Blue is the Color, sat on the floor of that dreary little laundry room, and wrote, and wrote, and wrote in my Pusheen notebook. He wrote through the wash and dry cycle. He was still writing when I'd folded all my gloriously clean clothing and put my T-shirt and shorts back on.

Since he was in another world, and I highly doubted I'd have another chance in my lifetime to witness the creative process of a musical artist, I stood there watching him for a minute. His pen moved furiously over the notebook paper, his handwriting like chicken scratch. I couldn't actually read anything he wrote, but still, there was something so damn sexy about the entire thing. How he'd been overtaken with inspiration from something I'd said. And the vision of him sitting there on the concrete floor, long legs encased in tattered jeans stretched out in front of him...it could have been an album cover.

I snapped a picture on my cell phone. I'd probably never show it to anyone, because this moment felt private, but I wanted to remember him like this when I went back to my regular life.

"Nick?"

"Hmmm?"

"I'm done."

He looked up at me, startling when he saw me dressed and holding my suitcase.

"I'm done," I repeated.

"Whoa." He shook his head, clearing it. "I guess it'd be weird if I stayed down here writing, huh?"

I picked up my suitcase. "Do what you need to do. Personally, I need to stretch my legs and find some real food."

He ripped several pages out of my notebook and handed it back to me.

"Want some company?"

"I...guess?"

He chuckled. "I need to stretch my legs and hunt down some real food too. Might as well do it together."

SIXTEEN
NICK

I HAD no idea what the hell I was doing. I just knew a week of avoiding Dalia had felt like the wrong thing to do. I also knew it'd been months since I'd been as inspired to write as I was in that laundry room with her watching me.

A night alone in an anonymous hotel room was the least attractive proposition I'd had in a long time. So there I was, walking down a dusty main street in Arkansas, the sun beating on the back of my neck, trying to find what the clerk at our hotel billed as the best southern soul food on Earth. With Dalia. We hadn't even asked the guys to come along, which was probably shitty, but I saw enough of their ugly mugs. Right now, I just wanted to sink my teeth into a piece of fried chicken while sitting across from a ridiculously pretty redhead.

That wasn't too much to ask for, right?

It probably was, especially given what an asshole I'd been to that pretty redhead—and was bound to be again. But today, I wasn't really asking. I was taking what I wanted.

Or...at least some of what I wanted. I wanted her company. I couldn't quite explain it. Wasn't sure I liked it. But I saw no reason to fight it. Not this time, at least.

Dalia pointed to the right. "I think it's over there."

"Nope, it's farther down."

"I really think that's it!"

"I don't."

She stomped her fucking cowboy boot. "Fine. You go your way, I'll go mine. We'll see who's eating mac and cheese first."

Not surprisingly, she didn't wait even a second for me. I was ninety-eight percent sure I was right and Dalia was damn wrong, but I followed her swaying, bouncing, stubborn ass anyway.

She turned down a small road that looked residential, and I was about to declare victory when she stopped and turned around grinning like she'd won the grand prize.

She held her arms out, showcasing the sign that looked like it'd been hanging in the same spot for decades.

"Alma's Kitchen."

That's all it said, but no more explanation was needed. One look at the converted shotgun house and the people exiting holding Styrofoam containers like they were filled with gold instead of down home cookin' told me we were in the right place. Oh, and that Dalia had been right. I'd have to eat shit.

She came up to the spot where I'd stopped on the sidewalk and poked my chest.

"Say it."

I feigned ignorance. "What?"

She flicked her finger under my chin. "Say that without me, you'd be wandering and lost."

"I'd have found my way sooner or later."

"But with me, it was sooner."

I laughed. "Fine, I bow down to your superior sense of direction. Can we eat?"

"Hell yes! I'm just telling you right now, if you judge how

much I eat, I'll take a picture of you drooling in your sleep and post it on Instagram."

I clutched my chest. "You'd ruin my rock star cred?"

"Will you judge my soul food consumption?"

"I'll judge a hell of a lot of things, but never that."

The inside of Alma's was bare bones, which, to me, was a sign we were in for amazing food. I'd traveled through the south a time or ten, and our old bus driver, Marvin, who was from Georgia, took me to a few of his favorite haunts. They all had been some variation of this place: no air conditioning, surly cashier, a couple tables with plastic tablecloths, paper plates, and plastic cutlery.

"Want to share?" she asked, gazing up at the handwritten menu on the wall.

"*Will* you share?"

She shrugged. "If we order enough. I'm gonna need hush puppies."

"Obviously."

"And black-eyed peas."

"Dalia, I'm not brand new. I know what I'm doing."

We ended up ordering half the menu, though we both agreed to skip the chitlins. More power to anyone who liked them, but one try was enough for me.

Since there weren't any tables available, we carried our food and sweet tea back to the hotel. It got kinda awkward when we stepped off the elevator on our floor.

"Your room or mine?" I asked.

She stared me down. "Nick, you and I both know you have a suite with a full dining room. You really want to go to my room and eat on my bed?"

I didn't mind the idea. Instead of saying that, though, I swiped my key card, letting Dalia into my room.

We set out our food—which was truly enough to feed ten

people—and sat down across from each other, taking turns scooping out pieces of fried catfish, okra, collard greens, corn bread, and....the list went on. Let's just leave it at our plates were full and I was fucking drooling.

I didn't know if I'd ever truly experienced the much lauded "comfortable silence" before, but Dalia and I fell into one. Okay, it wasn't completely silent. We both sounded like monsters chomping, crunching, gnawing. She wasn't a delicate eater, and I added it to the growing list of things I surprisingly liked about her. Mostly because I didn't feel the need to attempt to be delicate either.

She shoveled a forkful of collard greens into her mouth. "This is the best thing I've ever eaten."

I held up my drumstick. "Alma knows her fucking fried chicken."

She laughed. "Alma knows delicious. I think I might write her a thank you note."

"I might write her a song."

She slammed her hands on the table. "Oh my god, Nicky, let's write Alma a song!"

"I thought I was writing it."

"I'll be your ghost writer."

I groaned. "Fine. Got an opening line."

She rolled her eyes up to the ceiling as she chewed on a piece of okra and thought. I almost choked on my chicken when she suddenly belted out, "Alllllllllma! Oh, Alllllllllma!"

"How was that?" she asked.

I laughed. "Maybe the best opening line I've heard. How about after that, it goes, "Why your kitchen gotta be so faaaaaar-rrr?" I sang.

She gave me an indecipherable look. Like I'd confused her.

"Has anyone ever told you you have a lovely voice?" she asked.

I snorted. "Yeah, a time or two. I don't really buy it."

She shook her finger at me. "Ah, modest. I like it. With a voice like that, it'd be easy to get a big head. Stay humble."

I shook my head, finding myself grinning down at my mostly empty plate. "How can you like my voice, but not my music?"

"You're really stuck on that, aren't you?"

Leaning forward, I rested my elbows on the table, studying her. "Yeah, it's weird, but I kinda am."

She tossed her fork on her plate and propped her chin on her hand. "I just never got into it. I swear, it's not personal. I like what I like, and I can't really explain why I like something. I know it when I hear it."

"And you know it when you hear something you don't like?"

"Well, yeah. But I honestly haven't heard a lot of your music."

"So, let's listen to my music."

I couldn't say why I was so determined for Dalia to like my music. Maybe because no one had ever really said to my face they *didn't* like it. And maybe because this was my entire life. It was hard to hear someone—*her*—dismiss the one good thing I'd ever done.

"Okay, but I think I need to lie down. I'm *so* full," she said.

I waved at the bedroom. "There's a king-size bed in there *and* speakers. Sounds like fate."

While I set up my phone in the docking station, Dalia flopped on the bed with her arms over her head, exposing a slash of her soft belly. I didn't even bother trying to deny to myself how attracted to her I was. I still hadn't worked out whether I liked her or whatever I felt toward her was due to being trapped together every single day.

Probably the latter. Once this tour was over and I got my head on straight, she'd fade into a distant memory.

Only, I didn't believe that. I doubted very many people forgot meeting Dalia.

"Ready?"

"What am I going to hear first?" she asked.

"Some early stuff."

She raised an eyebrow. "Stuff you recorded when you were my age?"

"Yep. About fifty years ago."

I hit play, then joined her on the bed, lying down on the opposite side. Our music filled the room, and it made me smile. These days, we only played a couple older songs at our shows. Fan favorites. A lot of our early music had been forgotten, even by us. But I liked to listen to it from time to time, for nostalgia. Our production value had multiplied tenfold since we recorded that first album, but there was something to be said about the gritty realness it had to it.

I turned on my side, watching her. She had her eyes closed, and her hands on her stomach, one finger gently tapping. The song playing was called "Queen." David had written it about his daughter, Emma.

Under my breath, I sang along to the rawest, most bare version of David I'd ever witnessed. His girl did that to him. When he'd brought me the lyrics, I could tell from the way he wouldn't meet my eyes he'd been worried I'd laugh in his face. But when I read his words, saw the love for his daughter he'd set to music, the only thing I wanted to do was justice to his expression.

Pretty thing, never lie
Reach out, fill my sky
Oh, Oh, Oh, Oh, Oh
You don't know
Oh, Oh, Oh, Oh, Oh

That someday you'll go

I hold you
Trying not to wreck it
You hold me
I know you'll make it

And I told you that's your throne
And I told you to be kind
Rule with an iron fist
Rule with a gentle mind
I'll always be there
You'll want to leave here
And oh, oh, oh, oh
I'll let you go

"I love this one, Nicky," Dalia said.

"Me too. It's one of my favorites." She listened when I told her who David had written it about. We'd been these twenty-three-year-old punks, and he'd poured his soul out and given it away to the masses, so maybe Emma would see one day he'd always loved her, even when he couldn't be around most of the time.

"I saw him talking to her once. He seemed really private about her. I'm surprised he wrote this about her."

I chuckled. "Yeah, he's protective of her now. Not that he wasn't then, but she's fifteen, so his protectiveness is at a different level. Plus, David got her mom pregnant when he was eighteen and she was sixteen, so he knows firsthand what kind of shit lurks around the corner, you know? He'd probably hide her in a convent if he could."

She smiled at me. "Maybe he needs to listen to his own song again and remember he promised he'd let her go."

"He didn't say *when* he'd let her go."

"Play me another, maestro."

Sticking with our first album, I played her song after song. She didn't declare her love for all of them. I got the picture she wasn't into our harder stuff. But the slower, more soulful songs, she really seemed to dig. Kind of made me wanted to write an entire album of ballads.

Each time I'd gotten up to play the next song, I moved closer and closer to Dalia when I returned to the bed. And she'd scooted toward my side of the bed too. And that was how we'd ended up in the middle of the bed, side by side, listening to the last track of the album. A cover of Sade's "By Your Side."

"Damn, this is romantic," she whispered.

"It's a good song."

She rolled onto her side, her eyes meeting mine. "It is. But it's your voice..." she trailed off, mouthing the words.

I couldn't keep my eyes off her. I wasn't even sure I liked this woman until today. And now...well, I definitely wanted to kiss her. To finish what I'd started last week.

"Dal..." I traced my finger along her jaw, and she shuddered.

"Nicky, what...?"

She was propped up, her face above mine. My hands were itching—itching to dive into her wild hair and pull her face to mine. To lap at her lips and taste her tongue. To roll her over and sink into every inch of her softness.

Her tongue darted out to lick her top lip, and her face came even closer to mine. Her sweet tea breath was hot on my lips, and her pretty brown eyes were steady on mine.

"I should—" Whatever she was about to say got cut off by a steady, persistent, annoying knock on my door, followed by David and Jasper screaming and moaning my name.

"Stay, please."

I left her there on the bed, hopefully for seconds, to send my idiot brothers away.

Yanking the door open, I scowled at them. "What?"

"Dude. Did we catching you in the middle of jerking off?" David asked.

Jasper frowned. "What's up?"

"Just working on something," I said. "How can I help you?"

David threw his arm over Jasper's shoulder. "We're headed out for some dinner. You in?"

"Nah, I'm good here. I ate a little while ago."

David tried to see over my shoulder. "You're being weird. You got a girl in there?"

"Where would I find a girl?"

"Oh, I have no doubt you could if you wanted. Flash those baby blues around town—"

"My eyes are green," I corrected.

"Whatever. Point is, you've found a girl in a town much smaller than this."

Jasper pointed at me. "You didn't say no."

I pushed the door closed another inch. "Actually, you caught me. I was about to jerk off. Had to pause my porn to answer the door. Would you mind leaving me to it?"

That finally got them to leave. They knew all too well how precious private jacking off time was. It was done on the bus, of course, but there was nothing like doing it in the privacy of a hotel room after being two feet from each other for weeks at a time.

My plans were a lot more attractive than that, though.

Too bad my plan wasn't on the bed anymore. She was standing just outside the bedroom door, shoving her feet back into her cowboy boots.

"I'm going to go," she said.

"You should definitely stay."

She blew a curl off her forehead. "I really think that's a bad idea. Thanks for today. Can't believe we went all day without arguing. I'm definitely writing about this in my diary."

I knew what she was doing. Deflecting. Trying to dissipate the charge in the air.

"I want you to stay, Dal."

But she pulled her key card out of her back pocket. "I'll see you in the morning. Enjoy the room and...masturbation."

With that, she made a swift exit, and I was left with whiplash. That was two times she'd turned me down flat. I didn't want to be that guy who couldn't take a hint, but damn, I knew I wasn't the only one feeling it. There was something between me and that fireball of a woman. Something that was going to be damn hard to give up on.

Now that she was gone, and I was left in a big hotel room with an entire evening in front of me, I didn't know what to do. Making myself come in my fist didn't sound that appealing, so I did what I always did when my brain was muddled with too many thoughts: I wrote. And so what if every song could somehow be linked back to *her*? Didn't mean anything. Just meant she'd captured my attention momentarily. Wouldn't last. Tomorrow, we'd be back to fighting and she'd annoy the shit out of me.

A light knocking sounded on the door. It'd been a couple hours, but she'd come back.

I opened it, my smug smile at the ready, but Dalia's brow was furrowed seriously.

"I forgot to ask you something."

"Yeah?"

"Yeah." Her fingertips brushed over my arm. "Are you okay?"

"Am I okay?"

She nodded once. "This is me, checking in with you. Asking if you're okay."

I closed my eyes, exhaling heavily through my nose. No one ever asked if I was okay. That was my job. Not one I'd been hired for, but one I'd claimed.

Yet, here was this girl who barely knew me, tapping on my door to ask if I was okay after I'd made unwanted moves on her for the second time.

I opened my eyes, blinking slowly as I took her in. "I don't even know, to be honest."

"You don't have to be. At least not at every second."

"I'm okay today. I've been more okay today than I've been in a while."

Her fingers drummed on the outside of the doorframe. "I'm happy to hear that. Do you mind if I keep checking in every once in a while? For my peace of mind?"

My heart fucking ached. The little intruder being sweet like this, but completely out of reach, made me a little angry. Not at her, but at the situation. I didn't want to want her. She wasn't doing anything to encourage me with her kindness and concern. And my brain knew my anger was irrational, but my mouth wasn't having any of it.

"I'm good. I'm not interested in being babied. I never asked for it, and I don't want it. I'm a grown ass man, Dalia. Not some little boy." Leaning against the doorframe, I crossed my arms over my chest. No doubt a body-language expert would have had a field day with that. "Pretty sure you can find one of those on the tour, though. How about the one with the dimples you've got wrapped around your finger?"

She took a step back from the door, the concern in her eyes vanishing, replaced for a split second by hurt, then that pissed off look I knew so well.

"You sure as hell don't act like a grown ass man. I'm eight years younger than you, but I swear I have more emotional maturity in my pinky. I'm sorry for you if you can't be friends with a girl who doesn't want to suck your cock. Your loss, Nick Fletcher. Your fucking loss."

She stomped off down the hallway, but seeing her leave pissed off at me was a lot easier to take than her leaving because she didn't want me.

The bitter irony was I was aware enough to know exactly what I was doing and why, but I was stupid enough to do it anyway. My life was a bullet train, and I was the conductor, the villain with the twirly mustache and hapless victim tied to the tracks.

SEVENTEEN

DALIA

IT'S funny how easy it was to ignore someone who slept a couple feet away every night. But a lot of unhappily married couples did it every night, so maybe it wasn't all that funny.

I'd officially given up on trying to understand Nick. He was the exact kind of chaos I'd always been attracted to, but this time, I wasn't letting myself be swept up. Because he'd be the one I'd fall for. He was just wounded enough for me to want to fix him, but not so far gone he was unfixable.

My stupid heart saw him as a weekend project. I'd have him in ship shape with a couple fucks, a few snuggles, and several late-night, soulful conversations.

The ridiculous fantasy completely disregarded the fact that he was a famous musician who could have a no strings attached fuck at any port. Also, he didn't want to be fixed. And didn't seem to like me much.

I didn't like him a whole hell of a lot lately either. Because his cold shoulder was a lot icier than mine.

I wasn't on this tour for him, though. I was here to work and see parts of this country I'd otherwise probably never have a chance to.

Sadly, I didn't have enough time to see Nashville. I would have loved to have taken my cowboy boots out on the town in Music City, USA, but alas, the bus was leaving right after the last act of the night, so I had to stay put.

An absolute genius had created a makeshift line dancing bar in the bus parking lot, though, and one of the southern roadies taught us some moves. I mostly tripped over my own feet, but I attributed that to the bottle of Bud in my hand rather than my lack of dancing skills.

Malka laughed, throwing her arm over my shoulder. "Girl, I don't think either of us are meant for country dancing."

That wasn't really true. Or not completely true. Malka picked up the moves right away and danced like no one was watching. She had her own pair of cowboy boots, and with her tatts and bright hair, she looked like a rebellious country music star.

"You haven't seen my square dancing abilities. I learned in middle school, and I've still got the moves," I said.

She cocked her head. "What is square dancing? I think I need this in my life."

"I need a partner to demonstrate." Glancing around, my eyes landed on Mo, sipping a beer while he talked to the drummer from his band. "Mo!"

He glanced up, a smile already playing on his face. "Yo!"

"Come square dance with me!"

He sauntered over, chuckling. "Gladly. You're gonna have to take the lead, though."

I slapped his chest. "I don't mind being in charge, baby."

He waggled his brows. "Good to know."

"Are you two going to dance or fuck?" Malka asked.

"We're going to fucking dance!" I said.

Normally, square dancing required four people to make an actual square, but Mo and I improvised. We do-si-doed with the best of them. There was some promenading and a lot of swinging. Malka caught on quickly, then it was the three of us, swinging each other and laughing.

It was mostly ridiculous, but the kind of ridiculous I loved. Laughing and drinking and being silly without a care in the world. And no Nick Fletchers around to tell me just how ridiculous he thought I was.

When the night was winding down and everyone started heading back to their buses, Malka and I walked slowly back to ours.

"You're a month in now. How are you liking the tour?" she asked.

"I love it. I really don't know if I could do this long-term, but for now, it's perfect."

"Well, not every tour is like this. The Swerve is different because there are so many of us. I went along with Blue the last time they toured Europe, and it was pretty mellow."

I snorted. "Because they're ancient!"

She smacked my arm. "Hey, girly, I'm not too far behind them. I turn thirty soon."

"Really? What's your skin care secret?"

"Heavy drinking and swallowing a lot of jizz," she said dryly.

"Oooh. Note to self: swallow more jizz."

Malka laughed. "You know something weird? I'm always surrounded by guys, so I thought I just wasn't a girl's girl. Now, I think I am. I like having another girl to talk to."

"Same. Well, I mostly just hang out with my little sister. We had an exclusive club we never let anyone else join."

"Sounds healthy," she chided.

"Yep. Codependency at its finest! This is the first time I've really done my own thing."

"And?"

"I should probably do more of it."

We got to her bus and paused outside the door. "Can I tell you something?"

"Of course," I said.

"Ian and I broke up earlier. For good."

"*What*? When? Why didn't you tell me?"

"After my set. He was just standing there off stage, watching me like he always does, and I realized I can't keep doing this. I think he realized it also. And maybe we've got a little codependency thing going on too."

"How are you?" I asked.

She let her eyes wander up to the sky for a beat. "I think I'll be okay. The cord is cut, and that was the hardest part."

"How's he?"

She lifted a shoulder. "Who can say? I've known him for years, and he's still a mystery to me."

"Maybe I can ride on your bus to the next stop. I have a feeling my bus isn't going to be much fun."

She gave me a quick squeeze. "Sorry, girl. My bus is jam packed. You're going to have to deal with the grumpy men on yours."

"Ugh, fine. I guess I'm happy for you that you're breaking the habit."

"If only there was a patch for quitting bad decisions like there is for smoking," she said.

"If only."

We said our goodbyes, then I made my way to my home on wheels. There was already tension between Nick and me, and I wasn't sure I could take a whole lot more. We had an eleven-hour drive ahead of us, and I would have rather spent it sleeping peacefully than dealing with annoying men.

When I stepped onto the bus and saw the boys all sprawled on the couches, Jas and David playing a video game, Nick with his headphones on, and Ian reading a comic book, relief washed over me. Maybe if I tiptoed, they wouldn't notice me and I could collapse in my bed.

"Nice of you to join us, babydoll," David said without looking away from his game.

"I had some square dancing to do, but I'm completely wiped out, so I'm going to hit the sack."

"G'night," Jas called after me.

I grabbed a T-shirt and boxers and took them into the bathroom with me to get changed and brush my teeth. The bus started moving while I had my shirt over my head, and I almost fell out of the bathroom. Fortunately, I kept my balance and dignity.

When I came out, Nick was standing in the narrow walkway, rummaging around in his bunk.

"Excuse me," I said.

He stayed put, giving me a long and thorough once over, his eyes hardening at my chest.

"I don't like that shirt."

I hadn't even paid attention to the shirt I'd grabbed, and when I looked down, I saw it was my Unrequited shirt.

"It's comfy."

He turned fully, his back to his bed. If I wanted to get into my bunk, there was no way I could avoid touching him.

"You work for us. You shouldn't be wearing another band's shirt. Makes us look bad," he said.

I rolled my eyes. "Come on, dude. No one actually cares."

"They do. People talk."

"Let them talk!"

"I don't like it."

I waved my toothbrush at him. "I didn't ask. Now, can you please move so I can go to bed?"

"I'm good here."

Narrowing my eyes, I said, "You're not being very nice right now."

"Never claimed to be nice."

I moved closer, calculating whether I could climb into bed without pressing my ass to his dick.

"You should work on that."

Moving sideways, I slid in front of him and tossed my toiletries onto my bed. Before I could step onto the bottom bunk to boost myself up, Nick's hands gripped my waist, and I swore I almost melted from the feel of his heat so close behind me.

"I think you like it when I'm not nice," he growled next to my ear.

"You have too many personalities to keep track of. No thank you."

But then I did something mean. Only because he seemed to think he had the upper hand, not because I wanted to feel him. Arching my back, I pressed my ass into his crotch, swaying my hips side to side.

"Ooops. The bus moved. Sorry," I said innocently.

His hands slid under my shirt to my belly. He could have easily gone higher—and I probably would have let him—but he seemed satisfied with touching that stretch of skin. He rubbed his callused fingers along the soft curve just under my belly button, his dick hardening against my ass.

"I'll get you a Blue shirt," he said against my ear. "Don't wear this one again."

My eyes had started rolling back in my head just from the feel of his hands on my stomach, but they snapped back into normal position at his possessive demands.

"That's fine. I have an entire collection of Unrequited shirts. I *love* their music so much."

My final act of defiance was climbing into my bunk and sliding the curtain closed without giving him a single look. His growls were audible. I'd never had a man growl at me, but I couldn't say I didn't like when Nick did it.

His growls and hands on my skin had me holding onto my resistance by the very tips of my fingers. It wouldn't take much effort to send me over the edge, and that scared me. Nick hadn't gotten famous because he was unappealing. He had moves that inspired everyday women to throw their panties at him. Maybe in another life, if I wasn't working for his band and hadn't held him while he fell apart, I'd succumb and succumb hard. I'd walk away with a story to tell Melly and reminisce about when my tits were down to my knees and my hair was thin and gray. Now, though? If I gave into this lust...these feelings...there was absolutely no telling if I'd walk away at all. It'd probably be more of a limp or crawl.

When I walked out to the front lounge in the morning, I almost screamed at seeing Tali perched on one of the chairs, tapping away on her laptop.

She grinned at me when she saw me standing there. "Hey! Mind if I join you?"

I bent down to give her a quick hug. "You're back! I didn't know what time you were getting in today."

She sighed. "I got in super early. I actually beat the bus to the stadium. How have things been going?"

I sat down across from her, tucking my legs under me. Tali knew about the Arizona interview, and she'd ripped her contact at the station a new one—well, another new one, since I'd already ripped one.

"Pretty smoothly. With your daily emails, I've been able to keep track of schedules and press. I mean, obviously, without you we'd be lost."

She laughed. "I knew you'd be fine. You're the hardest worker we've ever had, honestly. We got lucky having you here with us."

Thus far, I'd held many, *many* service jobs, from barista to babysitter to bartender. I'd worked my tail off in those positions, even when I'd hated every second of it, but I'd never been complimented this way, and it meant more to me than it probably should have. Although I didn't quite have my life figured out, the one goal I had was to be reliable. And yeah, that sounded boring, but it was important to me that other people knew they could count on me.

"Thanks. I'm feeling pretty lucky myself. I've seen so many states and listened to some amazing music. It's like the road trip of my dreams, you know?"

"Well, maybe I can convince you to work for me once the tour is over. I'm certain I can find a job for you."

"That would be amazing, but I'm not sure..."

There was no way in hell I could be around Nick long-term. If he weren't in the picture, then hell yeah, I'd jump at the chance. But I doubted they'd fire their lead singer so they could hire me. That might have been a step too far.

She waved her hand. "We'll both think about it. And then, when we get back to Baltimore, I'll make you an offer you can't refuse, and there won't be any more thinking required."

I laughed. "When we get back to Baltimore, I'm going to take a lot of naps."

"Take a lot of naps today. Enjoy the music. Hit the beach. You definitely deserve the day off."

"Really?"

"Mmhmm. Really. I hate to do this to you, but when we get up to Jersey, I'm going back home to take care of my dad. He's doing okay, but I'd feel better if I could be there."

"Don't worry about us. I'll take care of the band, you take care of your dad."

She nodded gratefully, the fatigue behind her eyes evident. "I don't know what I'd have done without you, Dalia."

"You're Tali. You'd have figured it out without breaking a sweat."

That made her smile. "So, not only are you a talented website developer and skilled at merch sales, you're also a skilled pep-talk giver?"

I fluffed my hair. "What can I say? I've got it going on."

We went over the schedule of the upcoming week she'd be gone, including all the press the band would be doing. They usually did an interview at every stop, and fortunately, minus Arizona, they'd all been pretty routine.

"So, what are you going to do with your day off?" Tali asked as I poured a cup of coffee and turned on the kettle—a habit I couldn't seem to break, no matter how annoyed with Nick I was.

"God, I don't know. I might skip the beach this time since I've actually been to Virginia Beach before. I'll probably go listen to Malka's band, then see if she wants to hit some of the other bands with me. There are so many I haven't gotten the chance to see yet."

"Including Blue."

Goosebumps instantly lined my arms at the sound of the gravelly voice behind me.

"Hey, Nicky!" Tali said.

"Hey, Tali. Glad you're back." He stayed right behind me, his breath blowing the fine hairs on the back of my neck.

"Dalia, you should come with me to watch the band tonight," she said.

I stiffened. I could *feel* Nick's eyes boring into my back, waiting for my answer. "Oh. Yeah. Maybe. We'll see."

He scoffed. "You're not coming."

I finally turned around to look at him. Which was a mistake. He was shirtless, like always, and Nick shirtless could have been a deadly weapon. At least for me. One look at him killed the clever snark on the tip of my tongue.

My fingers were scrabbling, scrabbling, trying to hold on.

"How do you know?" I asked dumbly.

"You haven't yet."

"You haven't watched them play?" Tali asked.

I turned back to her. "No, not yet. I will, though."

He scoffed again and muttered, "Doubt it."

"Well, okay then!" I said much too brightly. "I'm going to go grab breakfast! I'll see everyone later!"

A day away from every single one of these people suddenly sounded like exactly what I needed. Maybe I *would* hit the beach, hang out on the boardwalk, and grab a giant ice cream. And maybe some distance would help me get a better grip on the edge I was dangling from.

EIGHTEEN

NICK

AS FUCKING PREDICTED, the little intruder never showed up. She didn't show up in D.C. or New Jersey or Connecticut either. She was around, doing her work and hanging out with either Malka or that little shit, Mo.

I'd left a Blue shirt on her bed, only to find it wadded up in mine that same night and her wearing an Unrequited shirt the last two days.

This whole thing was ridiculous. I was too damn old for this. There were so many less complicated, easier women around. The stack of reasons to get right the hell over this girl was a mile high. But I just...couldn't. And it grated.

Seeing her every morning was like rubbing sandpaper on my eyeballs. Not because she was unpleasant to look at. In fact, it was quite the opposite. Her kind of pretty grew every day. The vibrancy of her pulsed, like the world was her dance floor and she was the strobe light. I found I *couldn't* stop looking at her.

It pissed me off. Everything about her pissed me off. Her smart mouth, her crazy hair, her gentle way. Ian had been off for days, and I hadn't even talked to him about it. My brain had been invaded and was at capacity.

David clapped his hand on my shoulder. "Ready, dude?"

"Mmm...yeah. Where are we again?" I asked.

"Pennsyl-fucking-vania. Land of the Liberty bell, the Amish, and cheesesteaks."

"Ah, right. One of my favorite states."

"Rank?"

I scratched my chin. "Definitely top fifty."

David nodded. "Agreed."

Jas came up behind us, throwing his arms around both our shoulders. "Anyone noticed Ian is quieter than normal?"

"Malka dumped his ass," David said.

Jas inhaled sharply. "For real?"

"Who knows with them," I said.

The three of us tried to be lowkey as we glanced at Ian, tapping his stick on the hallway leading to the stage, but it was hard not to notice three grown men suddenly looking your way.

"No," he said.

David held his hands up. "Didn't say anything."

Ian scowled at him. "I can practically feel your concern in the air. Don't need it. I just wanna bang the shit out of my drums."

I'd known Ian since high school, and he still threw me. One day, I'd go around thinking I had a handle on him, then, the next, it was like we'd just met. I'd been around him long enough to know if Malka breaking up with him had broken his heart, he'd internalize it to hell. The only time I'd ever seen him visibly shaken was when Reinece died. And by shaken, I mean maybe two tears fell. That was Ian having a big reaction.

I loved the guy. He was solid. But even after all these years, on the road, sharing this crazy ride together, he kept himself just a little apart from the rest of us. I couldn't say if it was on purpose or unintentional, but I'd accepted he wasn't changing a long time ago.

"Let's do this thing, boys. I hear them calling our name," I said.

David cupped his ear. "Nah, I think they're yelling *show us Nicky's dick*! Gonna have to take off your panties for them, man."

Jas pushed David's shoulder. "He can't. They're all under your pillow!"

I sighed. "I thought we talked about this. Stop stealing my panties, Dave."

He threw his hands up. "Can't help it! They feel too good when I rub them all over my face."

A stagehand interrupted our cackling to tell us it was time. The food, the road, the cramped quarters, the press—it had all gone stale. But every time I stepped on that stage, no matter the size of the audience, with my band next to me and behind me, the experience was fresh.

I never got tired of performing. *Never.* And the songs we played, they'd meant something when we'd written them. Sure, over the years we'd evolved and our relationship to them had too, but I still loved those words, the rhythm, the melody.

And standing here, in front of this crowd who'd waited in the stifling heat all day to see us play, had me fucking wailing. I gave them a show like it was the first day of the tour, not the thirtieth, like I'd slept on a bed of feathers instead of a rocking tin can, like I'd just had the best fuck of my life instead of the bluest of balls. They ate that shit up, giving me back as much as I gave.

We'd been at this for years and years, and maybe we'd peaked, maybe we hadn't. But the people who loved our music *loved* our music, and tonight's crowd was packed with our true-blue fans. They were singing along to every song, even the B sides.

David and Jas played back to back, riffing off each other. From the giddy smiles taking over their faces, I knew they were feeling it just as much as I was. Ian was thrashing on his drums, but that was nothing new. He always went hard. On stage, behind his kit, he transformed into a machine, killing every beat with his sticks.

We played for an hour, and by the time I walked off the stage, I had sweat cascading out of every pore. Someone handed me a bottle of water, which I downed in twenty seconds.

"I could use a cheesesteak," David said after he'd demolished his own water.

"We're in Pittsburgh," Jas said.

"So? I bet there are cheesesteaks somewhere in this town. Who's coming with me to find one?"

"I'm in," Ian said.

"Fine. Let's see what Pittsburgh cheesesteaks taste like," Jasper said.

They all looked at me. "Nope. I'm showering and hitting the hay. I have no deep, dirty desire to experiment with cheesesteaks."

The three of them went their way, and I went mine, back to a blissfully quiet bus. Dalia must've been out with the cool kids —the bands who were actually her age, still bright-eyed and bushy-tailed like her. Blue was officially the old men on the tour, and I had to believe this would be our last hurrah. At some point we'd have to pass the baton, and this felt like the time. These guys were hungry for it, whereas I was well and truly satiated. We'd still tour, but our days at Swerve were coming to a close.

Once I'd taken a cold shower and pulled on a pair of sweatpants, my old ass went looking for a cup of tea and a Kit Kat. When I slid open the door to the lounge, the little intruder had yet again invaded my space. Dalia was kicked back on a couch, her bare feet crossed at the ankle. Her brows shot up when she saw me, and then, time slowed. She lifted her hand to her mouth —the hand holding what looked distinctly like a Kit Kat—and, her eyes locked on mine, took a bite.

"What the fuck?" I bit out.

"Mmmm..."

"Are you eating my chocolate?"

She chewed slowly, never looking away.

"Give it to me, Dalia."

She shook her head, offering me a smug smile as she chewed.

I opened the cabinet next to me, knowing my stash was low. And lo and fucking behold, the cabinet was completely bare. "You took the last one?"

She shook her head and took another bite.

It was too much. Weeks of looking at her, hating her, wanting her, and now *this*. Treating me like the punchline to her own private joke. Eating my fucking chocolate right in front of me.

I stalked toward her, no idea what my plan was. I just wanted my chocolate.

I held my hand out in front of her face. "Give it to me."

"Mmm-mmm."

"Dalia. Give. It. To. Me." I tried to snatch it, but she hopped up, holding the Kit Kat over her head.

"It's mine," she said.

I barely heard her. The way she waved that red wrapper over her head transformed me into a raging bull, Dalia my sadistic matador.

She ripped the last of the chocolate out of the wrapper and held it in front of her mouth.

I charged, getting right up in her face. "Give it to me."

Her eyes had gone wide, and her breath was hot on my lips. "You really want my chocolate, don't you?"

I could've sworn she took a step closer, because her tits brushed against my bare chest.

"Dalia..." She had me crazed in every way. My dick was hard. My brain had gone haywire. None of my thoughts were straight. The need to have *something* sweet in my mouth was almost overwhelming.

She hesitated. For a brief moment, she closed her eyes and pulled her bottom lip between her teeth. Then, her eyes opened, and it was like something had been decided. She tipped her chin up. "If you want it, take it."

I frowned at her, confused for a second, then she opened her mouth and placed the chocolate on her tongue.

All I could think was *mine*. I wasn't sure whether I was thinking about the girl or the chocolate, but I wanted both, so I threaded my hands through the back of her curls, yanking her against me, and I took.

Dalia's lips were open, pliant, and she pushed her tongue into my mouth, passing me the melting chocolate. It was a damn shame I had to pull away to chew because Dalia combined with chocolate was the sweetest thing I'd ever tasted.

I held her eyes while I slowly chewed. Her fingers dug into my shoulders, where she'd braced herself when I'd grabbed her. She licked her lips, and her eyelids went heavy, lowering to half-mast.

"I need more," I said.

"I'm all out," she whispered.

Bending, I traced my tongue over her lower lip. "Mmm. No, I don't think you're all out. I think you're holding back."

Her hands clasped behind my neck. "So taste me and find out."

She didn't wait for me to come to her again. Her lips were on mine in less than a breath, and she never paused. Her tongue dove into my mouth, tasting of chocolate and defiance. This kiss wasn't about falling in love. It was still the same bad idea as before, but as she sucked on my bottom lip and raked her hands through my hair, I pictured her giving common sense the finger.

This was inevitable. Fighting it was fun, but pressing my aching dick to Dalia's soft belly was even better. Slipping my hands under the back of her shirt and feeling the smooth curve of her spine was amazing. Sinking into her pussy for the first time was gonna be life changing.

She stopped kissing me and stopped touching me, but she didn't end this. Instead, she moved it along. She'd tossed her T-shirt behind her in another breath, her hands cupping her fucking beautiful breasts, the pink of her nipples peeking out between her fingers. The tattoo across her chest was on full display. A delicate branch with pink buds and a little blue bird perched on her shoulder.

"I'm throwing caution to the wind right now, Nick. You coming with me?"

I grabbed her hands, gently moving them away from her breasts, letting them fall free. My mouth watered at the sight of her. There were so many things I wanted to do to her. If we had time, a bed, and maybe some patience, I'd have done them all. As it was, I felt the need vibrating off her, and there was no telling how long we had to be alone.

I kept her hand in mine and started walking through the bus. "*You're* coming with *me*."

She did. For once, there weren't any arguments. We stopped at my bunk to grab condoms, then I pulled her to the back lounge.

"I need to taste you," I said.

"You did."

"Baby, I'm only getting started."

She was so soft in my arms. When I'd pictured this happening—because hell yeah, I'd pictured it on the daily—I'd imagined a battle for dominance. Fighting mixed with fucking. So it was surprising how pliant Dalia was as I held her, directing her mouth under mine.

As much as she let me take the lead, I knew that's what it was. She was *letting* me. I had no doubt if I made the wrong move, she'd let me know.

So far, so fucking good.

I ran my palm up her belly, between her breasts, and along her throat, pushing her chin back to give me access. Her head fell back, and I devoured her sweet neck, pulling the delicate skin between my teeth. Dalia's hands dug into my hair, both yanking me away and pushing me closer, like she couldn't quite make up her mind. But when I pulled her rosy pink nipple into my mouth, she stopped fighting whatever was going on in her mind and fully gave herself over.

Her tits were perfect. They spilled from my hands as I lifted them to my mouth, the weight of them sending my cock panting.

"Come here," I said.

"I'm here."

Backing up to the bench behind me, I sat down, spreading my legs so she could stand between them. She had on little boxers, and I licked a line from the elastic waistband to her belly button, then back again.

"Can I take these off?" I asked, hooking my fingers along the top of her shorts.

"Please," she said breathily.

I went slow, torturing myself, and from the quiet moans escaping Dalia, torturing her too. I kissed every inch of skin I revealed. She felt like silk under my lips. I'd never felt skin like hers. I dragged my nose and chin over her hips and stomach, reveling in her.

My attention was dragged away from her skin to the thatch

of red hair between her legs. I'd never been with a natural redhead before, and her trimmed triangle had my cock throbbing desperately.

I got down on my knees and kissed and nuzzled her there, making her gasp.

"Nick," she moaned.

"Lift your leg, Dalia."

She raised one leg up, resting her foot on the bench right behind me, giving me the most incredible view. God, I wanted to pause and look at her, to memorize every fold and line, but her scent hit my nose and there was no pausing. I buried my face between her legs, lapping at her. It wasn't artful. In fact, it was sloppy as hell. Later—and sweet baby Jesus, I hoped there was a later—I'd go slow, draw this out. Right now, though, I needed her pussy all over my face and Dalia screaming my name as I made her come.

Spreading her even farther with my fingers, I found her clit with my lips, and pulled at it, making her legs shake. She was so wet for me, so slick, and her clit throbbed between my lips. There was no doubt she was close. Hell, I was close, and my cock was still lonely in my pants. But this was Dalia fucking Brenner greedily grinding her gorgeous pussy against my face while I licked and sucked at her. My cock had never known the likes of this woman existed.

"Nick, Nick, Nick," she shouted, getting louder and louder each time. I held her hips as she rocked and shuddered. "Please, please, please fuck me now."

I sat back on the bench, my pants around my ankles, with Dalia straddling my lap before I'd taken a breath. Her eyes were glazed and hooded, sweat beaded on her forehead, and her hair was everywhere. I'd never seen anyone more beautiful.

My hands roamed the rolling hills of her body as she buried her face in my neck, kissing and licking my skin.

"You smell so good," she murmured right before she bit my shoulder.

I grunted, reflexively shifting my hips, causing my cock to slide between her folds. She moaned, then bit down again, and my cock went on the same slide.

"Like that?" I asked.

She rocked her hips. "Love that. But I think I told you I need you to fuck me. Why isn't that happening?"

"Lift your pretty pussy off my dick so I can roll on a condom and it'll happen."

She complied, raising up just enough for me to sheath myself, then she sunk down, taking me inside her slick heat, all the way to the bottom.

My head flopped back when she was fully seated with her inner muscles squeezing. "Jesus Christ, Dalia. You're about to turn me into a two-pump chump."

"Look at me, Nicky."

I raised my head, taking her in. "So pretty."

She traced a finger over my bottom lip, then she said the thing I'd never forget for as long as I lived.

"Hold on, because I'm about to ride the hell out of your gorgeous cock. Don't ask me to go slow. I need to go hard."

I gripped her waist, thrusting upwards. "Go hard, baby. I'm here. I got you."

She raised up and slammed down, her ass hitting my legs with a slap and her breasts swinging in my face. She did the same move again and again, her pace picking up each time. And I...I went along for the ride. This was the Dalia show, and damn if it wasn't the best thing I'd ever seen.

Each time her ass hit my legs, it sent a shockwave through her body, shaking the flesh at her hips and jiggling her tits. She had my cock in a vise grip, squeezing and sliding until I was ready to lose my mind. I pushed her down and thrust up at the same time, hitting her even deeper, eliciting a deep groan from her.

"Oh god, keep doing that and I'm going to come," she said.

Gladly.

I met her thrust for thrust, and she arched back, her face to the sky, her tits in my mouth. The urge to come was so strong, I had trouble thinking of anything else. I became this base being. Shooting my load and planting my fucking seed deep inside her was imperative. Nothing in this world could've possibly been more important.

Still, that part of me that hadn't let the caveman take over kept my eyes locked on her. She was more than a pussy and a pair of tits. This was Dalia, the girl who held me, the woman who challenged me. And here she was, naked in my arms, letting me have her. I took mental notes of every detail. The silk of her skin. The movement of her thighs. The smell of her arousal, the taste of that arousal—and her eyes, her eyes. There was a song written in those eyes. Or those eyes were gonna be written in one of my songs.

Brown. Glazed. Wide and full of heat. Open, present. Watchful, always watchful.

"Nick," she moaned weakly, just as her eyes rolled back and her inner walls clamped down on me. Seeing Dalia come, shaking in my arms, her breath heavy in my ear as she collapsed against my chest, was so fucking erotic. I held her through it, then I followed her over, planted myself inside her as deep as I could go.

She'd completely depleted me, taking my come, my energy, my will to do anything besides touch her skin.

We sat there for long minutes, not speaking, mostly just remembering to breathe.

Finally, she lifted off me, and I got rid of the condom.

"That—"

"I know, shouldn't happen again," she filled in.

I grabbed her tit and gave it a good, long suck. "Not what I was going to say."

Her hands were in my hair again, pushing and pulling. "Oh? What were you going to say?"

I pulled her back into my lap, sitting sideways, and growled against her neck, "I was going to say that needs to happen again and frequently."

"But you don't even like me," she protested.

"Oh, I like you. Sometimes you piss me right the hell off, but I like that too."

She squirmed in my lap as I licked a line up the side of her neck. I was already half-hard and fairly confident I'd be ready to go again any minute.

"You're not gonna be my boyfriend," she panted.

"No?"

"No. This is a tour thing."

We'd fucking see about that. "I'm not so sure I agree."

Dalia had just opened her mouth to reply when the sounds of several people tromping up the bus stairs reached us. She sprung out of my lap, finding her shorts, and I stood, pulling my pants up from my ankles.

"Impeccable timing," I muttered.

"I can't find my shirt," she said.

Our eyes met, and it clicked that her shirt was in the front lounge. "Shit!" she whispered.

"I'll go out there, you get another shirt from your bunk. Talk later?"

She pushed my shoulders. "Go!"

The boys were in the front lounge, stuffing their faces with cheesesteaks, completely oblivious to what they'd almost walked in on.

"Hey! What've you been up to?" Jasper asked when he noticed me lingering by the kitchen.

"Uh, just watching a movie in my bunk." I toed Dalia's rumpled shirt under the table.

"Did we interrupt your self-love?" David asked.

"Nah, I finished five minutes ago. I just googled your picture and I was good to go," I said.

"Aw, that's sweet," David said.

The door behind me slid open, alerting me to Dalia's emergence. I turned, and when our eyes locked, she blushed. And I'm not ashamed to say I felt the same flush heating my own face.

"Babydoll!" David yelled. "I thought you'd be out with your boyfriend."

She giggled. "I'm here. I'm going to sleep, though. Just wanted to say goodnight."

The guys all said goodnight, turning their attention back to their food. She was close enough I could sniff her neck. "You smell like me," I said.

She palmed my cock through my sweatpants. "Bet you smell like me too."

"Never washing my dick again," I whispered.

She snorted. "Sounds appetizing." Then she opened a cabinet in the kitchenette and pointed inside. "I went shopping earlier. Guess I put them away in the wrong cabinet."

I barked out a laugh when I saw the contents. She'd filled the cabinet—yes, the wrong one—with chocolate. Kit Kats and Hershey bars, and Snickers and Kisses. I reached in and picked up some in gold wrappers.

"Ferrero Rocher? You got me the good stuff. Must mean you like me," I said.

She lifted a shoulder and grinned. "It was on sale."

"You don't have to admit it. I can tell."

"Don't try to be cute with me, Nicky. Won't work." She wiggled her butt as she turned away. "Goodnight!"

"Night."

Flopping down in a chair, I slowly ate the chocolate hazelnut candy, laughing to myself. If Dalia had just told me to open the other cabinet in the first place, none of the best parts of tonight would've happened. But then, maybe that was the point. She'd been wanting this just as much as I had, no matter how many times she denied it.

Dalia was still complicated, but as it turned out, I'd been looking for a complication.

NINETEEN
DALIA

I SUCCUMBED.

Truthfully, I didn't want to resist anymore, and I wasn't sorry I gave in. I'd resisted until I couldn't quite remember why I was resisting in the first place.

The way he'd touched me by our bunks in Nashville had obliterated the rest of my defenses. Oh, I'd tried to stay away. And I'd succeeded all the way up the east coast. But when he came out to the lounge when we were parked in Pittsburgh, eyes flashing with anger, chest gleaming with droplets of water, I had to tease him, and then I had to have him. Not for a story to share with Melly. No, what happened on that bus was just for me.

I had no idea if Nick had a reputation of being a ladies' man, but damn. Just *damn.* He made every one of my past partners look like little boys. The man ate pussy like it was his job. Actually, more like a passion project. And that had been at an awkward angle in confined spaces. I had to know what he could do with a big bed and all the time in the world.

We wouldn't be staying at another hotel until we got to Chicago. We still had Ohio and Indiana to get through before my bedroom fantasies could come true. That was...if he wanted to. Which I thought he did. And if he wasn't sure, I'd steal all his chocolate again.

Our...thing might have had an expiration date, but now that I'd had a taste, I was definitely going back for seconds.

I spent most of our day in Ohio dealing with a massive merch shipment. There'd been a mix-up and we'd gotten tons of extra-smalls, but no extra-larges. So, I'd been on the phone all morning with our supplier, expediting the correct order after getting the runaround. Not my most fun day, especially when I would have liked to be flirt-slash-fighting with Nick instead.

Not that he wasn't busy himself. I was still in charge of the band's schedule with Tali being gone a few more days, so I knew they were at the Rock and Roll Hall of Fame for a press event, then they had a fan meet and greet back at the stadium, followed by their nightly performance. He probably wouldn't be back to the bus until I was in bed for the night.

We were pretty much always surrounded by nosy ass men anyway. We hadn't had much of a conversation after we'd had sex, but I was all for keeping this on the down low. I really didn't need David all up in my business. Jasper would have been polite about it, Ian would have ignored it, but David...oh David. He'd poke and prod relentlessly, and the only one I wanted poking me relentlessly was Nick.

I finally had a moment to breathe and *eat* a little after three. Lucky for me, I was able to scrounge up a sandwich at catering, and I settled under the tent outside the bus with my laptop and my lunch. And Mo. He'd spotted me when he was walking by and pulled up a chair beside me without invitation.

I wasn't the type of person who needed a lot of alone time, fortunately, because it was pretty much impossible to get on this tour.

Mo leaned over my shoulder, checking out the graphics I'd been working on for Unrequited's website. I'd done a complete rebrand, taking their old, tired logo and bringing it up to date. It looked pretty damn snazzy, if I did say so myself.

Mo pointed at the screen. "Isn't it too...gold?"

"Are you asking me, or telling me?"

"You're the expert. But what if you lightened this up a bit over here and added a drop shadow behind it?"

I actually laughed. *What the what?* "I can make some tweaks, but I truly can't spend a lot more time on it. You can't afford for me to spend more time on it."

He stared at the screen thoughtfully, leaning over my shoulder. "I just don't love it. Sorry."

I cocked my head back to get a good look at him, to see if he was messing with me. Sadly, he looked completely serious. "Should we just call it a day then? You can pay me for the hours I've put in, and then find someone else whose vision meshes with yours."

His eyes went wide. "What? No! Fuck, I'm sorry. I thought we were friends, you know, and I could be honest..."

"We are friends, Mo. But this friendship is gonna be short-lived if you can't respect my time. Where were these opinions when I sent you a mock-up?"

He had the decency to look sheepish. "I guess it was hard for me to visualize the final product. Just keep it how it is."

I sighed. "It's fine. I'll work on it a little more, then email you later. But this is *it*!"

"I like stern Dalia." He held his arm out in front of me. "See this? You're giving me goosebumps."

I pushed his arm away, laughing. "You haven't seen stern Dalia yet. Ask me to make more changes and see what happens."

"Oooh, will you get out your ruler?"

"Are you involving me in your dirty teacher fantasy?" I asked.

He batted his eyelashes at me. "I've been a bad boy, Ms. Brenner. Please don't hurt me!"

I burst out laughing, shoving his shoulders. He grabbed my hands to stop me, and then we were both laughing, especially when I told him he was my naughtiest pupil.

Because my life was my life, the band returned from their press event as Mo stuck his butt in my face, begging me to go easy on him.

"My fantasies usually involve two women in this position, but this is an interesting scene to come home to," David said.

Mo straightened, smacking David's offered hand.

"Whatcha up to?" Jasper asked.

"Would it be cliché if I said it's not what it looks like?" I asked.

Jasper snorted. "I didn't actually believe you were conducting a BDSM dungeon outside our tour bus."

"I did. And I'm next in line," David said.

"Careful. Ms. Brenner has a heavy hand," Mo said.

I laughed with the guys, but I was also avoiding Nick's stare. Because he *was* staring. I didn't have to look at him to feel his eyes boring into me.

My eyes met Jasper's instead, and strangely, he looked disappointed, making me want to explain what was really going on.

"Actually, I was just showing Mo the graphics I'm working on for his band's website." I turned my screen around to show them. "See?"

Jasper squatted down to take a better look, and even David bent down to check it out.

"That's pretty as shit," Jasper said.

"Right? But Mo doesn't like it," I said.

He held his hands up. "I didn't say I didn't like it!"

"Whatever. Just admit you're very demanding considering the steep discount I'm throwing your way," I said.

"That, I do admit. Which is what led to my ass being spanked."

"Fucking hell," Ian muttered before disappearing onto the bus.

"Why is Mo getting a discount?" Nick asked.

I couldn't *not* look at him. His hands were at his hips, his shoulder tense. I'd seen Nick angry, but this was different. He looked ready to knock some heads, and it inexplicably turned me on.

"Friends and family," I said.

He jerked his chin up. "So, I'd get a discount too?"

I shook my head slowly. "No."

"I'm not a friend?"

"Not sure yet. But that's not why."

His brows drew together, forming a deep line between them. "Why?"

"Because I know you can actually afford me."

His eyes studied mine as he rubbed the scruff on his chin. A flash of a memory of that scruff buried against my pussy had me crossing my legs.

"And I'd never ask to pay less than you're worth," he said.

Jasper clapped Nick's shoulder. "Come on, man. Have you forgotten what it was like just starting out? Sometimes you gotta hustle."

Mo frowned. "I'm not hustling her."

I waved him off. "You're fine, Mo. I wouldn't have said yes if I didn't want to help you out. And you're going to tell everyone you meet—or at least the bands you meet who *can* afford me—how awesome I am to work with. Right?"

"You bet your pretty ass I am."

"Not cool," Jasper muttered.

I clicked my laptop shut. "All right. I think I'm done here. Mo, I'll email you later. I'm going to eat my sandwich in peace."

I left the guys to measure their dicks or whatever egotistical men did when they got together and climbed on the bus. Ian had settled in at the small table, working on a puzzle with a million pieces.

"I'm going in the back," I said.

"Okay."

"Okay. I just thought it'd be weird if I walked by you without saying anything."

He looked up from the puzzle, the corners of his mouth barely quirking up. "And this isn't weird?"

"Maybe less weird?"

His eyes returned to his puzzle. "I can't find the last fucking corner piece."

Scanning the pieces strewn on the table, I found it almost immediately. "There!" I pointed.

He snatched it up and sighed with what looked like relief. "Thanks. Sometimes it takes a pair of fresh eyes to see the forest for the trees."

"This is the most I've heard you talk," I said.

"Now I've reached my quota."

"Let me know if you need any more help. I like puzzles."

He barely nodded, so I took myself and my sandwich to the back of the bus. Before I even sat down, I took a huge bite out of it. This not eating all day business was for the birds. When I graduated, my ass was finding a sedentary job with built-in mealtimes. Although, the thought of working in a cubicle day in and day out made me shudder. There was something to be said for days filled with sunshine and fresh air.

As I wadded up the wrapper, the door to the back lounge slid open and Nick stepped inside, closing it behind him.

"Hey," he said.

"Hey, yourself. How'd the Hall of Fame go?"

"Nothing unexpected. I wish you would have come with us. It's a cool place."

"Next time, definitely. I just had a lot to do around here today."

His brows pinched together. "Looked like it."

"Right. Because that two seconds you witnessed was the entirety of my day."

He sat down next to me on the bench, and I threw my wrapper at his face, and like the cool cat he was, he caught it midair and tossed it over his shoulder. He grabbed me, pulling me against him. "I don't like that...that kid."

"Are you actually jealous right now?"

"It's possible."

"Why?"

I knew why. I'd have been jealous as hell if I'd walked in on a similar scene. Nick wasn't really mine, but I couldn't say I wanted him to be anyone else's either.

He shook his head and looked out the darkened windows. "Because that kid doesn't deserve any of your attention or time. In Vegas, he left you out there, asleep, while he went off to god knows where. That's not something a friend would do."

And suddenly, my vague memory of floating clicked with reality. Nick had saved me. Of course he had. He took care of everyone around him, and I'd somehow become part of that circle.

"You were the cloud?" I asked.

He chuckled. "Yeah, I think you mumbled something about that. And you told me I wasn't magnificent."

"That sounds like something I'd say. But Nick, are you saying *you* want my time and attention?"

"Was that not made clear last night?"

"We fucked. Your big dick and talented tongue were the only things made clear."

He rubbed his thumb over my bottom lip. "You have a dirty fuckin' mouth, Dalia."

"Still not clear."

He grinned. "Yes."

I wrinkled my nose. "Yes?"

"Yes, I want your time and attention."

My heart was doing crazy hops and skips in my chest. "I can't give it all to you."

He cupped my jaw, tipping my head back. "You gonna give it to *him*?"

"I'm committed to building his website, so yeah."

"I need you to commit to fucking me again," he rumbled.

"Throw me in a padded cell and commit me. As crazy as it is, I want you."

He growled and took my mouth hard, licking at my tongue and biting my lips. I dove at him, knocking him flat on the couch, clanking our teeth together. He didn't pull away, though. His arms wrapped around my back, pressing me against him. He was hard against my stomach, and I was slick between my legs—and we had to stop.

"Nick..."

He licked my neck. "Dalia..."

"We can't," I moaned.

"I can't kiss you?"

"The guys." My eyes rolled back as he bit my shoulder.

"I don't want to kiss the guys."

"But they might come back here," I whimpered as he continued his trail of bites on my neck and shoulder.

"Dalia, *you're* on top of *me*."

My head popped up from where it had been buried in his neck. "Oh." I blew a curl off my forehead. "Right." With very little grace, I rolled off him and moved a good two feet down the couch.

Nick sat up, adjusting the front of his jeans and full-on grinning at me. "Am I your dirty little secret?"

"Yep. Imagine the damage to my rep if people found out I'd been making out with a hot rock star. I'd never recover."

He scratched the back of his head. "I'm pretty sure the guys'll figure it out. Especially when I'm nice to you."

"You've been a lot nicer to me than you think. And I have a hard time believing we'll stop arguing just because we've had sex."

He leaned his head back and kicked his legs out. Even just him relaxing on the couch was sexy. The bulge tenting his pants probably had something to do with it, but mostly, it was just Nick. He had swagger that couldn't be taught. He owned the skin he was in, and damn, if I was in that skin, I'd own it too.

Oh jeez. That sounded a little skin suit-y. The point was, Nick was gorgeous and confident, and he had every right to be.

"You coming with us to the meet and greet?" he asked.

"Yeah, Tali asked me to go to make sure everything runs smoothly."

He turned his head to look at me. "You staying for the show?"

I lifted a shoulder. "Maybe. I haven't decided."

His eyes darted all around my face. "What's up with that?"

"Nothing's up with it," I said defensively. "I'm just not sure what I'm doing tonight. I might just want to chill."

I was spewing bullshit. I didn't want to watch Nick perform. In fact, I'd been actively avoiding it. At first, I'd skipped Blue's shows out of exhaustion and disinterest. Now, though, I was being stubborn. I'd dug my heels in, convincing myself it was better not to see him up on that stage. I could still see him as a regular guy now, but if I witnessed thousands of people worshipping at his feet, I'd have to look at him differently. We wouldn't just be the hot guy and fucking adorable girl making time with each other. We'd be superstar famous dude slumming with poor college student. I'd rather us be on the same plane, even if that plane was mostly made of lies I told myself.

The look of disappointment on Nick's face almost had me. He wanted me to be there, and I felt like a dick for *not* wanting to be there.

He shook his head, smiling ruefully. "Okay. Enjoy your chill time."

He got up and slid the door open, but I grabbed a handful of his shirt, stopping him from leaving.

"You're not going to fight with me?" I asked.

"Not today."

"What if I promise to come see you play before the end of the tour?"

He fingered one of my curls, twirling it around his pinky. "Twice."

"Watch you play twice?"

"Yep."

"Okay, twice."

He nodded. "You have three more weeks."

"I keep my promises."

He cupped my jaw, rubbing his thumb over my chin. "I know you do, so I'm not going to ask again." He held my eyes with his for a long beat. "See you later, Dalia." His hand dropped, and he sauntered through the open door, heading toward the front of the bus.

I slapped the button on the wall, closing the door again.

Well, that was a trampling. I'd gone from planning on never seeing Blue is the Color on stage again to agreeing to see them twice. Nick wasn't famous without reason, though. Aside from the obvious musical talent, the man had charm. He made me want to agree to things. He also made me absolutely crazy.

Which was my only explanation for downloading every album Blue is the Color had ever recorded and laying there on the couch, listening to their music. Listening to *him*. Maybe I didn't hate his music so much anymore. Maybe I even kinda liked it.

Thank Freddie Mercury—aka my god—I only had three more weeks with him. Any more time than that, and I'd no doubt be swept up in him, and this time when it ended, instead of pretty tattoos of flowers covering my arms, I'd end up with "I Heart Nick Fletcher" tattooed on my forehead. I liked tattoos as much as the next girl, but that wouldn't be a good look on anyone.

TWENTY

NICK

"LET'S GO FOR A DRIVE."

"I'm down," I said. "Where to?"

Jas shook his head. "A cornfield or something? I don't know. What is there in Indiana?"

"There's always food," I said.

He smacked my shoulder. "Yeah, let's find food. Genius plan."

I stood by the bus waiting as Jasper went to find someone who'd loan us a car. I had no doubt he'd accomplish his goal. People looked at Jas and just trusted him. He looked like a fine, upstanding citizen who'd give you the shirt off his back. And he absolutely was those things. He was the fabled good guy who never let fame go to his head, and the same kid I'd met twenty years ago. Even losing his mama hadn't hardened him.

When he came back into view, shaking keys over his head, I laughed. "Who'd you con outta giving up their car?"

"Some poor schmuck in catering. By the way, we have to stop for a six pack of beer on the way back. That was my payment."

"Sounds fair. Should we catch David and Ian?" I asked.

"Would it be really uncool if I said let's go without them?"

"Nah. Let's go."

Jasper and I hadn't had any time alone together since the tour started. And even before the Swerve tour, we'd been out on the road pretty much right after the funeral, playing surprise shows at small clubs. None of us had wanted to sit around and mourn. I'd begged Tali to get us out of there, to keep us busy, and she'd worked a miracle, booking us last minute at every club that'd take us.

This was good. Jas was my brother, and I'd missed this. Our friendship beyond the band. I liked to think if our lives had gone in another direction, if we hadn't made music work and had to have taken office jobs, we'd still chill on the weekends, bitching about our coworkers and playing video games.

As we walked toward the parking lot, my eyes were drawn toward a glint of bright red approaching. The sun was in my eyes, so I couldn't really make her out, but that red was unmistakable. Dalia was walking with Malka, talking and laughing. Jas was probably still talking, but he sounded like Charlie Brown's teacher at that point.

Ten feet away, she still hadn't glanced my way.

"Hey, you," I called out.

Her head turned, and the smile she was wearing grew when she saw me. "Hey, yourself."

Her eyes stayed on mine as she approached. When we were side by side, she reached out, brushing her fingers over mine.

"See you later, Nicky," she murmured as she passed. And damn if I wasn't too proud to turn around and watch her go. At the last second, before she disappeared around a corner, she looked back, giving me the barest of waves, and I was sunk.

I'd been sinking, falling, floating since the second I laid eyes on her at my door. But right now, I was panting for her. I'd *never* had this feeling before. It was disconcerting, but at the same time, I wanted to bottle it to splash on my face whenever it wore off.

I turned and started walking again, pretending I hadn't just tripped over my own feet at the sight of a pretty girl. Beautiful girl. Dalia.

"Saw that," Jas said.

"Saw what?"

"Nope. What you're not going to do is pretend like that didn't happen."

"Not sure what you mean."

"Oh, just Dalia, the girl you've been lusting over for more than a month, touching your hand and calling you 'Nicky.' And you, looking all giddy and shit."

"I don't look giddy," I mumbled.

I sure as shit didn't look giddy anymore, asshole.

"You did. You're good at hiding some shit, but not this."

We stopped at a non-descript black sedan and hopped in. We were driving for a few minutes before I responded.

"Not sure I want to talk about her," I said.

He sputtered. "Not sure if you noticed, but the subject had been fully dropped. I think you actually do want to talk about her."

I stared out the window, watching the blur of scenery as we sailed down a highway.

"Maybe I just wanna talk."

Jas nodded. "Let's talk."

We were quiet for a while, though, long enough for the scenery to change from strip malls to cornfields. Jas exited the highway, winding the car through narrow, sleepy streets in a town that looked like it'd stopped progressing in the fifties. We drove by a corner store, complete with an old man rocking in a rocking chair out front, houses with red white and blue bunting strung from their wraparound front porches, and a drive-in restaurant.

"Think they welcome my kind around here?" Jasper asked as he pulled into one of the drive-in parking spots. He'd had to ask that questions many times over the years as we traveled through certain parts of the country. In towns like this one, which, at first glance, was quaint in how it clung to the ways of the past, Jas, with his mix of black and Filipino heritage and waist-length dreads, stuck out like a sore thumb. And sadly, he hadn't been welcomed into every town we'd stopped in. In our early years, David had punched some hick in the face for calling Jas a word even *I'd* never say—never even think, for that matter. And I damn well knew David would have no problem throwing down for Jas even now, as would the lot of us.

"Hope so, man. 'Cause now that we're here, I need a malted," I said.

He glanced at the menu next to his side of the car. "Have we ever figured out what exactly a malted is?"

"Nah, the details aren't important. Order me a breaded tenderloin too."

He leaned out the window, yelling our order into an intercom that had seen better days. Considering our car was the only one in the parking lot, we probably wouldn't have to wait too long. I turned up the music on the radio—only three channels seemed to get reception out here, and thankfully, one was a classic rock station.

"So...Dalia," Jasper started.

I leaned my head back on the seat. "Yeah. I'm into her."

"No kidding. You've been less than subtle in your appreciation."

"But it's more than that. Maybe. I don't know. Could just be a tour hook-up."

His brows shot up. "You're hooking up? Don't let David get wind of that, he'll never leave you alone."

"Once. And we're keeping it quiet. Whatever this is."

He twisted in his seat to face me. "I like her for you. You've needed someone who'll call you out on your miserable shit."

"True. But she's young."

"Not *that* young. And you're immature as hell."

"Very emotionally stunted," I said.

He snorted. "Aren't we all?"

"Not you."

He dug his thumb into the leather console, leaving shallow tracks in its wake. "I don't know. I've been on the road non-stop since Mom died. And I actually dread the tour ending. Don't you?"

"Yeah," I agreed quietly.

"It's like if I go home, and I don't see her, then it's real. But if I keep moving, keep traveling, then maybe she's just at home, waiting to tell me what she thought of our latest track."

That dread I thought I'd mostly left in the dust, surged back, filling my gut with such force, the wind was knocked right out of me. Then I remembered what Dalia had said. *It's grief, not dread. Grief.*

"I feel it too. Every time it's quiet, I start thinking about her, and I just can't bear it. It hurts, so all I want to do is fill up the quiet."

"And see, I *can't* stop thinking about her. You know how they say missing someone makes you forget all their flaws? Not me, though. I remember the bad shit, her perfectionism, her impatience, how she made me roll my ass out at seven, even on the weekends."

I grinned. "And there weren't any secrets around her. She was like a private detective. She'd figure out who I was with, where, and exactly what I did."

He slapped his knee, chuckling. "Yep. Sounds about right. She'd say it was to keep us safe, but the truth was she was nosy as hell."

I closed my eyes, picturing how Reinece's eyes lit up as she cross examined me. "She was."

"The thing is, even her flaws make me miss her. That pedestal she'll always sit on is high, but she built it herself, with blood, sweat, and laughter. And I just..." He shuddered. "How can a woman who was so alive be dead?"

His voice broke on the last word, and my heart broke for the hundredth time since Reinece finally confessed her diagnosis. The one she'd hidden until she couldn't hide it anymore. She'd been able to keep the effects of her brain tumor from us because we'd been caught up in our own lives, too busy to see her vision fading and her constant headaches. She'd also been steeped in denial—her medical training alerted her to the seriousness of her symptoms, but she refused to get them checked out until it was much too late.

We lost her, almost two months from the day she'd confessed. Reinece hadn't gone down easy. She carried on normally until she couldn't anymore, and even then, she fought. When she was taking her last breaths, we'd think *this is it, this is the last one*, then she'd take one more. When she stopped breathing, when it had been minutes since she'd last inhaled, Jas and I watched her, waiting for one more.

"Are you okay?" I asked.

"What?"

"This is me, checking in on you," I said, echoing Dalia's words. "Are you okay?"

He dug the heel of his hand into his eye and sighed. "No. I'm really not. I will be—I really feel that—but I'm not there yet."

"Me either."

His eyes opened, and he really looked at me. "But you're so...steady."

I held out my shaking hand. "I'm crumbling a little here, man."

"We need to go home," he said.

"Think that'll do it?"

"I'm hoping. Get back to our roots. Face the new reality. Just slow down and feel what we need to feel."

"Feeling what we need to feel sounds fucking horrifying," I said.

There was a tap on Jas's window, interrupting the trip down misery lane. Our food had arrived.

He rolled down the window, and the waitress hooked a tray laden with junk food to the side of the car. She bent down, smiling at us, but when she made eye contact with me, she gasped.

"N-Nick?" Her eyes darted to Jas. "J-Jasper?"

He waved. "Hey. What's your name?"

"Holy Moses! I'm Melanie."

"Nice to meet you. I'm assuming you're a fan?"

"Are you kidding me? You're looking at the lead singer of Indiana's best Blue is the Color's tribute band!"

Jas laughed. "No way! Name?"

"You'll think it's lame!" Melanie said, blushing all the way up to her forehead.

"Never," I said.

"Okay!" She covered her eyes. "It's Pink is the Color. We're an all-girl tribute band."

"Holy shit, I love it!" Jas said.

"We play every month at the church's spaghetti dinner. We've turned the entire town into fans of your music. I bet if you looked at your record sales, you'd see a mysterious spike in Wikahache, Indiana," Melanie said.

Jas shook his head. "I gotta hear this."

I couldn't say exactly how it had happened, but within ten minutes, we'd followed Melanie to her house after she'd made a bunch of phone calls. And then, we were sitting in her driveway, our sandwiches and milkshakes from the restaurant in hand, surrounded by half of Wikahache, watching Pink is the Color perform in her garage.

They were actually pretty good. I'd seen a few of our tribute bands over the years, and this one sat firmly at the top of the bunch. It was surprising to see Melanie, a woman in her forties, whose look screamed "mom," rasping out our lyrics with all the soul of Stevie Nicks and Shirley Manson. And her band was made up of pretty talented musicians.

I enjoyed myself thoroughly, but even more, I took a second to count my lucky stars. Here was this woman, full of talent, performing *our* songs at her small town's spaghetti dinner. Maybe she was completely fulfilled by that, by where she'd ended up. Or maybe, if her life had gone just a little differently, she'd be selling out stadiums and have her own tribute band.

When I met people like Melanie, it was hard not to want to kick my own ass for letting myself get so apathetic about this whole thing. My career, the fame. It had changed my life, and it meant something, not just to me, but the people who wrote us letters or knew our songs so well, they could sing them backward and forward.

Jas and I made eye contact, and I didn't even have to say anything. He felt it too.

Before we left, we signed a hundred autographs and posed for every requested picture. And I got Melanie's contact info. There was no way we weren't having Pink is the Color on stage with us the next time we came to Indiana. In fact, I was more than a little obsessed with the way my words sounded coming from Melanie's mouth.

Back in the car, on the highway, I let out a loud laugh. "Holy shit, did I just dream that?"

"Shit, I don't know, man. That was surreal, but like good surreal. Did *not* expect that when I drove into that town."

I shook my head, the smile on my face refusing to budge. "So crazy."

I hadn't felt this good since...that day Dalia and I spent together in Arkansas. And before that? Jesus, I couldn't pinpoint a time where I'd felt so fucking light. Talking about Reinece with Jas and admitting I wasn't quite okay probably had a lot to do with it, along with just reveling in the pure joy of making music.

I wasn't okay. But I was getting there.

TWENTY-ONE
DALIA

I SORT OF fulfilled my promise that night.

I had the bus to myself while the band was performing, so after checking in with my parents and Melly, I retreated to my bunk, ready to hang up my proverbial troubles and regroup. Part of me was nervous to see Nick tonight. I'd chickened out of going to see Blue is the Color play yet again, even though I'd wanted to. Every time I thought about doing it, just sucking it up and going, panic set in and I couldn't.

Instead of going to the concert, I laid in my bed and listened to my carefully curated list of Blue songs. Ones that sent shivers down my spine. Ones that made a lump form in my throat. Ones that made me cross my legs and squirm.

Let's be real, I still didn't like all their songs. I never would. But since the beginning of their career, they'd put out an album almost every eighteen months, so their catalogue was massive. The list of songs I *did* love was extensive.

At first, I tried to read as I listened to the music, but Nick's rough velvet voice distracted me from doing anything else. Instead of fighting it, I pictured our mornings in the front lounge, bickering, bantering, *being* together. Nick's golden torso, stretched out as he kicked back on the couch, the early morning sun hitting his eyes just right, and oh god, his feet.

My hand traveled down my belly and under the waistband of my shorts. I hesitated just outside my underwear. There was no coming back from this. If I touched myself to Nick's voice, I'd always associate it with making me come.

My hips arched to the sound of Nick holding the last note of the song for an unreal amount of time. His voice got all breathy at the end, sliding along the note until there was nowhere else to go but silent. And still, the recording didn't end. There were endless seconds of Nick panting into the microphone.

I was panting too.

I pushed my hand into my underwear, parted my folds with a finger, and slid to my entrance. As Nick reached the chorus in the next song, I thrust my finger home, deep and hard.

He sang me to the edge. His voice had my clit throbbing even before I touched it. But then I did touch it, and my gasp was louder than it had any business being, but I couldn't hold back. His voice had invaded me, it was inside me, it turned me upside down and twisted me into knots.

I was so wet, so aching, my fingers became frenzied and my moans couldn't be contained. Nick crooned, and I clenched. He rasped, and I rocked. He wailed, and I—

The curtain of my bunk flew open, and there he was. In the sweaty, steamy flesh. His eyes looked absolutely crazed as they raked over me. I had no time to be startled or embarrassed before he was pulling down my shorts, yanking my body sideways so my legs dangled over his shoulders, and burying his face in my pussy.

I'd already been close before he showed up, so all it took was one lick up my center and a few swirls of his tongue on my clit to send me flying. I had no idea if the other guys were on the bus or not—my earbuds were still firmly in place—but I knew I was loud. I knew it, but I couldn't stop it. It didn't seem particularly important at the moment to be discreet. Especially when Nick kept licking and sucking, even as my orgasm subsided.

His face was deep in my folds, and from the vibrations of his lips against my skin, he must have been humming or groaning. I dug my hands in his hair, holding him in just the right spot.

He stayed there, but when he thrust two fingers inside me, I let go of his hair and my arms flopped back. I was boneless, completely at his mercy. And thankfully, he was merciful, but his lips around my clit, pulling and sucking, and his fingers, curling and sliding, had me cresting for the second time in minutes.

If possible, I was even louder. The music in my ears was loud, but I still heard myself over it.

When my hips fell back on the bed, Nick nuzzled his nose and lips on my thighs and pubic hair, then laid his head on my lower belly. I stroked his hair dazedly, the music keeping me slightly apart from the real world of the bus. I wasn't quite ready to come back.

Nick straightened, and pulled one of my earbuds out, slipping it into his own ear. Realization of what I'd been listening to as he ate my pussy slowly washed over his face.

Without a word, he pulled my other earbud out, tossed it aside, and held out his hand, which I took without hesitation.

He pulled me out of my bunk and slung me over his shoulder, massaging my bare ass as he carried me. The music had ended, but I was still in Nick-land. I could have lived there, in the upside-down world filled with pleasure and beautiful man.

He took me to the tiny shower, barely big enough for one person, and turned it on before he set me down, leaning against the plastic wall. His eyes never left mine as he stripped all his sweaty clothes off and sheathed himself with a condom before stepping under the spray.

My Unrequited T-shirt clung to my tits, completely drenched. Nick took one look at it and ripped it off me, throwing it down like a piece of trash, then his mouth was on mine. He was savage in his kisses, hard and rough. His tongue lapped at mine, pushing and exploring my mouth...and then he tilted my head back so he could go even deeper.

He palmed my breasts, kneading them and plucking my nipples, sending me writhing against his dick pressed heavily on my belly.

The first time we were together, Nick was the hot guy I'd been flirting and fighting with forever. There was something about the way he touched me now, the utter confidence and claiming in his hands, that made me realize this was Nick Fletcher, Rock Star. There was a chance the change was partly in my mind, since his lyrics were filling my brain, but whatever it was, I'd never been so hot for a man.

Grabbing my shoulder, he spun me around, pressing me to the wall. He leaned against me, his dick nestling between my ass cheeks and his hands sliding over my sides. He kicked my ankles apart, and I spread my legs as wide as they could go in the small space, arching my ass back. Nick growled in my ear, then slammed into me, filling me completely.

This wasn't making love or even having sex. Nick was fucking me hard and dirty. Our skin slapped as the water sprayed wildly between us. His breath was hot in my ear and his hands were possessive on my hips, digging into the flesh, holding me just how he wanted me so he could pound me hard.

My body was already on fire, primed and ready, so all it took was a minute to have me clenching around him, scrambling for purchase on the wet shower wall, but of course finding none. I was out of control as I came, grunting and pushing back on his cock, needing more, or less, or *something* to relieve the helpless ache between my legs and in my chest.

Nick's hand left my hips to slide up my belly to my throat, holding me firmly as he turned my head and took my mouth. It was just what I needed, his tongue and teeth anchoring me, tying me down to the moment so I didn't fly out of my skin. I kept my eyes open, watching him kiss and fuck me. That line between his brows appeared, and all I wanted to do was press my lips along its path to smooth it out. The sweetness of that instinct was completely incongruous to the current situation, but the feelings he brought out in me were never straight-forward.

His mouth left mine, but his hand stayed at my throat, squeezing gently while he bit my shoulder. His pace sped up, uneven and frantic, the hand on my hip gripping me like a vise. He was marking me in a place that was only for him and me to see. The kind that said, *you're mine, and I don't need to tell the world as long as you know it*...and I knew it. In the span of half an hour, Nick had absolutely ruined me. I refused to believe I could ever have something so intense with anyone else.

Finally, *finally,* he grunted as he bit down hard and stilled inside me. I had no idea how my legs were supporting me and a grown man leaning the entirety of his weight on my back, but I stayed standing. Thank god for the flimsy shower wall—though, I wouldn't have been surprised if Nick had fucked me right through it and out into the aisle. And he probably wouldn't have stopped even then.

Nick pulled out, but instead of leaving me, he kissed a path along my shoulders, his lips heartbreakingly soft on my skin, and wrapped his arms around me, holding me close.

My knees *did* go weak then, from the way he held me and breathed against my ear, so tender and affectionate. After a few long moments, he shut the water off and spun me around, still holding me.

His eyes searched mine, and that line between his brows

formed again. This time, I reached up and smoothed it with my thumb. He caught my hand on the way down, kissing the inside of my wrist, then my mouth. It was too perfect, being fucked senseless, then absolutely treasured. I didn't know what to think, how to react. It made me nervous. It made me want to fall.

"Shit," he whispered. "We don't have towels."

Hearing his voice jarred me, and I realized we hadn't exchanged a single word until now.

"Or clothes," I said.

Instead of moving, though, he kissed me again. This time, I threw my arms over his shoulders and kissed him for every beautiful word he'd written and sung. I hadn't gone to see him play in person, but his music meant something to me. The music *he'd* created meant something to me. And lord help me, *he* meant something to me.

Breathlessly, he leaned against my forehead, and said, "If I had another condom, I'd be inside you right now."

"I want to reply, but I can't really think."

He laughed and kissed me one more time. "Okay, stay here, I'll find towels and clothes."

When he left, I blinked slowly, finally catching up to reality. I'd planned on a little self-love and an early bedtime, *maybe* a goodnight kiss if I got lucky and the guys weren't around.

Holy shitballs, the guys!

I pictured them sitting in the lounge, smiling all smugly when both Nick and I came out of the back soaking wet. Earlier, in the throes of everything, discretion had been the last thing on my mind. Now that my brain was slowly becoming functional again, I wanted to throttle old me. I wasn't particularly shy, but I wasn't an exhibitionist either. And I definitely wanted to keep...whatever was happening between Nick and me separate from my job.

Good thing I didn't run from complications. I usually ran to them, and I was finally ready to admit to myself Nick was no exception. He was my current complication, and he was a big one.

He slipped back in the bathroom holding folded towels and clothes, handing a pile to me. Covering my hand with his, he said, "Wait."

I blinked up at him. "What?"

He pushed my hand to the side. "Let me look at you."

There truly wasn't enough room for the two of us, and for sure not enough for him to get a good look at me, but I backed up the half-step available and let him look. Instead of taking a perusal of my own, I watched his eyes drink me in. My nipples puckered at the hungry look in his eyes, and there was no doubt he saw.

He shook his head slowly. "Jesus Christ, this isn't fair. Now that I know how you feel and what you look like under those ridiculously tiny clothes of yours, I'm not gonna be able to stop thinking about it. And we're stuck on this fucking bus with three other guys and I can't touch you. Not fair."

"Plus Buddy."

He snorted. "Plus fucking Buddy."

"And soon Tali."

His hands looped around my waist, and he pulled me against him. "Too many obstacles."

"Nothing lasts forever."

He pulled back, frowning down at me. "What do you mean?"

"The obstacles. They won't always be there."

He exhaled. "Seems like there's always something."

I smacked his chest. "Ever the optimist, huh?"

He grabbed my hand and kissed my fingertips before letting me go. "Get dressed or be prepared to put on a show. No way David won't barge in here."

Laughing, I pulled on the boxers he'd brought me, then unfolded the T-shirt—and threw it at him.

"You punk!" I exclaimed.

"What?" he asked innocently.

Grabbing the Blue is the Color shirt back from him, I waved it around. "This! Really?"

"It was the first shirt I found."

"In your stuff?" I asked.

He smirked, and I simultaneously wanted to punch him and kiss him. Instead, I pulled the shirt over my head and held out my arms. "Satisfied?"

The smirk was wiped out, replaced by renewed hunger. "Why do I want to rip it right off you now that I finally got it on you?"

I lifted the hem. "I'll take it off if you want..."

He grabbed my arm. "Nope. Keep it on."

The distinct sound of noisy rock stars tromping up bus steps interrupted our playful bickering. Nick quickly opened the door and we both stepped out of the bathroom and into the aisle between the bunks.

"I should go out there," he said.

"I'm going to sleep. It was a super long day."

He patted my bed. "Hop up. I'll tuck you in."

I pushed him. "You're not tucking me in, you weirdo."

"I am, and you'll like it." He caged me in so I couldn't get away...not that I really wanted to. "Hop. Up. Dalia."

"So bossy."

I climbed into my bunk, but not without a little grope from Nick on my way. I pulled my covers up to my chin and grinned. "I'm having deja vu."

He grinned back at me. "I never knew the top bunks were perfect pussy eating height."

I kicked at him through my covers. "Go away! You're going to make me blush."

He pushed a wet curl off my forehead, his eyes moving over my face. "You gonna spend the day with me in Chicago?"

"Do you want me to?"

"I kinda have a thing for you, Dalia. I'd like to spend a lot of days with you."

"Okay then. Tomorrow."

He tapped my chin. "Tomorrow."

Then he walked away, and I watched him go. If he'd turned back, he would have seen how pink my cheeks were. Not from sexual innuendo or filthy fucking, but from the quiet open affection he just shown me. No games. No beating around the bush. He liked me and wanted to spend the day with me.

What the ever-loving hell was happening? I'd made it clear this was a tour thing, but Nick sure wasn't acting like it.

TWENTY-TWO

DALIA

NICK HELD his hand out to me, and for a split second, I hesitated. Oh, I wanted to take it, but it was a terrible idea, because where there was hand holding, there was also bound to be attachment. I slipped my hand in his anyway. His warm, dry hand holding mine was achingly good. And when he winked down at me, I almost tripped over my stomach, since it had dropped right down to my feet.

Jesus, he looked so cute in his shorts and T-shirt, with a baseball hat on his head and flip flops on his feet. He could have passed for a grown-up frat boy if not for the ink covering his arms and neck. We were catching a few eyes as we strolled down Michigan Avenue hand in hand, but in my mind, it was people staring at the hot guy with the adorably tatted girl beside him rather than trying to figure out if he was *really* Nick Fletcher.

"Do you ever get mobbed?" I asked.

"Nah, not really. I get recognized a bit, but nothing scary. Since I live off the paparazzi grid in Baltimore, my face isn't splashed all over the place these days. Plus, I'm boring. Fans meet me, get my autograph, and are thoroughly disappointed I don't...I don't know, snort a rail of coke or do shots with them. I'm not *that* rock star."

I knocked my head against his shoulder. "You're such a goody two shoes. Who knew?"

He chuckled. "Never claimed not to be. Reinece pretty much cleaned up my act back in the day. Any time I was tempted to pull some bullshit, I thought of her disappointed face and reined myself in."

"Bet she would have been pissed about the Twitter thing," I said.

His head dropped, and he squeezed my hand. "No fuckin' doubt. She would have ripped my ear off for even knowing that word, let alone calling a woman that. And then she would have yelled at Jasper for letting himself get that sick."

I put my free hand on his abdomen. "You know I'm not still mad about that, right? Now that I know the extenuating circumstances, I get it. Plus, I'd been meaning to shut down my Twitter account anyway."

He groaned. "God, I'm such an asshole."

"Yeah, why do I like you?"

"Hot?"

"Bet that's it."

He pulled me to a stop in the doorway of a bank and looped his arms around my waist.

"Do you know how much I hate that we started that way? I can't seem to find it in myself to regret it, though," he said.

"I could have gone without being called that, but I can't deny I'm glad to be here."

"Here *here*? Or here on the tour?" he asked.

Raising up on my tiptoes, I murmured, "Both," against his lips, ending the word with a soft kiss.

He sighed and kissed my temple. "Me too. So, what should we do *here* here?"

A short laugh burst from me. "I'm following you around! I've never been to Chicago."

"Should we just be tourists?"

I nodded. "Yes, please. We have to take a selfie in the reflection of the Bean. Oh! And eat pizza. And a Chicago dog." I gripped his arm. "I need to go up to the Skydeck! Can we do that?"

He laughed hard at my enthusiasm. "I thought you didn't know what you wanted to do!"

"Well, when you said you wanted to spend the day together in Chicago, I was picturing hotel room activities. But now that I'm out in the city, I want to see everything I can. Who knows when I'll be back here?"

He shook his head, his mouth turning down at the edges. "You'll come back. I have no doubt you'll go wherever you want."

"That makes one of us."

We started walking again, and I took in the sights of Chicago. I lived in a city, and all cities were inherently similar, but Chicago was so very different from Baltimore. Everything was *bigger*. Taller buildings, thicker pizza, gorgeous, expansive parks. Baltimore would always and forever have my heart, but Chicago intrigued me. I wanted to do everything all the characters on TV shows and movies did, like ride the El, or go to a Cubs game, or work in an emergency room. Scratch that. They probably frowned upon tourists reenacting George Clooney scenes from *ER*.

I stopped in front of little girl heaven—the American Girl store. "I need to go in here."

"You want a doll?"

"Wasn't there one toy you would have killed for as a kid, but didn't dare ask for because there was no way your parents could afford it?"

Nick's eyes went skyward, and his brow furrowed as he thought about it. "Most everything I wanted was music related. Guitar lessons, or you know, a *guitar*. I would've killed to learn how to write music, even as a little kid. But toys? I guess I wanted laser tag."

My heart ached for little Nick's inner musician. No wonder he'd gotten into trouble before he met Jasper and his mom. To have all that creative energy pent up with no outlet must have been torture. The fact that he was mostly self-taught was crazy. I couldn't even imagine what kind of musician he'd be had his talents been fostered from day one.

"I can say a lot of bad things about my parents, but they sacrificed everything they could so Melly and I could play sports and take dance classes. Of course, as an adult, I know not paying the electric bill and having a month of candle-lit nights to send kids, who were mediocre dancers at best, to ballet lessons wasn't a normal or responsible thing to do. But as a child? The candles seemed whimsical, and I loved twirling in front of the wall of mirrors in my tutu."

"I'm glad you had that, candle-lit nights and all."

"Yeah. Me too." I pointed to a doll through the window. "And I wanted Samantha. She was so classic and came with the cutest little accessories. I wanted to shrink myself so I could read her tiny books and sleep in her little wooden bed."

"How did you know about all that if you didn't have one?"

I leaned against his solid chest and stared into his eyes intensely. "The catalogues, Nick. They sent them to our house, and I studied those things with a fine-tooth comb. I could probably tell you what was on every page of two-thousand-four's issue."

He cupped my face tenderly. "You're a little scary right now."

I cackled, pulling him into the store. "Oh, you haven't seen anything yet!"

AN HOUR LATER, I left the store carrying the latest catalogue in my purse, a shell-shocked Nick trailing behind.

"There's an actual doll salon in there," he said.

"I know. I'm going to have to have a kid just to bring her or him here."

"And a restaurant...with little high chairs for the dolls," he said dazedly.

"If I wasn't craving pizza and a hot dog, you better believe we'd be eating there right now. Where to now?" I asked.

He stopped in the middle of the sidewalk, eyes darting wildly. "I'm not sure I ever want to go back there."

I laughed and threw my arms around his neck. "You're a surprisingly good sport, Nicky. Let's do what *you* want to next."

He nuzzled the side of my neck, nipping it with his teeth. "I think I'm done with Chicago. I need a nap."

I would have made out with him right there, on the center of Michigan Avenue, if someone hadn't bumped into us, almost sending me sailing down the sidewalk. Nick held onto me, keeping me upright. "Nap?" he asked.

"I'm not done with Chicago yet, and if we go back to the room, we'll never leave."

"I'll bring you back," he said.

"Ha. You're funny."

"Wasn't trying to be funny."

I tilted my head to the side, trying to figure him out. Something had changed recently. Maybe it was as simple as us sleeping together relieving the tension and making him less cranky. Or it could have been something else entirely.

I had trouble not finding him delightful, which obviously

worried me. Malka had explicitly told me not to let my heart get involved on the Swerve tour. But today, walking around Chicago together, my heart felt involved. It didn't seem to understand Nick Fletcher had an expiration date, which was barreling closer. Soon, he'd be touring Europe, meeting some sophisticated French girl in a beret, and I'd be in Baltimore with my nose in a book, holding down a slightly above minimum wage job, hoping and praying to all that was holy I could afford to pay all the vital bills that month.

As much as I wanted to get caught up in Nick and believe we'd come back to Chicago together one day, the pragmatist in me said enjoy it while it lasts, because it won't last long.

"Should we get lunch?" I asked.

He sighed. "Sure."

Once I'd devoured my first Chicago hot dog, we went to the top of Willis Tower to check out the Skydeck. I made him take pictures of me laying on one of the glass ledges, hovering one hundred and three stories above the ground.

He held his hand out. "Come back now."

I turned in a circle in the glass box, checking out the views all around me. "Never. I feel like I'm floating out here. Why don't you join me?"

"That can't possibly be safe."

I stomped my foot on the thick glass, and Nick winced. And I was just wearing flip flops. I couldn't imagine his reaction if I'd had on my boots. "It's just as safe as the ground you're standing on."

"You don't know that."

I scanned him from his ticking jaw to his clenched fists. "Are you...are you scared of heights?"

He took off his hat and shoved a hand through his hair, glancing around at the crowd of tourists milling about, then back to me, and grimaced.

"Come here, Nicky," I said softly, holding out my hands.

He took a step forward, but it was reluctant.

"I won't let you fall," I said.

His lips curved up, and he finally stepped onto the glass with me. I wrapped him in a hug, and I could feel him shaking slightly in my arms. "You're really scared, aren't you?"

"Yeah, I really am. Not very attractive, is it?"

"Being vulnerable is always attractive. Overcoming your fear is fucking sexy as hell," I whispered. "Now, take a picture with me so we can get outta here."

After the Willis Tower, we made our way to Millenium Park and took goofy pictures of our reflections in the Bean, a huge, reflective sculpture shaped like...well, a bean. Nick was normally so scowly—and, you know, I didn't mind that about him—but happy, selfie-taking Nick was a whole other ballgame. His face bloomed when he smiled. It was open, showing the most gorgeous parts of him. And I just...felt this pull. In my heart, in my belly, like a tether had formed between us, and it was yanking me closer and closer to him.

There was no way I was walking away from this with an intact heart.

There was also no way I was putting a stop to this before it ended on its own.

REACHING ACROSS THE TABLE, I wiped the corner of Dalia's mouth with my thumb.

"Do I have pizza all over my face?" she asked.

I shook my head. "No, you're good."

She wiped her mouth with her napkin anyway, smiling at me from across the table. I'd barely eaten my pizza. I'd been too busy staring at the glow of candlelight on her freckled, colorful skin. She was gorgeous in daylight, but something about the warm glow of the votive in the center of the table gave her an ethereal quality, like she wasn't quite of this world.

She wasn't of *my* world, of this I had no doubt. Dalia could have told me she'd come from another planet, and I really wouldn't have been surprised. She had invaded Earth, but mostly my thoughts. I saw the world from a new perspective. With a sense of adventure and newness.

Hell, just eating a hotdog with her had been an event. She'd researched the best place to get the most authentic Chicago dog, then she'd eaten it with peppers on it, even though she didn't like peppers, because if she took them off, she "wouldn't be getting the full, authentic experience." I'd looked down at my hotdog with just ketchup on it and felt like I was missing something. Like maybe I'd been missing something for a long, long time.

"Did you have a good day?" I asked.

She exhaled slowly, a small smile playing on her lips. "There have been so many good days since I started this tour, but this has got to be in the top three."

I leaned forward on my elbows. "What do I have to do to make it into the top spot?"

"Take me on a boat ride, captain," she said in a low, sultry voice.

"I want that to be a euphemism, but I'm pretty sure it's not."

She winked. "It's not. But play your cards right, and we can go on a euphemistic boat ride later."

I tapped her hand resting on the table. "Just so we're on the same page, we're talking about sex, right?"

She snorted with laughter. "I hope so. I don't think I want to know what else 'boat ride' could be a euphemism for."

We made our way to Navy Pier and bought tickets for a boat ride on Lake Michigan. We were the first on the boat, since it didn't leave for a little while, so we found a spot in the back corner and huddled together. The sun was making its initial descent, and the wind had picked up, so the air had taken on a chill. I didn't mind it. It gave me an excuse to hold Dalia close without looking like the needy bastard I was.

She rested her head on my shoulder, and I buried my face in her hair. She smelled like oranges, and even though it was probably just her shampoo or something, it didn't stop me from inhaling her sweet scent whenever I got near.

When the boat started moving, we had to speak into each other's ears to be heard over the wind, so eventually, we just gave up talking and enjoyed the ride. The sun was setting, the view was perfect, and I had this crazy girl in my arms. It was so good, it was almost unbelievable. I had a twinge in my gut—not exactly the dread from before, but similar. I'd had good things happen in my life, but they were never just mine. And they always involved sacrifice.

But this thing with Dalia, it was only mine. I didn't know what sacrifice I'd have to make to keep her—but I was pretty damn sure I'd make it.

When we docked at the pier just off Michigan Avenue, the sky behind Dalia was flaming orange, almost the exact color of her hair.

"I thought I liked you in candlelight, but damn, I'm not sure I've ever seen anything more beautiful. I need to write a song about your hair at sunset."

She ran a hand over her curls. "Oh god, please don't write songs about me."

I pulled her against my side as we strolled down the sidewalk to our hotel. "Not a chance I won't."

She worked a hand under the back of my shirt, slowly rubbing along the waist of my shorts. "Can you keep it vague? No details about my orange hair or tits?"

I laughed into her hair. "I'd accuse you of never listening to my music, but I know you...listen."

"I even like some of it."

"Did it bring you pleasure?"

Tilting her chin up, she held my eyes with hers. "Your voice does. I'll never try to deny that."

"Where's the fucking hotel? I'll sing to you while I'm inside you if you want me to. I just *need* to be inside you—now."

"Let's go then!" Dalia took off running, pulling me with her. The sidewalk was too busy to be doing this, and I seriously should have been trying to keep a low profile, just in case, but I ran anyway.

If she ran, I'd chase her...probably right off the edge of the earth. I now understood Ian just a little bit better.

Today was my lucky day, because she let me catch her in front of the revolving doors of our hotel.

"Think we'd catch any looks if I tossed you over my shoulder?" I didn't, but now she had to pump her short little legs to keep up with my long strides across the opulent lobby.

"What's up with boys and slinging me around? First David, then you. I'm not exactly dainty."

I slid my hand in the back pocket of her jean shorts, squeezing the curve of her full ass. "Thank fucking god for that. And don't let David sling you. You're mine to sling."

We stepped into the elevator, and she looped her arms loosely around my waist. "I'm yours, huh?"

I gripped the point of her chin. "Damn right you are."

She blinked up at me, not replying, just studying me like I was some mystery. I thought what I'd said was pretty straightforward. She was mine, and the only arms she'd be in for the foreseeable future would be the two attached to me.

"Stop looking at me like that before I take you right here," I said.

When the elevator door opened, I bent down and hauled her over my shoulder, carrying her through the hallway to our room. Dalia's hands went straight into the back of my pants, gripping my bare ass, so I gave *her* ass a spank. She squealed and wiggled so much, I almost lost my grip on her, so I spanked her again.

"Stay still."

"Stop spanking me." She went limp, despite her protests.

I rubbed her cheek. "Sorry, baby. I don't want to hurt you."

I let us into the hotel room and slowly lowered Dalia to the ground. Running my nose along the side of her neck, I murmured, "I need you on that bed, spread out and ready to be devoured."

She moaned and let her head flop to the side as I sucked on her earlobe. "Nick...give me a minute, okay?"

I backed off, but didn't let go of her waist. "I'll give you a minute, but don't you dare wash your pussy. I want to taste the day we just had when my face is between your legs."

She agreed, so I relented and let her go to the bathroom while I sat on the edge of the king-size bed, kicked off my flip flops, pulled my shirt over my head, and undid the button on my shorts. Holding Dalia had gotten me so hard, I needed more room for my dick to breathe.

The bathroom door opened, and I leaned back on my hands, watching my girl come out. She'd lost the shorts, leaving her in sheer panties that stopped just above her pubic hair and a belly baring T-shirt.

She tugged at the bottom of her shirt as she walked toward me. "I thought you might like me in this."

I drank her in, starting at her pale, pale legs, then traveling to the exaggerated flare of her hips and the dip of her waist. That dip, fuck. I could write a song about it. Hell, I could write an entire rock opera about it.

Finally, I tore my eyes from her waist and moved up to the little blue T-shirt she had on. It was so small, it could have fit one of her American Girl do—

"Holy shit, baby, what are you wearing?"

She bit her lip, trailing her hands down her sides. "Like it?"

"Come here," I growled.

She moved to stand between my legs. Grabbing the top of my hair, she tipped my head back. "Like it?" she repeated.

"Like it? Are you kidding? I'm never letting you take this off." Starting at the soft skin of her stomach, I ran my hand up to her chest, where the words "Blue is the Color" were emblazoned and bedazzled on her chest. She had on a tiny, sparkly T-shirt with my goddamn band name on her gorgeous tits.

"Sure you don't want me to take it off?" She pulled the bottom of the shirt away from her body, and from down below, I got a pretty glorious view of her round, full breasts.

"Do you have any idea what you do to me?" I asked.

She captured my hand and guided it to the heat between her legs. "The same thing you do to me, Nick."

Wrapping one arm around her back, I used the other to push her panties to the side, leaving her slick heat bare on my waiting fingers. I teased her folds, rubbing back and forth, but not making contact with any of the *good* places.

"I wore this T-shirt for you," she whimpered. "The least you could do is touch my clit in appreciation."

I watched as her head fell back and she leaned more and more into my hand. "I'm gonna take care of you." I found her swollen clit and circled it with my thumb while I teased her entrance with my other fingers.

"Wasn't there something about spreading me out on the bed?" Her voice was all breathy and sexy.

I rubbed my nose side to side over her belly button. The softness of Dalia's skin had become an obsession of mine. Under the rough pads of my fingertips, she felt like the finest silk. Under my lips, she was warm cream. Against my cheek, she was the downiest pillow.

Pulling her even closer, I pressed my face to her skin and thrust two fingers inside her. Her body jerked, and her stomach tightened. "Nick..." she whimpered.

"You're so sweet." I kissed her stomach softly as I slid my fingers in and out of her. Her hips rocked with each slide, her channel tightening and breath becoming more shallow. "Come for me, Dalia."

She clenched around me, and her fingers dug into my scalp

as she rode the wave, coming until her knees gave out and she dropped into my lap. I kissed her long and hard, lapping, sucking, exploring her pretty mouth and down the side of her neck.

"I can't decide if I want to take this shirt off you or attach it to your body." I slid my hand underneath, cupping her breast.

She pulled it over her head in a flash, tossing it behind her. "I'll wear it again whenever you ask."

"In public?"

Her eyes were heavy lidded as she bit her bottom lip. "If that's what you want."

"Oh, that's definitely what I want."

I laid her down on the bed, using my tongue to blaze a trail down her neck to her tits. Her nipples were rosy and tight, begging to be sucked, and I obliged, pulling each peak into my mouth. She arched, her hands yanking at my hair, as always. It was like she wanted everything I was doing to her, but she had to file a protest just because it was who she was.

Settling between her thighs—truly my favorite place I'd ever been—I inhaled her musky, distinct scent. "Mmm...our day smells delicious on you. Wonder how it tastes."

She tilted her hips up, and I caught her ass, pulling her onto my waiting tongue. She coated me, and I devoured her. I couldn't get enough of her taste, the feel of her. She was just as soft and silky between her legs as the rest of her.

I brought her to the edge, then forced her over, with her clit held tight between my lips and my fingers deep inside her. Her plush thighs clamped down on my head, offering me no escape. But I never wanted to leave. I could live here, pleasuring her, tasting her, hearing her scream for the rest of my life. I'd never get bored, never go hungry.

"Come up here, Nicky." She pulled at my hair, but her thighs were still clamping me down.

"Baby, you gotta let me up."

"Oh. Right." Giggling, she let her legs fall to the side, and I crawled up her body, nestling my hips between them. She tried to reach between us to take my shorts off, but I grabbed her hands, pressing them flat to the mattress above her head.

"Stay."

Her fingers twitched, but she didn't move once I let go to take off my own shorts. She watched me, her lids heavy and eyes darker than normal. Just the way she looked at me had me feeling out of control. Like if I didn't get inside her right then, I'd never recover...and even then, I still might not.

Sheathed in a condom, I pushed the head of my length against Dalia's clit, making her back bow and mouth fall open. I did it again...and again, torturing myself, torturing her, prolonging the inevitable blissful moment when I finally lived inside her for too short a time.

"Oh, god, Nick, *please!*" Her hands lifted from where I'd put them, so I grabbed her wrists in one hand and guided my cock inside her with the other. She never took her eyes off mine as I slid all the way home.

Because this was home. *She* was home. The second she let me kiss her, the homesickness I'd carried faded away. I couldn't be homesick; I was already there.

"Dalia," I whispered.

She raised her legs, squeezing my sides with her knees. "Move. I need you to move."

I moved for her. Pushing in deep, then sliding back out. Our other times together had been rushed and frenzied, but I intended to draw this out. The time we had tonight was a luxury we wouldn't have a lot of for a while.

Every time my hips hit hers, she let out little mewls, her inner muscles tightening, pulling me farther in.

I kissed her everywhere. Her lips, her eyes, her neck, her

chest. I couldn't keep my mouth off her. I needed to feel every part of her with every part of me.

She was quiet, apart from the moans and whimpers she let out, and she kept her hands where I'd put them, not pushing me away this time, but holding me closer with her legs.

"I'm going to stay here all night, Dalia. I'm going to fuck you slow—so slow but so deep. We're both going to ache tomorrow."

Her neck arched, and she moaned. I cupped the top of her head, keeping her like that so I could lick her jaw and throat. "Fuck. You feel too good."

I nuzzled her tits, burying my face between them. I could live here too. Or maybe die. It didn't much matter if I got to stay.

"I want to touch you too," she said.

I lifted my head, meeting her hooded eyes. "Touch me, just don't push me away."

Her arms immediately looped around my shoulders, rubbing down, then back up my arms, squeezing my straining muscles.

"I won't push you away. It feels too good to have you close." Her words were almost inaudible, but I picked them up and held them, tucking them away for later. They were a promise, whether she truly meant them that way or not.

I groaned, curling into her neck, my arms sliding between her arched back and the mattress, moving faster, plunging deeper. Dalia clung to me, her legs hooked around my waist and arms circling my neck.

She was too sweet, too soft, too...*everything*. There was no holding back anymore. I breathed hot and heavy against her throat as I pushed into her as far as she'd take me.

"You ready to come for me?" I panted.

She bit the meat of my shoulder hard. "Yes, *yes*! Please."

I swiveled my hips, grinding against her clit and pressing myself as deep as I could go. I murmured all kinds of things in her ear. Dirty things. Song lyrics. All my plans for her body. How hot she was. How good she felt. I talked her right over the edge, sucking on her earlobe as she came.

I lost it then. Seeing her come for the third time, *making* her come for the third time, was more than my self-control could handle. I rutted against her, fucking her down and dirty. She moaned my name, clawed at my shoulders, writhed beneath me, but I didn't stop. My arms were brackets to her face, so she couldn't turn away, but she didn't try. Her eyes were no longer at half-mast. They were wide open and watchful. It was the vulnerability I saw there that took me over. I grunted and lost everything inside her.

Dalia, the little intruder who'd stormed into my life, had opened herself to me in a way I'd never had. It was times like these I wanted to learn to live again. And in this shining moment, I thought maybe I could have that without burning it all down.

THE NIGHT WAS STILL SO VERY young, so after taking an extremely friendly shower together, Nick and I curled up on the couch in the living room, my legs braided with his. We settled on watching an action movie, but neither of us were very interested.

"How did you guys pick the name for the band?" I asked.

He gave me a closed-lip smile. "You mean, you didn't Google?"

"I didn't. Besides, I imagine hearing the story direct from the horse's mouth might be more accurate."

"Accurate? Yes. Interesting? Probably not. David likes to tell people it came to him in a dream, but that's complete bullshit. It was Reinece who came up with it."

I leaned my head toward his, not wanting to miss a single word. I loved hearing about Reinece. Nick was never softer than when he talked about his true mama.

His focus fixed on his fingers, tracing gentle lines on my bare thighs. "She walked into our rehearsal one day—she liked to pop in, keep us on our toes, so we knew not to have drugs or chicks there—looked at the four of us, and said, 'I guess blue is the color today!' We hadn't even noticed, but we all had some shade of blue T-shirt on. Course she walked in and saw it right away, because she was always taking note of our details, checking in with us. Ian is the most closed off motherfucker in the universe, but Reinece never failed to get him to talk."

I let my head rest against his. "I love that story. I love that this facet of her, the way she cared about her boys, is always gonna be at the forefront of your mind because it's the name of your band. She must have been tickled fucking pink when she heard the name, huh?"

He chuckled softly, his fingers now making swirls on my skin. "She told us it was silly, but she couldn't stop smiling. And I'll be damned if she didn't wear her Blue T-shirt every chance she could."

"And now I feel just a little bit guilty for refusing to wear mine."

"Nope. Don't. If you'd given into me easily, you wouldn't be you."

I decided to go down a different, bumpier road. "Do women normally give into you easily, Nick?"

"There's no 'giving in.' They either want it, or they don't."

I hooked my pinky around his, stilling his roving hand. "And do they always want it?"

He exhaled heavily. "Not sure what the right answer is here, Dal."

"The *real* answer is the right answer. I'm not picking a fight or fishing. I'm curious. You can ask me anything too. I might punch you, but you can ask."

He picked up my hand and nibbled the tips of my fingers until I was squirming to get away. "You're nuts, you know that?"

I kicked his leg. "That is neither here nor there. Answer!"

He held my gaze. "There've been women. Quite a few women."

"Never wanted to settle down?"

"I never saw it as a choice for me. At least, not in the way I wanted to settle down."

"Why wasn't it a choice for you? Do you see yourself as unsettled?"

He glanced down at his hand on my leg again. "Yeah. I'm home maybe twenty-five percent of the year. The rest, I'm on tour, or in L.A. or New York doing press shit. And I guess...I don't know how to get off the track I'm on."

"Do you want to?"

His eyes shot up to mine. "I think so. I feel old. And tired. I wanna stay home long enough to remember where I keep my mugs. And I want a damn dog."

I perked up. "What kind of dog?"

"I like your dog."

I narrowed my eyes at him. "You're not thinking of stealing *my* dog, are you?

He let out a gravelly laugh. "Nah, don't think he'd go with me anyway. He's devoted to his pretty owner."

I smiled dreamily, like I always did when I thought of my gorgeous boy. "He is. But I'll let you visit him."

"Thanks for throwin' me a bone." He spread his hand out on my leg, squeezing gently. "Don't I owe you a question?"

"You didn't tell me what kind of dog you want." I was absolutely deflecting. I *did* want to know so much more about Nick, but I was also appreciating the side benefit of delaying discussing the horror show of my past dating life.

He rubbed the scruff on his jaw. "I haven't gotten that far. It's gonna be a couple months before I can even think about it."

"Do you leave for Europe right after Swerve?" I asked.

"There's maybe a week in between." His eyes sparked. "You should come."

I laughed. "If only. I have one more semester before I'm the proud owner of a bachelor's degree and shit ton of debt."

"Don't laugh when I bring up us doing something beyond Swerve. It's giving me a hell of a complex. I never know where I stand with you."

This time, I picked up *his* hand and nibbled his fingers. "I told you this was just a tour thing. I swore you were in agreement."

"Then you have a terrible memory. You made a statement, which was completely wrong. I was just too kind to correct you at the time."

"Or you're sex drunk on me right now and thinking things that aren't realistic. We were just enemies a few days ago. How did we get from there to here?" I asked.

He grasped my chin. "We were never enemies."

I leaned into his hand, the pads of his fingers rough on my jaw. "Oh, I don't know. Pretty sure we were."

"Maybe. For five minutes."

"At least ten."

He frowned at me. "We're about to be enemies again if you don't stop being so difficult."

"Oooh, you know how much women love being called difficult by the men they disagree with. Next you'll tell me to calm down."

"Shit, Dalia, you actually planning on punching me this time?" He nodded down at my balled-up hand.

"I warned you it was a possibility."

Letting go of my face, he held his hands up in surrender. "I give up. We'll do things your way, but let the motherfuckin' record state I want more, mmkay?"

Leaning his head back on the couch, he closed his eyes and

clasped his hands over his stomach. I was always mesmerized by how effortlessly sexy and cool he was. How could one be so relaxed and scowly at the same time? Even when I was rankled, I couldn't help pausing and taking note.

I blinked at him. "More me?"

"Yep."

"Sex?"

"Always."

"Talking?"

"Love hearing your voice."

"Cuddling?"

"Into it." The corners of his lips quirked, but his eyes stayed closed.

"I'm into all those things too," I said softly.

He turned his head and slowly opened his eyes. "So, let's do those things and not put a time limit on it."

I twisted on the couch to face him fully. "I know I come across as a flighty bird, but I'm an overthinker from way back. I plan and plot. I research before I make decisions. Do you know before I agreed to take Flamingo from my neighbor, I found out everything I could about Frenchies? Life expectancy was a big consideration. It's shorter than I would like, not that Mingo will ever die."

He pulled on one of my curls. "So, you researched, didn't find the answer you wanted, but you took him anyway. And now he's the love of your life, weird ears be damned."

"He *is* the love of my life, and he's terribly insulted about the ear comment. I *do* get your point, though." I leaned in and kissed his rough cheek. "Ask me your question."

He chuckled. "Oh, that's it? Done with that topic?"

"You dissed my dog, dude. You're lucky I'm still speaking to you."

He pulled my legs into his lap, and started that slow,

torturous stroking he'd been doing earlier. "Tell me about tattoo guy. Why'd you stay?"

"If I say it was for the free tatts, can we move on to the next question?"

He drew infinity symbols on my kneecap. "Nope."

I groaned, pulling at the sides of my hair. "I have this...tendency to go big or go home. I can't just get one tattoo, I have to be covered in them. I'm in Texas? Gotta have cowboy boots. If my hair is gonna be curly and red, it's also going to be big and wild. And if I love someone, it's gonna be stupidly fierce."

"You loved the guy?"

"I was twenty-three. I thought I did. I convinced myself of it. Looking back, no. I barely liked him. He sucked in a major way."

He grinned. "Now, *this* I need to hear."

I kicked at him, but he trapped my legs under his arms. "I'm glad my suffering brings you such joy," I said.

"Not joy. More like amusement."

"Wait until you're asleep. Ever tried to wash Sharpie off your face?"

He stared at me like he couldn't quite figure out whether I was serious or not. That made two of us.

"Give me a rad porn 'stache, okay?"

"I was thinking more like kitty whiskers, but porn 'stache works too." I scribbled over his lip with my finger, nodding at my pretend handiwork. "The guy, Bastian, didn't get me at all. He had this idea he could tame me. I was like this project for him. He thought he could mold me into his perfect, tatted-up Barbie. The truth was, though, he just didn't like me much either. We got stuck in an endless cycle of fighting, him saying horrible things to me, and yeah, I said a lot back to him, then apologizing and making up. It was exhausting."

"Tell me where this guy works."

A laugh burst out of me. "Why? Are you gonna take him out?"

"He probably should know what a fuck up he is."

"Oh, I told him that when I caught him fucking his receptionist. Melly told him when he picked up some stuff from my place. And Mingo growled at him. He knows."

He scrubbed his hands over his face. "He cheated?"

"At least the one time. Although, the two of them looked mighty cozy." I shrugged. "Maybe they lived happily ever after. She was more of the Barbie he was looking for, and girlfriend was mighty flexible."

"I'm getting kinda pissed off," he growled.

"At me?"

"Yes. No. I don't know! Why're you acting like it's no big deal?"

"The cheating?"

He swept the air with his hand. "All of it."

"Because I already did the devastated, blubbering mess thing. You should have seen me then."

He yanked my legs until I was sideways in his lap, then cupped my cheek with his hand. "Do you know how helpless I feel right now?"

I leaned my forehead on his. "Because you can't make it better?"

His other hand came up, and he held my face, smoothing his thumbs over my cheeks. "Hell yes."

I rubbed my nose back and forth against his. "You can't make everything better, Nicky."

"I want to."

"You're so good."

"Not me," he said. "I'm not good."

"You are. You take care of everyone else. But who takes care of you?"

I want to. I want to take care of you. I want to wipe away your hurt the same way I smoothed the line between your brows.

"I don't need to be taken care of," he said.

I wrapped my arms around his shoulders, hugging him. "Everyone does sometimes. And that's okay."

His hands slipped from my face to my waist, pulling me even closer. How we'd gone from talking about my asshole ex to this quiet moment was beyond me, but I liked it. Probably too much.

"You want this to end?" His voice was muffled, his face buried in my neck. The way he said it made it sound like ending what we were just starting would be the craziest decision in the world. And maybe it would be.

I stroked his silky hair, letting it fall from between my fingers. "Not anytime soon."

"Nah, not anytime soon," he agreed.

And then he lifted me, carrying me to our bed, where we had the kind of slow, easy sex that made me feel like I was in a lava lamp, oil and wax swirling languidly, shapes coming together and breaking apart, colors glowing as the heat built and built.

Even after it was over, we laid tangled together, talking about nothing and everything. No matter where this went, I'd always remember the little details of this day. Nick shaking when he stepped out on the ledge with me. The tang of the pepper on my Chicago dog. Sunset over skyscrapers. Racing down the busy sidewalk.

If I were a songwriter, this day would be my signature song. People would yell it out like they do "Freebird." Hell, maybe it *would* be Nick's song one day.

"Go to sleep, Dalia," Nick rumbled.

I was curled on my side, with Nick wrapped around my back. "How do you know I'm awake?"

"I hear you thinking."

"Write about today," I said.

He smiled against the back of my neck. "Not a chance I won't."

WE HAD to get back to the bus early, but our feet were dragging. It was like neither of us wanted to break the spell of the last twenty-four hours. I'd never experienced anything like it, the intensity and intimacy, and even though Nick had been around the world a hundred times, he'd admitted all of this was new to him too. But today, it was back to secret glances and rushed encounters all while trying to do my damn job.

When Nick signed a few autographs in the Starbucks we'd stopped in on the way back to the bus, reality set in before I expected it to. I'd dropped his hand when a teenage boy approached with his phone, asking to take a selfie with him. After that, he'd had to sign autographs for the baristas while I waited in the background. We'd gotten lucky yesterday, walking around Chicago more anonymously than we had any business pretending to be. Nick wasn't Dave Grohl, but he also wasn't too far behind him.

When we settled in the back of the car Nick had ordered us —my first and probably last limo ride—he laced his fingers with mine.

"I lost you for a second in there," he said.

"Yeah, that was weird for me," I admitted. "I don't think I was quite prepared for that."

He ran a hand over his hair, his lips pressed into a flat line. "I always forget it's not normal to have my picture taken with strangers multiple times a day. It's crazy what we can adapt to."

"I don't think I could ever adapt to it."

He chuckled. "Wait until the first time someone calls your name and asks for your picture."

I snorted. "I doubt that'll happen when I'm working in my cubicle."

He frowned. "I meant when you're with me. People are going to notice us together pretty quick. You don't exactly blend."

I twisted my lips to the side for a beat while I stared out the window. "I'm not...we're not telling people we're together. I don't think I'm comfortable with that, since I work for you."

He captured my chin, turning my face toward him. "People —the guys—are gonna know. Especially after we spent the night together."

"They don't know where I slept."

"They'll figure it out, Dal. And so what if they know?" That line between his eyebrows was a mile deep. Nick was *not* happy with my reluctance.

"So, it's not very professional, is it?"

"I find it hard to believe that's what this is about. I saw you fuckin' spanking Mo in broad daylight. I carried you back to the bus when you were high as a kite. You're telling me those things were professional?"

I tried to let go of his hand, but his grip was too firm. He wasn't letting me go.

He sighed. "I'm sorry. That was low."

"It was. But the difference between me getting high and me having an open sexual relationship with you is I work for you. Your band literally signs my paychecks. It's a bad look for me."

"Bullshit."

My eyebrows shot up. "*Excuse* me?"

"I say that's a bullshit reason. This is a summer job. This thing between us is worth a lot more."

"Okay, no. You don't get to decide that, Nick. I like you, and I'm willing to see where this goes, but I won't sacrifice my career. You might think I'm a ridiculous perso—"

"I don't." He rubbed his thumb back and forth on my hand, as if that would calm me. It did, a little, but I wasn't done talking. Or ranting.

I cleared my throat. "You might think I'm ridiculous, but being a dependable, hard worker means a lot to me. I come from parents who never held a job longer than a year. They'd quit on a whim. My dad's had so many careers, I couldn't even tell you what he does now. And my mom's been involved in every fad multi-level marketing out there. She nearly got them evicted when she spent all their money on leggings."

He touched my face gently. "Dal—"

I held up my free hand. "No! I'm not done! I have worked every menial job you can think of since I was fourteen. I've scrubbed toilets and changed shitty diapers. I've waited tables and served coffee to dimwits. All while paying for college on my own. So this might be 'just a summer job' to you, but to me, it's something real to put on my resume. It's a reference I desperately need. It's experience in a field I would love to go into. And I know you haven't seen it, but I work my ass off for you. Tali even offered me a job after we get back."

"You should take it," he said.

"That's exactly what I'm not going to do! Especially if this thing between you and me continues after Swerve—"

"It will."

"Fine. If it does, then I can't work for you. I need my own thing."

He stared at me, stroking my hand as I calmed down, all talked out.

"Dal, you know I didn't know any of that, right?" I nodded. "We're just getting this thing going, but as you are well aware, I have the propensity for being an asshole. I'm working on it. And I hate that you want to keep us quiet, but I get it. After Swerve, though, I'm branding my name on your ass."

I forgave him in a heartbeat, but my wariness was heightened. I'd been down the road of bitter words followed with "I love you" or "I'm sorry." I didn't want to go there again. Nick and I had started with a cruel word, but as pragmatic as I tried to be, sometimes my heart was bigger than my head. My heart wanted Nick. After a day and night with only him, I was well and truly swept up in his dervish. I only hoped when he set me down, he'd do it gently.

"And you want me to walk around with my ass out so everyone sees?"

"Uh, let's chuck that idea."

I scooted closer and hooked my arm around his neck. "You're an asshole, but you're my asshole."

"And you're my little intruder."

I cocked my head back. "I'm *what*?"

He smiled sheepishly, and I had to stop myself from swooning in his arms. Nick wore sheepish well. "It's what I've called you in my head since we met."

"Hmm...I think I like it."

He pulled me closer and kissed my neck. "Now that we're friends again, can we discuss your feelings on limo sex?"

I was about to tell him my feelings were very positive when we pulled into the stadium parking lot, filled to the brim with tour buses.

"Kiss me really dirty so I have something to think about all day," I said.

"Happy to," he murmured.

His hand wrapped around the side of my neck, thumb pressing into the tender spot under my jaw, then his mouth covered mine. His other hand slipped under my shirt, groping my tits, as I straddled his lap, pressing myself to his chest.

One day on our own, and I was already spoiled. God, it was gonna suck not being able to kiss him whenever I wanted. Nick was supremely kissable, even when he was a scowly ass. Because I'd seen the man behind the scowl and stardom, he was just Nick to me, but he wasn't *just* Nick. I couldn't separate him from his music. It was who he was, and I liked that part of him. But I also like the guy who'd step out on the ledge with me, even though he was scared.

We kissed until there was a tap on the glass and we had no choice but to break apart.

He cupped my cheeks in both hands, giving me an intense stare. "You coming to my show tonight?"

I lifted a shoulder. "Maybe."

His thumb rubbed my bottom lip. "You're running out of time to fulfill that promise."

I wanted to, but the stubborn part of me—which was the biggest part of me, if I was being honest—resisted. I'd wait just a little bit longer.

"I'll definitely come when we hit Maryland. Melly's spending the day with me."

"That's in a week."

I rolled off his lap and reached for the door. "Yep. That'll give you plenty of time to practice so you put on a good show for me." I opened the door, making my escape, but not before he smacked my ass and called me a little shit.

· · ·

THAT NIGHT, while the guys were doing their thing on stage, I spent some time on the bus with Malka. Neither of us really felt like joining in with the big groups hanging out in the parking lot. I was ready for a quiet night, and Malka...she was more subdued than I'd ever seen her. The fact that she was wearing sweatpants disturbed me most. Girlfriend normally decked herself out in leather and lace, so seeing her in baggy cotton was disconcerting.

"What's up, lady?" I asked.

She held up a hand. "Nothing much. Before I came over, I ate one of the edibles I smuggled out of Colorado. It's got me more mellow than weed usually makes me. No giggles tonight."

"I'm offended you didn't share!"

She gave me a lazy smile. "It was my last gummy. Sorry, honey."

"Forgiven. I wouldn't have shared my last gummy either."

"You should kick me out. I'm terrible company."

"Grumpy?" I asked.

"*Ja*. Sad too."

"Wanna talk about it?"

"No. Just cheer me up."

"Should we call my dog?"

"Hell yes!"

Melly answered quickly, a happy smile brightening her face. "Hey, sissy!"

Her smile made my chest tighten. As much fun as I was having on tour, I couldn't wait to wrap my arms around her. "Hey, babe. Having another thrilling night at home?"

"You know it!"

Malka leaned her head into the shot. "Aw, she looks like you."

Melly waved. "Well, hello there. You've got to be Malka. You're even prettier than Dalia said."

She fluffed her hair. "Oh, please, do go on."

I pushed her aside. "Where's my man?"

Melly waggled her eyebrows. "Which one?"

"The small, furry one. Mingo!" I called.

I heard the jingling of his collar before I saw him hop up on the couch with my sister. He put his face right in the screen, giving it a lick as I baby talked him. My heart squeezed. I missed him almost as much as I missed Melly.

"Oh. My. God. He is so adorable!" Malka squealed.

I beamed like a proud mama. "Flamingo, meet Malka."

His head tipped to the side as he studied her on the screen. He was used to having colorful women in his life, so her tatts and pink hair didn't faze him. He was pretty judgey, though, and particular about who he liked. He let out a short *ruff* followed by nudging the phone with his nose.

"That means you're a-okay with him," I translated.

Malka fanned her face excitedly. "I just want to smoosh him! How do you get anything done when he's around?"

"He's really lazy and naps a lot," Melly said.

"Like a king should," I proclaimed.

"Aw, I want a dog." Malka gave Mingo a wistful smile through the phone, and he hopped off Melly's lap to prance around on the floor, showing off just how adorable he could be, then flopped on his side, exhausted from all the effort.

"You sound like Nick," I said.

"Oooh, yes. Let's talk about Nick." Melly leaned so close to the phone, all I could see was her nose and part of an eye.

"He has a lovely singing voice," I said.

"Why are we talking about Nick?" Malka asked.

"You didn't know they're sleeping together?" Melly asked.

I slapped my forehead. "Hello! That was told in confidence. Some sister you are, brat!"

"Oh, I totally knew you were fucking. Didn't know why it was a topic of conversation."

My eyebrows pinched as I turned to Malka. "How did you know we were fucking?"

She shrugged lazily. "It's obvious."

"I still can't believe my sister is having sex with the lead singer of my favorite band. And you don't even like their music!" Melly exclaimed. From the floor, Mingo lifted his head to see what all the fuss was about. When he saw it wasn't about him, he flopped back down, completely disinterested.

"He's just a guy to me," I said quietly.

"Aw, so sweet," Malka said.

"Well, whatever. I can't wait to meet him," Melly said.

I arched a sardonic eyebrow. "And see me?"

She waved me off. "That goes without saying."

"Everything good there?" I asked.

Melly blew a curl off her forehead. "It's fine. My boss cut down my hours, so now I'm going to have to scramble to find a second job."

"Starbucks. They have the bennies," I said.

She nodded. "I'll sell out to Big Corporate for benefits any day of the week. Which reminds me, you got a message today from that bank that interviewed you for an internship."

I scrunched my face. "What? That was at the beginning of the summer and I never heard anything back. I took that as a sound rejection."

"I'll text you the number. They want you to call them."

"Well, damn. That's gotta be good news, right?"

I didn't need an internship to graduate, but it was an unwritten requirement. I'd half-heartedly applied to a couple, but they were unpaid, and nobody's got time for that. Well, the twenty-year-olds on Mommy and Daddy's dime did, but not me.

The bank had been the one paid internship I'd applied for, and I'd been bummed when I never heard back after my stellar interview. I'd tamed my hair, covered my tatts, and been utterly charming.

I said goodnight to Melly and Mingo, then got a bag of chips to share with Malka. Setting it between us, I crunched on a chip while she stared at me.

"What?" I asked.

"You're going to work in a bank?" She asked this like the idea was vile, like I'd said my favorite food was boogers.

"It would be in the marketing department."

"But still. A bank."

"It pays. There's no shame in taking a job that pays the bills."

She stuffed a handful of chips in her mouth, crunching loudly. "I guess not. Can't see you working in a bank, though. You'll drown there."

"Beggars can't be choosers. I'm not going to bust my ass in a coffee shop just because I can dress how I want to. If I have to conform for part of my day for experience and a paycheck, you're damn well right I will."

"I don't see that making you happy."

I rolled my eyes. "It's an *internship*. It doesn't have to make me happy."

"But it's a track you're starting on. Sometimes those are almost impossible to hop off of."

That reminded me of what Nick had said—that he was stuck on this track of never-ending tours and press and couldn't see a way off. I was stuck on another track, but I was swiftly approaching a divergence, and if I pulled the lever at just the right time, I'd have a chance to stop living paycheck to paycheck and actually...relax. It was hard to explain to someone who'd never feared not having *enough*—who'd never lived the reality of not having enough. I'd do a lot of things not to live that way anymore. Maybe that wasn't the cool answer, to not pursue my creative side, but there was time for that in the future.

So, if I was offered the internship, I wouldn't hesitate to take it, even if I had to wear slacks and button-down shirts every day. My principles were important, but they didn't revolve around the clothes I wore or the fulfillment of my job. If I could take care of myself, my sister, and my dog, that's what I'd do.

"Enough about me," I said. "Tell me why you're sad."

"Boy trouble."

"Ian?"

"No, I've barely seen Ian since we broke up. I...have feelings for someone who doesn't return them. It's truly an impossible situation anyway." She looked absolutely miserable. High, but miserable.

I rubbed her arm. "I'm sorry, babe. I can't picture any man not wanting you."

She snorted. "It's happened once or twice. It *just* happened."

"I thought Swerve wasn't a place for getting your heart involved?"

She patted my hand. "I'm very good at doling out advice. I'm shit at taking it. Also, I'm not too sure you listened."

"I listened and tried to set limits, but Nick is really pushy."

She smiled at me. "You're so smitten."

I rolled my eyes and ate another chip, because yeah, I kind of was—or *definitely* was.

Malka left after a while and I went to bed, snug in my baggy Blue is the Color T-shirt—the one Nick had given me after our shower. I had to admit, the cotton was softer and more comfortable than my Unrequited shirts.

I tried to wait up for him, if only to say goodnight one last time, but I must have dozed off, because my eyes drifted open slowly at the sound of my curtain sliding.

Nick stood there in the dark, scowling until he saw me looking back at him, then his face just...lifted. Like seeing me had changed his entire demeanor.

"I just wanted to tuck you in," he whispered.

I was basically tucked, but I pushed the blankets off so he could do it properly.

"Like your shirt." He slid his hand underneath, up to my breast briefly, and then back down to my belly. "Love your skin."

"Tuck me in, Nicky. I'm tired."

He pulled my blankets back up to my chin, then pressed an achingly sweet kiss to my lips. If my arms hadn't been trapped under the covers, I would have tried to keep him there, but he straightened and cupped my cheek for a moment before whispering goodnight and retreating to his own bunk.

This man didn't play fair. If he kept this up, I'd *never* want to let him go. Not at the end of the tour, not ever.

WE SLOWLY MADE our way through the Midwest, with Tali rejoining the tour in Wisconsin. I needed to sit down and talk to her, and to the band—to really hash out our plans for the future. Because, while they'd always be my boys, I was sick of their faces. Pretty sure they were sick of mine too.

We spent the morning doing press and meet and greets and I'd barely caught a glimpse of Dalia before she was running out the door to get to work. It was funny. When I first met her, it was clear she contained a determined spirit in her colorful body. What wasn't clear was the single-minded drive to be successful.

I'd never had an office job—shit, I'd have probably burned the place down the first time someone took my red stapler. I'd had to hustle for a while there, but I'd been living on easy street from a pretty young age. We landed our record deal back when people still bought CDs, and the money started rolling in fast. I still had plenty of pressure and stress. More than enough. But money wasn't something I'd worried about in years. Even before the record deal, I had Reinece to back me up.

Dalia didn't have that. Her parents barely made their own

ends meet. All she had was her determination, insane work ethic, and sister.

I had this...this tightness in my chest when I thought about the fact that she was going back to that and there was nothing I could do about it. Or that she'd let me do about it. Because that voice in my head—the one that had me up at night worrying about Jas, Ian, and David—was urging me to *fix it*. Write a check. Take the burden. Don't let her go.

It'd never fly. She'd probably flay me with her eyes if I tried. But, Jesus, knowing that didn't stop me from wanting—no, *needing* to help.

My mind was full of this crazy little intruder. The first spare minutes I had, I retreated to the bus to write. I wrote about her, our day, the invasion she'd successfully completed.

Intruder, Invader, in her I can fade or
shoot like a comet, burning hot
through the heavens
not ever gonna tame her

FEEL like a soldier
one curl for my locket
as I march off to war for
this girl who don't want it

I'd told her there wasn't a chance I wouldn't write a song about her, but the bigger truth was, there was hardly a chance any songs I wrote in the future wouldn't have some piece of her in them.

If she believed this would be over at the end of the tour, then she was even crazier than I realized. I wanted her like I'd never wanted anything in my life—more than music, more than this career, more than all of it. I wouldn't say I'd give it up tomorrow for her, but there were no guarantees I wouldn't the next day.

Tali climbed on the bus just as I scratched out the last line of a song.

"Working hard?" She smiled down at me.

"Got a lot of thoughts I had to get out."

She sat down across from me, leaning forward with her elbows on her knees. "I feel so out of touch with everyone since I've been in New York. How's the tour been?"

I rubbed my thumb along the spirals of the notebook. "Decent. The fans have been on fire."

She arched a brow. "But...?"

"I'm tired. We're the grandpas out here in this young man's game. I think this'll be it for us."

"No more Swerve?"

"Do you disagree?"

She tapped her fingers on her chin, measuring her words. "No, I don't disagree. Too bad we didn't bill this as your farewell Swerve."

"Yeah, but Swerve was never about one band. It's giving a platform to the new guys, finding fans, getting close to the people who love your music."

"You're right. I get caught up in all the business stuff, I haven't even been to see any of the bands play besides you guys. Have you?"

I rubbed my chin. "Nah. Can't say I have."

"I just passed Dalia heading to see Malka's band, Sadie. We should go."

I shot to my feet. All I'd needed to hear was I could spend some time with Dalia and I was in. "Let me grab a hat."

She laughed throatily. "Your magic disguise. How does no one ever recognize you when you wear a ball cap? It's like your Clark Kent glasses or something."

I pulled my Washington Mystics hat down low on my forehead. "What are you talking about? This is a boss disguise."

She slapped my bicep. "Come on, Clark. Let's go listen to some music."

THERE WERE four stages at Swerve, and the one Malka performed on, along with the few other female acts on tour, was...intimate to put it generously. The stage was only elevated a few feet off the ground and always tucked in a quiet corner away from the main action. There were maybe a hundred people surrounding the stage as we approached. I stutter-stepped when I spotted Dalia swaying her hips to the slow, sultry beat. Of course she wasn't alone.

Tali clutched my arm. "Oh! I see her. Pretty sure that's Moses Alvarez next to her." Absently, she added, "I wonder if they're having a tour thing?"

"No. They're not," I growled.

Tali's side-eye was epic, but she didn't ask questions. She would, just not right this second. Instead, she marched over to Dalia and Mo, tapping them both on the shoulder. I hung back, watching them, watching *her*, waiting for her to see me.

When our eyes met, the world stopped. The sweaty, writhing mass of people surrounding her disappeared. We were alone, the stars of our own movie, Malka's scratchy, low-pitched wail the soundtrack. I stepped toward her, and the corners of her mouth lifted. She held her hand out, beckoning me closer, so I went.

Our fingers twined loosely between us when I stood next to her. I knew she wanted to keep this on the DL. Wasn't my idea, but it was temporary. I could handle it.

I tipped my chin at Mo. "Hey."

He shot me a friendly smile. Fucker was always friendly,

but I couldn't stand to look at him. Or, more accurately, I couldn't stand the way he looked at Dalia. Like she was an option for him.

She squeezed my hand and bumped her hip against me. "I can't believe you're here with the commoners."

"I used to always come out and see the shows. I missed it. And Malka always puts on an amazing set."

Her attention was drawn toward the stage for a long moment, and she nodded to the beat. "She does. I've been to a lot of her shows on the tour. She's too good for her band, though. She needs to be the star." I couldn't say it wasn't a twist to the gut to know she'd taken time out of her days to watch Malka, but she'd always claimed she was far too busy to watch us...me. It made me wonder if she'd ever even hear the songs I wrote for her.

Malka stalked back and forth on the stage, periodically bending down and singing in the faces of the audience. Mostly lovesick-looking dudes, but also a lot of women and young girls lapping up her female empowerment anthems and slower, heartbreakingly relatable ballads.

"Don't know how she isn't a bigger deal," I said.

"She wants to stay indie. Can't give up that control," Dalia said.

"I feel that. I feel that a lot," Mo interjected.

I leaned around Dalia to look at him. Jesus, when had all these guys gotten so damn young?

I scoffed. "You feel that and you've been signed for five minutes?"

He shrugged. "I have to ask my label for every little thing. I'm sure you forget what it's like to be the newb."

"Nah, I'll never forget those early days. That was soul-shaping." The crowded dressing rooms, the beginnings of excess, having a boss for the first time, the drugs, the women, the feeling of my creativity being stifled, the pressure, the goddamn fun of it all. I wouldn't go back if you paid me, but I'd always look back.

Tali and Mo started talking about the specifics of his contract, so I was off the hook to just enjoy the music and Dalia. If I had my way, I'd be behind her, wrapping my arms around her, moving to the beat together.

"Care to get outta here?" I asked.

She glanced down at her bare wrist. "Yeah. But not for long."

We'd see about that.

We went back to the bus—the only place I could think of where there'd be a chance to be alone. The boys were usually off working out or hanging out with friends from other bands. None of them really liked spending a lot of time on the bus.

Wouldn't you fucking know it, though, when I climbed to the top of the steps, three sets of eyes blinked back at me. I cursed under my breath and dropped Dalia's hand. She must've known we weren't alone, but she also knew the guys couldn't see her yet, so she pinched my ass, hard.

I yowled like an angry cat, and the guys looked at me like I'd grown two heads.

"Stub your wittle toe?" David mocked.

I rubbed my sore ass cheek. "No, motherfucker, I was attacked."

Dalia stepped into the lounge behind me. "Hello, everyone. The attacker has arrived."

"Better than the first name he called you," David mumbled.

She laughed lightly. "We can probably never speak of that again."

Jas patted the spot next to him on the couch. "Come sit down. Stay a while."

Dalia started for the couch, but I grabbed her elbow. "Didn't you want to show me that thing? On your laptop?"

She turned and winked at me. "Oh, right. The thing on my laptop. Yes, let's go look at that thing."

I practically carried her to the back, ignoring the looks of the guys. There was no way they didn't know, but I was playing Dalia's game, being a good sport and all that.

I slid the door shut behind me and rubbed my chest. My heart had suddenly started hammering, being in that confined space with my beautiful girl. "Come here." My voice came out even rougher than normal.

She bit her bottom lip, looking almost nervous. "I'm not having sex with you with all the guys right out there."

I held my hands out to her. "I'm not asking for that. I just want to feel you for a little while."

She walked into my waiting arms, her head settling under my chin, and I pulled her close. Her sweetness, the orange of her shampoo, the summer sun on her soft skin, engulfed me. She was all I knew right then. She was the island the storm had carried me to. Battered and bruised, but fucking alive. And she fed me, nourished me, brought me color and comfort, all while having no clue how important she was to me. How vital she'd become.

She was the island. She just did what an island always did, and I was lucky enough to wash up on her beaches. If she'd let me stay was the question. If she'd let me build a house and settle in and care for her the way she'd cared for me without a thought.

With my fingers under her chin, I tipped her head back to look at her pretty face. Pointy chin, doll lips, scattered freckles on a button nose—I'd never known those were the exact ingredients that made the most beautiful women I'd ever seen, but damn if they weren't.

"I'm going to have to kiss you for a while," I said.

She raised up on her toes, her arms circling my neck. "Just for a while."

We kissed softly, in a way that was meant to make us ache. Not for sex, but for each other. When I left this bus, left Dalia, there was no doubt I'd ache for her. I'd think about the fineness of her skin, the plushness of her lips, the way my hand fit exactly in the curve of her lower back. Like maybe we were made for each other. An island seeking its castaway.

If I lifted her shirt, it was only to touch her skin. If I cupped her breasts, it was only to memorize the way they filled my hands. If I pressed my erection into her stomach, it was only to show her the power she had over me.

Mostly, I concentrated on her mouth. It was truly the only delicate, dainty part of her, but the feelings she brought out in me when I kissed her there were big and brutish, like I'd smash anything or anyone that got between us.

"Nick," she hummed against my lips.

"Dalia," I growled back.

"I want you so bad," she said.

I froze. I was the one who was always wanting with her, chasing her. To hear her say she wanted me...I swept her up. Not sure what I was going to do with her, but I needed her in my arms.

"I'm always wanting you, baby."

She wrapped her legs around me and held my face in her hands. "How can I miss you when we're together all the time?"

"I don't know, but I'm wondering the same thing."

"We should go out there."

I nipped at her chin and jaw. "I don't wanna."

"I still have to work."

"You're fired."

She wiggled around until I let her down, but I didn't let her go. "Let's go out there. Say hi to everyone else."

"I hate them."

She laughed. "You so don't."

"They're obstacles. I'll obliterate them."

She grabbed a wad of my T-shirt. "You love them and would do anything for them. And I kinda like them and would do several things for them. Let's go."

I laid my hands over hers. "I just gotta kiss you a little while longer."

She sighed. "Only a little while."

MY DEFINITION OF "A LITTLE WHILE" was probably not the technical definition. By the time we went back out to the front lounge, Ian was deeply engrossed in a puzzle, and Jasper and David were in the middle of a game of MarioKart.

Dalia brought her laptop out, like that was some ingenious cover. Like it explained why we'd been in the back for twenty minutes or her lips were red and swollen.

"How was the thing on the laptop?" Jas asked without taking his eyes off the screen.

"Oh, good. I couldn't get it to turn on, so that's what took so long," Dalia said.

David and Jas tore their eyes away from the screen for a second to look at each other and cackle.

I leaned in and whispered in her ear, "I don't think they believe you."

She scowled at me. "If they don't, it's your fault. Now, can I actually show you something on my laptop?"

"I'd love to see whatever you have to show me."

She pulled up the website she'd made for Mo's band and took me through all the pages she'd programmed and graphics she'd designed. I had no idea how to even begin doing any of it, so I was incredibly impressed. And kinda jealous.

"Our website is shit," I said.

"That's because I didn't design it," she replied.

"So, let's hire you."

She rolled her eyes. "I told you I'm not working for you anymore. Anyway, I won't have time if I land the internship I'm interviewing for when we get back to Maryland."

"*What?* You didn't tell me about that."

She clicked her laptop shut and twisted on the couch to face me. "I just set it up this morning."

"I thought you were spending the day with Melly at Swerve."

David threw his remote down and came to sit next to Dalia on our couch. "I get to meet the other Brenner sister?"

"Yes, and she's basically a baby, so don't even look at her," Dalia said, then turned back to me. "I'm interviewing at the bank in the morning. I'll be at your show."

"Promise?"

She nodded, and David groaned. "Don't be such a needy asshole!"

I threw up my hands. "You know me, constantly asking for shit."

Jasper gave up on the video game too. "I can't believe you still haven't seen us play, Dal. What gives?"

"I'm the actual worst," she said.

David slung his arm around her shoulder. "You're the actual best. You just hate Nicky with a passion. I get it."

She looked at me, grinning. "Yep. You caught me. I just loathe him. I'm coming with Melly in Maryland. I'm just giving you guys lots of rehearsal time."

"Dalia, I need help with the edges," Ian quietly called out.

She patted my leg, then went over to where he'd set up the puzzle on the table. Jas, David, and I watched her stand over him, moving the loose pieces around, then putting a few in the right spots. The three of us exchanged stunned looks. No one touched Ian's puzzles. He never asked for help, and we weren't allowed to tell him where pieces went, even if he was stuck. But he sat back and let her take over for a minute, like they'd done this before. Like he trusted her.

This gorgeous woman hadn't just invaded my life, she'd invaded all our lives. Even Ian, the toughest nut anyone ever cracked. Hell, we'd been friends since high school, yet he trusted Dalia with something I'd never even asked him to trust me with.

"Okay, I think you're on track now," she said to Ian.

He bent over the puzzle, checking out her work. "Impressive. Thanks."

"Okay...well, I have to head back to merch. See you guys tonight!"

When she left, all four of us watched her go.

"Huh," said David.

"Yeah, huh," agreed Jas.

I shook my head back and forth. "Dalia fucking Brenner."

TWENTY-SEVEN

DALIA

TALI and I were huddled in the back of the bus, going over the plans for the final week of the tour. Damn, it was hard to believe this thing was almost over. I'd call it a fantasy if I hadn't spent most of it in scorching heat, sweating my ass off.

Even still, I'd made more friends than I had in my entire life. I'd done something big, something adventurous, entirely on my own, without my sister. Not that I didn't want to do everything all over again with her, but it was empowering to know I could, and did, rock this solo.

The thing was, since I'd spoken to HR at the bank, I'd been keeping something to myself. Mostly out of denial, but I also dreaded disappointing Tali. And Nick. I so didn't want to see his face when I told him.

"Tal, you might kill me."

She quirked her head. "I'm not normally homicidal."

"Well, I told you about the bank interview..."

"Right. Seems like a good opportunity."

I just had to rip the Band-Aid off and tell her. "They actually basically offered me the internship and the interview in

Maryland is mostly a formality. I need to start next week. I'll have to leave the tour early. Please don't hate me."

She laid her hand on mine. "Breathe, Dalia."

I sucked in a breath, watching her reaction to my shitty news. She didn't really look homicidal, but my nerves were still simmering.

"I have to tell you I'm disappointed, but you have to do what you have to do. You know you can call me whenever you need a reference or if you're looking for a job. You saved my ass this summer, for real."

I blinked back grateful tears. I'd never had a boss like Tali, one who made me feel valued. I doubted I'd be getting any of this at the bank.

"Thank you so much, Tali. I know I kind of stumbled into this job, but I've loved every sweaty, dirty, exhausting minute of it."

"Swerve kind of sweeps you up, doesn't it?"

It had. Swerve was just my kind of chaos. The throngs of drunken people, the creative hum that buzzed incessantly, never quite getting comfortable, yet fitting in like I'd always been there. I'd miss it. I'd probably be dead by thirty if I kept up this insane lifestyle, but I wouldn't mind heading out on the road for a couple months each year. Of course, soon, I'd be spending my days in a windowless cube, so this had definitely been my last hurrah.

"Yeah..."

We went back to working on our own laptops, and I clicked open an email from Mo.

Dalia,

Are you kidding me with this website? It's fucking gorgeous. I know I gave you the hardest time, but you did amazing work. You should do this for a living or something.

I sent the link to Jamie Rosen at Tone. He's head of digital marketing. I'm pretty sure you're going to be getting paid your normal rate. He was like head over heels with all the organic interaction you got going on our Facebook page. I gave him your number, so I'd expect a call if I were you.

Your boy,

Mo

Holy shit. Unrequited's website had been live for two days, and Mo hadn't mentioned it. I was working under the assumption he hated it, but I'd washed my hands of it anyway. I put hours of labor into a complete overhaul *and* I'd managed their social media for the last couple weeks. If I were actually charging them for all the time I'd put in...well, let's just say if I got sick this winter, I'd be able to afford actual human antibiotics.

Tone was their record label, and if the digital marketing guy liked my work...I couldn't let myself get excited. Daydreams were for people with a safety net to catch them when they inevitably fell. The only thing under me was my scuffed combat boots and grit.

Instead of dreaming, I replied to Mo's email.

Mo,

Glad you love it. I was worried for a sec there when you didn't mention it the other day at Malka's show. Even though I knew it was awesome. I just didn't know if you knew it was awesome.

Thanks for passing my name along to Jamie. If I actually hear from him, I'll give you a big ol' smooch and a nice hard spank.

Happy I met you this summer. You're gonna go far, kid!

Dalia

We'd be in Maryland tomorrow. There was a very high probability this was my last day on tour. My last night on this bus. No more traveling, sleeping in a coffin, or having the time of my life. No more Nick. I mean, I hoped there was more Nick, but I couldn't wrap my head around that possibility. I kept it at arm's length, so if I did have to let it go—let him go—he'd already be halfway there, and maybe it wouldn't be so hard. Which was why I didn't go with Tali when she left for Blue's show. I should have. It might've been my only chance to keep my promise of watching them play twice. But what little bit of self-preservation I had urged me to stay away.

Instead, I had one last dinner in the catering tent with Malka. She still seemed like she had the weight of the world on her shoulders, but she wasn't ready to unload, so I didn't pry. We slowly walked back to her bus together, and I took everything in as we went, snapping mental pictures of all the little details to store in my imaginary scrapbook.

Her bus wasn't nearly as luxurious as the one I'd been riding in all summer. There were twelve bunks instead of eight, and they shared with another band. The seats in the front lounge had seen better days, and more often than not, they were used as beds by random musicians hitching a ride to the next city.

We had the bus to ourselves for the moment, so we sat across from each other, a bottle of beer in our hands.

"This might be my last night," I said. "If I get the bank gig, I'm staying in Maryland."

"Girl, you know what I think about that job. And now you're ditching out early?" She shook her head. "Is Nick furious?"

"Nick doesn't know."

"Oh, Dalia. You're playing with fire."

"I just don't want to say anything until I know for sure."

She used her beer to point at me. "Are you lying to me or yourself?"

"Can't it be both?" I took a long swallow of my beer in an attempt to soothe my fraying nerves.

She laughed. "We both have no idea what the fuck we're doing, do we?"

"I am absolutely making it all up as I go. If someone could tell me how we went from *no way, bad idea* to *pining for him every night,* that'd be swell."

"Aw, *mauschen*, you're pining?"

"Are you telling me you're not pining for your mystery man?"

She turned toward the window, the dark just starting to set in outside. "I don't know what I am. I don't know where I'm going after this tour. In a way, I'm a bit jealous you have plans. I just keep floating, and I'm getting too old for this. I gotta get my personal shit together before I can figure out the man shit."

I moved to her side of the bus, giving her knee a squeeze. "You're performing on a fucking tour, Mal. You've traveled all over the country and the world. Your band kinda sucks, but you're amazing."

She let out a teary laugh. "That was a terrible pep talk."

"That was what they call a compliment sandwich."

"Do they teach you that in your fancy college classes?"

"Maybe. I'm clearly still perfecting it."

She gave me a quick hug and kiss on the cheek. "Will you still be my friend when I'm homeless and bandless?" She asked it like she was joking, but I didn't miss the vulnerability behind her question.

"Abso-fucking-lutely. And you can always crash on my couch if you need to."

She wiped her wet eyes. "Can I snuggle with Flamingo?"

"He'll insist upon it."

I stayed there for a little while longer, talking about music and life, but then a couple of the guys who shared the bus climbed on, and I took that as my cue to leave.

My friendship with Malka had taken me by surprise too. Back at home, I stuck to my sister pod, not needing anyone else. And it was okay. It worked. Only maybe it didn't work so well. Melly and I were each other's glue, and while it felt good to be attached, we'd also gotten stuck. Neither of us could really move on because we didn't have anyone to move on *to*. Or with.

When I approached Blue's bus, I saw the guys sitting around in chairs outside. We still had a couple hours before we headed out, and they were probably as reluctant as I was to spend it cooped up on the bus.

They weren't alone, though. There were a couple guys from Unrequited—including Mo—and a few members from some of the bigger name bands.

Nick sat sprawled out in a folding chair, his long legs crossed at the ankle in front of him, a beer in hand. He seemed to be deep in conversation with a guy I recognized as the lead singer of a death metal band. I'd been to see them once on tour—for about five minutes. Death metal was never going to be my scene.

Mo noticed me first, hopping out of his seat to give me a hug. He smelled strongly of weed and beer—a smell I'd always associate with Swerve.

"There's the most talented web mistress in the land," he said.

I stepped back from his embrace, laughing. "And there's the most difficult client in the land."

"I have a secret."

"Tell me."

He pushed my hair aside to whisper in my ear. "Tone's paying your rate."

I pulled away, scouring his face, checking for lies. "No shit?"

He nodded proudly. "Yep. You should hear from Jamie tomorrow. He's digging on you."

I was speechless, so I pulled Mo in for another hug. "Thank you *so* much. You don't even know what that money means."

I ran through the things I'd use it for. It'd be gone in a blink, but fuck, I could buy my books without hyperventilating—and that was *everything*.

I didn't even notice Mo still had his arm around my waist until everyone was looking at us—including Nick.

"Aw, you guys are cute together," said David. "Like two little puppies."

I mimed putting on lipstick with my middle finger, flipping him off. Then my eyes were drawn back to Nick, like they always were. He looked miserable. Kind of like he had at the beginning of the tour.

All I wanted to do was make him feel good. To wipe that frown from his face. It may have been a byproduct of the two beers I'd had with Malka, but suddenly, it didn't matter who knew we were together. Actually, I *wanted* these people to know. Okay, maybe not death metal guy, but the Blue boys and Tali.

I broke away from Mo and crossed the semi-circle of rock stars to get to my man. His eyes traced my steps, and he sat up when I stopped in front of him.

"Hi."

He tipped his chin, not giving me an inch more.

"There are no more chairs," I said.

His eyebrows raised slightly. "No?"

"No, but you look comfy."

He patted his thighs. "Feel free, doll." From the looks of him, he didn't expect me to feel free, but I'd never felt freer than when I was with him.

Turning, I sat on his lap, my back against his chest. He didn't move. He barely breathed. His chest was a solid wall of marble. I grabbed his arms, wrapping them around my waist, and scooted back until I was even more firmly against him. Once I was in the right position, I turned my head and kissed his jaw.

He sucked in a breath, his hands spread wide on my stomach. "What're you doing?"

"Staking my claim."

Across from us, David hopped up and howled. "I fucking knew it!"

Jasper thumped him on the leg. "Sit down, you fool. We all knew it."

Ian nodded. "Definitely common knowledge."

Tali raised her hand. "I didn't know."

"Me either," Mo said.

Nick's hold on me tightened, and I turned my head to kiss his jaw again, but this time, he caught my lips with his, lingering there sweetly. We didn't respond to all the catcalls, so pretty soon, they lost interest in us.

"How was the show tonight?" I asked.

"Damn good." His hand slipped under my shirt, resting on my stomach. "Think we're ready for you to see us."

"You're only going to play my favorite songs, right?"

He chuckled, low and husky next to my ear. "Give me a playlist, and I'll see what I can do."

"I can't wait."

His hands felt so good, I melted into him. His gravel voice vibrated from his chest to mine as he talked to death metal guy again, and I went limp in his arms. I was also terrible company. I attempted to keep up a conversation with Jas about Flamingo, but my mind had shut down to everything but Nick.

We'd gone the last week without sex, but we found pockets of time to kiss ourselves silly. I wanted him inside me again, but tonight, being in his arms, was something special all on its own. I almost wished we'd gotten over ourselves together earlier in the tour so we could've had more nights like this, but then I thought, no, it wouldn't have been this sweet if we hadn't worked for it.

During a lull in conversation, Nick whispered in my ear, "I wrote a song about you. I'm gonna sing it tomorrow."

Before I could respond, death metal guy—his name was actually Donovan—started talking about some venue in New York he'd heard was closing. One of Nick's hands stroked back and forth on my belly, and I squeezed the other.

My heart barely fit in my chest. A song? For me? It was too much. I was having trouble accepting I was worthy of a song.

Tipping my head back, I whispered, "Is it about my tits?"

His hand tightened on mine, but he didn't answer. It was a shit question anyway. If he *had* written a song about my tits, I'd be honored. Nick was a master of words, and he could've made any topic sound beautiful.

When Buddy announced it was time to hit the road, everyone trudged on the bus. I would have gone to bed, but Nick grabbed my hand, stopping me in the front lounge.

"Stay out here with me for a few minutes," he said.

David stood waving from the door dividing the lounge from the bunks. "Goodnight, lovebirds." He slid the door shut, and we were alone. Sort of. It was pretty hard to actually be alone on a bus we shared with four other people plus Buddy.

Nick moved to the kitchenette and plugged in his kettle. "Want some tea?"

I leaned my hip against the counter. "I'll take some chocolate."

He chuckled, low and rumbly. "I like you, but that's asking a lot."

I opened his stash cabinet. "I restocked you today."

He looked inside the loaded cabinet. "Whoa. I'm flush."

"Just making sure you don't run out."

He poured hot water into a mug. "You know, there are grocery stores on the way to Florida."

I almost told him I might not be going to Florida, but I didn't want to spoil the moment. And there was still a chance I *would* be going. Nothing was set in stone.

I reached in and grabbed a bag of Hershey's Kisses. "Please, sir, may I have just one tiny kiss?"

Grinning, he leaned down and kissed me. "Never say I didn't give you anything."

"I would *never* say that. You've given me...not the world. But the U.S."

"You're a sweet talker." He groaned and grabbed the bag from me, ripping it open. "Fine, you can have one."

I held my hand out. "Three."

"Two, and that's my final offer."

When he placed the two silver wrapped chocolates in my hand, I stole a kiss from his lips. "There. That makes three."

He brought his mug and a couple more Kisses to the couch, and I snuggled next to him with chocolate melting on my tongue.

"What was up with that display out there?" he asked.

I swallowed. "I told you, staking my claim."

With his finger under my chin, he tipped my face back. "Really."

"Yeah, really. I missed you today and we barely get a chance to be alone. Seems silly."

"I gotta admit, I like being claimed by you. Especially seeing the look on that little shit's face."

I snorted. "Mo? He's a friend."

"*You* might think that. He'd fuck you in a heartbeat if he thought he could."

"Well, he can't. He's not my type. I like them older—and grumpier…"

He nipped at my mouth and chin, growling at me. "And apparently I'm into smart-mouthed women who don't like my music."

"Women?"

"One in particular."

"That's better."

He sipped his tea quietly for a minute, and the bus started moving. It was raining now, and as we sped up, streams of water streaked the windows, blurring the outside world.

"I want you to come on tour with me."

I startled, almost choking on my chocolate. "What? No. We talked about this."

"We did, but again, I don't agree. I need you with me. And now that everyone knows about us, I can't see any reason you shouldn't come."

"There were a lot of 'I's' in that statement. *I* have a semester left of school I'm *going* to finish. *I* have bills to pay. *I* have a sister and dog I've been missing something fierce. I'll miss you, but I won't follow you around at the expense of myself."

He sighed, scratching his chin. "I shouldn't have asked."

I chuckled. "You didn't really ask." I grabbed his hand, threading our fingers. "I don't want to be without you either. I've never had a rock star for a boyfriend, but I do know you're going to have every opportunity to fuck around and—"

He slammed his mug down on the side table with a *thunk*. "Don't even say it. I'd *never*. That's not who I am."

Our eyes met, and his were brimming with intensity. I took a deep breath and nodded. "Okay. I know. Can we just savor this and ignore what's coming?"

"Yeah, although there's no way in hell you're going to get me to stop thinking about not seeing you for two fucking months. I'm kinda ready to pack it all in and just tell them no."

"Who?"

"The record company. Tali. The tour managers. The band. Everyone. Fuck it all."

I rubbed his hand with mine. "Not for me, Nicky."

He huffed. "No, god fucking forbid I give something up for you." He scrubbed at his jaw again. "It'd be for me mostly anyway. For my sanity. Sometimes I just want to run away and leave it all behind. It's not gonna happen, though. Too many people counting on me."

"You can't take care of everyone. You have to be on the list somewhere too."

"That's a thing I'm working on. As you can see, I don't know how to add my name to my list without burning the whole thing down."

I looped my arms around his neck, and he buried his face in mine. "You've got me to remind you."

"Do I really have you?" he murmured.

"You do." I yawned and snuggled into Nick's shoulder. "I'm sleepy."

"Stay here with me."

I let my eyes close. "I think I just might."

I really, *really* hoped I could.

I WOKE up in the dark, but not in my coffin-slash-bunk. The fact that Dalia was curled against me hit me immediately, even before I realized I'd fallen asleep in the front lounge, before the sound of the rain met my ears, before the movement of the bus speeding down a highway shook out some of my grogginess.

Dalia was asleep too, her back to my front. The little spoon. I ran my hand over her jean-clad hip, letting it slide down the dip to her waist and over her ribs.

Jesus Christ, I love this girl. This fucking gorgeous woman.

It hit me like a bolt of lightning, completely wiping out my memory of a time before Dalia.

She let out a little whimper, and I held her closer. The word "mine" echoed through my brain. I was an ass, and didn't deserve her, but fuck if I wouldn't try to be worthy.

If she insisted on working at some bank, I'd stand at the front door with her coffee and briefcase and send her off with a kiss. I'd be back at the front door to greet her after her grueling day with a cocktail and her favorite dinner on the table. This was all metaphorical, of course. I wasn't a fucking fifties house-wife. Point was, I'd support her however she needed. I'd be there. I couldn't see myself without Dalia in my life in a significant way. The next two months in Europe were going to be complete hell, but maybe I'd convince her to hop on another plane and join me for a long weekend. And have a lot of phone sex.

Jesus, my hand was already tired from thinking of all the jacking off I was going to be doing.

"Mmm...Nicky, I was dreaming about you," she murmured.

"Not a nightmare?" I whispered, pushing her hair away from her face.

She turned her head, smiling drowsily. "Never. What time is it?"

I stroked her cheek slowly, studying her face. "I don't know. Middle of the night."

She reached up and cupped my face with her hand. "You're so beautiful. Even when you scowl."

I didn't have an answer to that, so I kissed her, slow and thorough. It started that way, but she made me crazy. Frenzied. Like I had to have her and have her and have her or she'd slip away. Even though she didn't seem like she wanted to go.

Kissing turned to touching turned to slipping inside her from behind, in the dark, the only sounds our breathing and the rain. I held her close, my hands tracing over her soft curves as I moved in and out of her.

I wanted to turn her over, see her face, see if she was feeling what I felt. At the same time, being behind her felt safer. Less vulnerable. I fucking hated being vulnerable, and Dalia had stripped me of my armor. She could've carved out my heart at any moment if she chose to.

I kissed her neck and shoulders, breathing her in, taking her softness inside me. There was no way I'd ever get enough of her. Not in a week, when Swerve was over, not next year, not in a century. She was my island, and I was her castaway.

The only way I'd leave was if a fucking tsunami dragged me out to sea.

She twisted her face around to kiss me again, and right before our lips met, I saw the same pain on her face I was feeling. The rawness of it all. Falling like this, being open to it, it hurt so good.

"You've invaded me," I rasped.

She pushed back against me, soft to hard. Smooth to rough. She held me inside her just as much as she'd climbed inside me. I couldn't stop taking her, fucking her, making fucking love to her.

She mewled and cried out, reaching behind her to claw at my ass, pulling me closer. I wrapped her in a vise-like grip, my hand at her throat, pressing her head back against my shoulder, still not close enough even though there was nowhere else to go.

She came with a trembling cry, her body arching in my arms and walls tightening around my cock until I had no choice but to let go inside her. I didn't want to. I never wanted this to end. This togetherness, in the rainy darkness, speeding between places. I'd been moving between places for a long time, but always alone. This was new, having her with me in the in-between. I didn't want to do it without her.

We didn't talk much. Just drowsy mutterings, the things people say right before they fall asleep that don't really make sense. Like when Dalia said she was sorry she wouldn't be able to go to Disney World. No sense.

I CRACKED AN EYE OPEN, and at first, I thought it was still dark, but then I realized David's fucking face was actually blocking out all the light. He loomed over me with a devious smile.

"Wake up, lovebird!"

I patted the couch next to me, but I was alone.

"She's in the shower," David explained, plopping on the couch across from me.

I sat up, rubbing my eyes with the heels of my hands. "We here?"

"Yep. Pulled in an hour ago."

"Fuck. How did I not wake up?"

He shrugged. "You two looked pretty cozy when I came out here."

I scowled. "Keep your eyes to yourself."

He laughed. "I didn't see anything, man! Just you and your girl all snug as a bug in a rug."

I shook my head, trying to hold back a grin. "You're such a fucking dad."

"True. Although, if I said shit like that to Emma, she'd cut me."

Dalia came out of the back, looking fresh as a fucking daisy with her wet curls and shiny, clean face. She had her backpack on her back and combat boots laced to her feet. My stomach sank. This looked like goodbye.

I tipped my chin. "Mornin'."

"Hey. I have to head out. Melly's picking me up"

I stood, stretching my arms over my head. "I'll walk you out."

She followed behind me, and when she stepped off the bus, I pushed her against the side and kissed her hard. She whimpered, then melted, her arms looping around my neck. God, I would have fucked her right there in the broad daylight, but she was mine. Her pussy and tits and ass were for my eyes only, not some pervy roadie to see.

I cupped her jaw, breathing hard on her lips. "You'll be back?"

"Mmmhmm. In a few hours."

"Promise?" *So damn vulnerable with this girl...*

She smiled softly. "Yeah. I do."

"Come find me before the show."

She nodded. "I will."

I smacked her ass. "Good luck at your interview." I shook my head. "Can't believe you wanna work at a fucking bank."

She held her hand up. "A job's a job. And if I don't have to pour coffee and deal with Ronald..."

"Who the fuck's Ronald?"

She laughed, and I glowered. "See ya, Nicky!"

I watched her walk away, hips swaying, backpack bouncing, and I wanted to follow her. To swoop her up and keep her. But I had to let her go, and work like hell to trust she'd come back.

I THREW my mug against the dressing room wall, watching tea stream down to the floor. "Fuck!"

Jas grabbed my shoulder, but I shrugged him off. "She's coming."

I glanced wildly around the room, full of three fuckers I could have done without seeing and Tali. No wild red curls in sight. My stomach knotted with dread and anger.

"Nick. Calm down," said Tali.

I yanked at my hair. "Not gonna happen until someone tells me why the fuck Dalia's not here."

Jas took out his phone. "I'll call her."

He held his phone to his ear, and I held my breath. When he shook his head and slid his phone back in his pocket, I looked for something else to break. I knew something like this would happen. I fucking *knew* I couldn't have something so good. Not me, the poor kid from Baltimore not even a mother could love.

Oh, I was sure she'd come rushing in with some explanation about why she'd missed yet another one of our shows, but it'd be bullshit. I loved her, and she couldn't even be here when I asked her to. I would've climbed mountains on my hands and knees if she asked me to.

"The interview must have gone better than expected..." Tali murmured.

I reared around to face her. "What does that have to do with why she isn't here?"

"Well, she was going to leave the tour anyway..."

"What the fuck? No she wasn't!"

Tali's hand shot to her forehead. "Damn. I can't believe she didn't tell you."

"Stop speaking in code, Tali."

"Dalia's internship starts right away. She said she was probably leaving the tour here."

"What? That's bullshit. She wouldn't do that without giving us a warning," David argued.

"She gave me notice," Tali said. "But maybe she didn't want to say anything until she got the official job offer..."

My gut clenched like a knife was twisting in my intestines. Dalia might as well have been the one holding it. I couldn't believe she hadn't said anything. She'd lied to my face. Made promises she hadn't intended on keeping. I should've been used to that by now, but coming from her, it cut me down to the bone.

They all tried to talk me out of my anger. Even Ian. She'd wrapped them all in her spell, convinced them she was here for us, but she was here for herself. She wasn't Blue. She was red—a raging fire—beautiful, tempting, but burned me right the fuck to ashes.

I RAGED through the entire show. The crowd lapped up my screams and guitar thrashes, but I felt like I'd left my guts on that stage.

I searched the audience. I looked for her red, but I never spotted her. She let me down, and I shouldn't have been surprised, but I was. I fucking was.

I climbed on the bus like a man possessed. I threw the curtain to her bunk open, but didn't know what the fuck I thought I'd find. Seeing her packed bag and folded sheets wasn't it, though. I lost it. I grabbed her shit and stormed toward the steps, intent on tossing it off.

That's when I was surprised again. I'd say gutted, but my guts were long gone. At the base of the steps, I finally saw the red I'd been looking for. I had to blink to make sure what I was seeing was real.

Dalia was laughing and hugging Mo, right there, next to *my* bus. Like she hadn't just broken her promise. Like she wasn't about to get fucking fired and thrown off my tour.

I tossed her bag at her feet, making her jump. "Nicky!"

I stood on the bottom step with my arms crossed over my chest. "Go."

Her face crumpled, and I almost faltered. But I knew, from the second I met her, she used that sweet face like a weapon. I'd forgotten for a while there, but my shields were back in place. "Get the fuck outta here, Dalia. You were going to anyway, right?"

Her eyes widened. "No! I mean I was, but—"

"Nope. Don't want to hear excuses. I'm done. I. Don't. Want. You."

"Nick..."

My eyebrows drew together. "Didn't you hear me? You're not wanted. It was fun while it lasted, but it's over. I'm bored of all this."

"Nick, come on, man, don't talk to her like that," Mo said.

I turned to him, glaring hard. "You want her? You're

welcome to her!" The words were like knives on my tongue, excruciatingly painful to say and eviscerating to imagine.

Dalia picked up her bag and slung it over her shoulder. "You're an idiot, you know that? A cruel and stupid man." She kicked a rock in my direction. "I'd tell you I was running late, but made it to your show. You don't want to hear it, though. I'd tell you I wasn't going to leave, that Mo helped me get an amazing job I can do on the road, but your head is too far up your ass to hear me." She tipped her chin up, eyes shining with tears, and my heart broke at the sight of her. "I'm not doing the whole 'I'm sorry, I love you' merry-go-round with you. Because I could have loved you, Nick, but I've been on that ride. It lost its charm when I was twenty-three. So, I'm done. I'm not going to stand here and be your punching bag. Enjoy Florida and have a wonderful life. Tell the boys bye for me."

She stomped off before I could get my mouth to function and a girl that looked a hell of a lot like her wrapped an arm around her and steered her away.

"Dalia!" I called. "Dalia, get your ass back here!"

The girl flipped me off. Had to be her sister.

"Dude, what are you doing?" Mo asked.

"I don't fucking know!" I roared.

He shook his head at me. Guy was a decade younger than me, but he saw what a mess I was.

"She's the one good thing I have," I mumbled.

He laughed, and I balled my fists. "Are you kidding me? She's not a thing, and you sure as hell don't have her. She's a woman working her ass off to stay on her feet. She's never gonna be a doll you can position how you want. That's not Dalia, and if you don't know that, then you *are* stupid."

He wandered off, still shaking his head like I was the dumbest fuck he'd ever met. And I pretty much agreed with the little shit.

"I'M BURNING all my Blue is the Color CDs!" Melly pounded the steering wheel as she drove.

"I don't want to talk about it, Mel." I stared out the window, completely numb. I'd gone from the highest of highs to crashing on my face in moments. The way he looked at me, like he really hated me...it was just like the day I came to his apartment—as if the last two months never happened. One misunderstanding, and all the moments we shared, everything we told each other, was wiped out.

If this were Bastian, I'd lock myself in my room, holding my phone, waiting for him to apologize. He inevitably would, and I'd forgive him. Not because I particularly liked or loved him, but because I wanted to know he was sorry for the shitty things he said. That he didn't actually think I was slutty or a loser.

I'd grown up a lot since then, and I'd never sit around and wait for a man to apologize to me. Even if I loved him. And I *had* been falling in love with Nick. But the things he said, handing me over to Mo like I was his to give, wrecked me. What he said was a reflection of who he was on the inside and really didn't have anything to do with me, but even knowing that didn't help.

I loved his insides and couldn't stand to know he had so much pain, he had to lash out, and I was the target.

I'd let myself believe he was just a little broken, nothing a little glue and affection wouldn't fix, but the cracks in him needed more than I had to offer—more than I was willing to offer. I would've loved him big, but like I told him on the bus, I wasn't willing to do it at the expense of myself.

There would be no tears shed over him. Like the tooth fairy and Santa Claus, I no longer believed in crying over stupid men. I'd definitely be eating ice cream, which I could easily afford now with my loaded bank account.

Thanks to my payday from Tone Records and my decent summer paychecks, I actually had four figures in the bank. Now, it was a very *low* four figures, but I was richer than I'd ever been. Ice cream for everyone!

When we got back home, all I wanted was to see my baby, do my laundry, and starfish in the middle of my bed. I'd think about the rest of it later.

Flamingo was at the door, ready to love me like I hadn't abandoned him for two months. I laid down on the floor, letting him walk all over me and lick my face. He was the only man I'd ever let do that, because there'd never be anyone more handsome or forthright. He told me how he felt, and it was as simple as that.

Melly laid down on the floor with us, rubbing Mingo's back. "Ready to talk?"

"I'd rather eat ice cream and forget."

"Can I be pissed on your behalf then?"

I rubbed Mingo's sweet cheeks and stared into his deep, black eyes. "You're welcome to it."

"I can't believe that fuck-wit talked to you that way. Obviously I knew he had a temper from how you two started, but I thought he'd reformed. You know, from the love of a good woman and all that jazz." She stood, pacing the living room. "And he didn't even give you a chance to tell him why you were late! I hate him. I'll never listen to another one of their songs again. They sucked last night anyway."

She sat back down again, giving Mingo another rub. "But you told him. You were amazing, Dal. I'm so proud of how you didn't take his shit. You just said, nope, not gonna do it, and walked your ass on outta there."

"I sure as hell didn't feel amazing. Right now, I don't feel much of anything except glad to be home with you and my baby." I scratched Mingo's ears. "You'd never say horrible shit to me, would you? You're a little gentleman."

He licked my wrist and nuzzled me in response.

It was late, but Melly dished us bowls of ice cream anyway. I threw my buzzing phone face down on the ottoman and shoveled a spoonful of salted caramel into my mouth.

"Mmm...you got the good stuff."

She picked up her own spoonful. "Now that I got the job at Starbucks, I'm basically going to be rolling in dough," she joked.

"See? Selling out is worth it."

After a couple minutes of eating and watching the latest *Real Housewives* fiasco, Melly nudged me with her foot. "Can I be happy for you yet?"

I gave her a pained smiled. "Now I feel like I should just work at the bank."

"The fuck you should! You're not bank material!"

I snorted and threw my spoon down in the bowl. "Well, talk to Sheila Dumphrey in HR. She certainly thought I was bank material when she offered me the job."

"I will not talk to Sheila Dumphrey—which, by the way, is such an HR person's name. Did her parents take one look at her when she was born and decide her fate? I'd rather talk to Jamie Rosen."

"I haven't even been able to wrap my head around the fact I got not one, but two job offers today. And neither involve cleaning toilets."

I was offered the internship at the bank after a soul-sucking interview, but I found myself saying I'd get back to them. I just couldn't say yes without talking to Nick about it, no matter how hard-hearted I'd tried to be. Then, when I was on my way back to the venue, Jamie Rosen from Tone Records called, and by some crazy alignment in the planets, was in Baltimore with a few social media big shots and wanted to meet with me.

I went, because I still had plenty of time to get back to Swerve, and at that point, I would have done anything not to work at the bank. Jamie was impressed with my meager portfolio, but even more impressed with the way I'd organically attracted thousands of people to Unrequited's social media pages.

He offered me a freelance position and had work for me right away. He told me if freelancing went well, once I graduated, we could discuss a permanent position. The most amazing, beautiful part of the offer was I could do it from anywhere. I could stay on the tour and work in my off hours. I could visit Nick in Europe and still get my shit done.

I hated admitting it, but he'd been the first thought in my mind when Jamie offered me the job. *I can be with Nick. We don't have to be apart.*

But he never even gave me a chance to tell him. Because I had a fucking flat tire and a dead cell phone and almost missed his show. Luckily, a dodgy-looking truck driver who turned out to be a really nice guy with terrible dental hygiene helped me change my tire and I made it. I should've known something was wrong when I saw him on stage, but since it was my first time seeing him perform an entire set, I hadn't known what to expect.

He didn't sing even one of my favorite songs, nor did he didn't sing *my* song.

So, now I had a job I could do anywhere, but not a single place to go.

Before I went to sleep, I braved checking my phone, knowing exactly what I'd find. Dozens of "I'm sorry, I love you" texts and who-knows-how-many voicemails. I'd heard this song, done this dance. My ears were tired, and my feet were sore. I couldn't find a single reason to respond, so I cuddled with my dog and fell asleep in my big bed.

THIRTY

THAT FIRST NIGHT without Dalia was a blur of booze and weed. I'd called her about a hundred times, but thank god she didn't pick up, because my "I'm sorrys" would have been slurred and mixed with anger.

When we left Maryland, heading south, I felt like my actual heart had been left behind too. I was as hollow as I'd ever been. I was in as much pain as when Reinece died.

We were parked in one of the Carolinas or Georgia—fuck if I knew. It was all the same to me.

Tali'd cancelled all our press, because there was no chance I'd answer a question without either hurling cuss words at the reporter or sobbing like a little baby.

Everyone was mad at me. I swore I even saw Buddy giving me some serious stink eye. *I* was mad at me. I was fucking furious with myself.

And yeah, I was mad at Dalia too. Not for the show, but for withholding. Keeping one foot out the door when I'd thrown myself in head first.

I should have known. I'd been chasing her from the beginning. I was the fucker lost at sea, drowning, and she was the island paradise. She didn't need to chase anyone. She was content and beautiful where she was.

And now, here I was, washed away on a deluge of angry words. My own personal tsunami.

Ian slammed his fists down on his puzzle. "Shit!"

"What's up, man?" Jas asked.

"I can't find the damn edges. Why isn't Dalia here?"

I scrubbed my face and drew in a shaky breath. "Can I help?"

Ian stared at me. Really studied me, like he was looking for something before he decided. Then he gave me a barely perceptible nod.

I sat with him at the table, moving pieces around. I wasn't nearly as good at this as he and Dalia were, but I found a few pieces and he got rolling again. I started to get up, but he muttered, "Stay," so I did. We worked quietly together, and when the picture came into view, I had to laugh.

"Chicago?"

Ian nodded. "Dalia bought it for me when we stopped there."

"Holy shit, I love that woman." I leaned over, covering my face with my hands, and had a good cry. I swear, I never cried, but something in me had been unleashed. I knew it was Dalia's doing. Some closed off part of me where I'd stored a lifetime of hurt had been cracked open and there was no stopping the flood. Sometimes, it came out as tears, sometimes anger, and sometimes songs that were better than any I'd ever written.

Jasper came over and slung his arm over my shoulder. None of them gave me shit for my very open display of emotion.

"You're gonna fix it," said David. "There's no way she's gone for good. I refuse to believe you fucked up that badly."

I wiped my face on the hem of my T-shirt and laughed

bitterly. "Nah, I think I did. I said some really horrible shit to her. I can't be the guy who does that. Not to her."

"So, don't be that guy," Jasper said.

"I don't want to be. But I've got a lot to work out right now. I'm so fucking angry. And I just...I need time off. I can't keep up this endless cycle. I don't wanna leave you guys, the band, but I can't—I can't do it anymore."

Everyone was quiet for a minute. Long enough for me to get control of myself and take a glance at all of them. Ian was the first to speak.

"Let's take a break then. A year?" Jesus, a year was more than I'd ever ask for, but the thought of having all that time lifted this huge weight off my chest.

David nodded. "I could use a break. Spend some time with my kid while she's still a kid."

Jasper tapped his fingers on the table, then nodded too. "I'm good with a year. I just want to make sure we're not breaking up for good. I'm not done making music with you fools."

"Fuck it. I'm planning on jamming with you people until I croak. You're gonna have to file a restraining order if you want to get rid of me," David said.

I laughed. "Message received. No, I think we have a lot of music left in us, but there's no reason to go so hard anymore." I thought of what Dalia had said, and added, "Not at the expense of ourselves."

"I've been wanting to get into composing. For movies, or anime, I don't know..." Ian said.

"For real? That's cool, man," David said.

"We're doing this? After Europe?" Jas asked.

"Who's telling Tali?" I asked.

"Telling Tali what?"

All four of us turned to see Tali climbing the bus steps. Shit got real.

． ． ．

I TEXTED Dalia that night after our set. I doubted she'd read it, but I needed her to know I wasn't giving up.

I'm not saying sorry anymore, because you deserve more than that.
I had a major talk with the guys today.
Ian let me help him with his puzzle.
Dalia: *WHAT?!?!?!*
I choked out a laugh. I was not expecting that.
Dalia: *I'm not actually talking to you, but please elaborate on Ian. Or have him text me.*
Me: *I'm not having Ian fucking text you. He did your Chicago puzzle and needed help with the edges.*
Dalia: *I love doing the edges.*
Me: *That fucker has never let any of us help with the edges. But he did today.*
Dalia: *Did he finish it?*
Me: *Yep. I can't believe you bought him a puzzle.*
Dalia: *I saw it when we were in that gift shop and it made me think of him.*
Me: *I miss you like crazy.*
Dalia: *I'm not talking to you about us.*
Me: *I just had to state it for the record.*
Dalia: *It's been filed. I'm going to sleep. Tell the boys hi for me.*
Me: *If I text you tomorrow, will you reply?*
Dalia: *If it's about anything other than us, maybe.*
Me: *Goodnight.*

I'd talk to her about fucking geometry if it meant she'd reply. If she replied, there was hope, and I wasn't gonna give up hope.

． ． ．

SHE DIDN'T REPLY the next day. I had a conversation with myself, telling her how grumpy Buddy was since she left, and how my chocolate stash was running low, and I strongly suspected he was the culprit, but he kinda scared me, so I didn't ask.

We were having an ongoing discussion with Tali about our plans for the future. Taking a year off affected her too. We had to decide what a year off really meant. Did it mean no band business at all, or just no touring and recording? We hadn't quite figured the details out yet, but we told her explicitly we weren't touring. Press and appearances were a maybe, but they'd be few and far between.

When we got to Florida, Jas and I hit the beach. Normally, I would've just stayed at the venue, but if Dalia had been here, she'd be splashing around in the ocean. It killed me she wasn't here in that polka-dot bikini. She would've made me take a picture of her in the water, so I made Jas take a picture of me to send to her.

"Want me to send it?" he asked.

I eyed him sharply. "Is she talking to you?"

"Yeah, man. I've checked in with her a few times."

"And?"

He twisted his lips. "And? She got her heart broken, but she's still truckin'."

I flopped back in the sand, hanging my head in my hands. "God, I'm such a fuck up."

He sat next to me, clapping me on the back. "Correction: you fucked up. It doesn't define you. But have you thought about *why* you got so angry at her?"

"I've done nothing but think about it. I've got a thing about being left. Shit, you know my mom up and moved without even telling me in high school. And then Reinece...*Jesus*, Jasper, I'm so mad at her. How could she not tell us? How could she not give us that time with her when she knew she didn't have much of it?" I jerked my head up. "Fuck, I'm sorry, man. I shouldn't be talking about your mom that way."

His eyes were on the ocean, arms wrapped around his knees. "I've had a lot of the same thoughts, if we're being real. It was her life, but god, I feel like she owed it to us to stick around as long as possible. I hate thinking that. I'm not mad at her. I just miss her so damn bad. But I get your anger. I get it, man." He turned to me. "And you know she'd throttle you for saying 'your mom,' like she hadn't claimed you as her own twenty years ago."

I let out a short laugh. "She sure as hell would." I paused for a beat, watching the waves crash and crash and crash. "I'm going to fix this. I'm going to let it all go and fix this...not be the guy who calls a girl a cunt on Twitter or throws the love of his life out for not doing exactly what he wants when he wants it. I'm going to be Reinece's son."

He nodded at the waves. "You are. You just got lost there for a while."

"You okay, Jas?"

"Getting there. I didn't know how much I needed that year off until we decided on it."

"I've known. Didn't know I could actually have it, though."

He exhaled slowly. "Nick. *Ask*. Ask for what you need. Tell us. Tell *me*. You're not a fucking island. We're in this together."

Not a fucking island, just a castaway. But that didn't feel true. Not entirely at least. I was still at sea, but I wasn't so lost anymore. My destination was Dalia, even if I didn't know exactly how to get back to her.

"Send her the picture, will you?" I asked.

He tapped a quick message on his phone. "Sent."

"Thanks. Let's go back."

Dalia: *Did you swim?*

SHE WAITED two days to message me after Jasper sent her the ocean picture. I was laying in my bunk, and I should've been sleeping—we were speeding down the highway to our last stop of the tour—but it wasn't happening. All I wanted was some morsel of Dalia. A signal there was a chance.

And then, a text. Fucking finally.

Me: *I'm still alive, so no, I did not attempt to swim. How are you?*
Dalia: *Did you see Mickey Mouse?*
Me: *Not this time. He doesn't just wander around Florida.*
Dalia: *Have you ever been to Disney World?*
Me: *Can't say I have. I'd go, though, if you wanted.*
Dalia: *Think you could wander around Disney World in your magic hat without being recognized?*
Me: *That hat is like my cloak of invisibility.*
Dalia: *I'm glad you're having a good time.*
Me: *I'm not. There's nothing good without you.*
Dalia: *I don't want to talk about us.*
Me: *That's okay. We can talk about anything.*
Dalia: *Goodnight, Nick.*

I tossed my phone down and growled. I was pissed, but not at her. Only myself. I had a lot of work to do to deserve more of a response.

Me: *I'm in Baltimore. Can I see you?*
Me: *I miss you.*
Me: *Just tell if you're okay.*
Dalia: *I'm fine. Busy with work and getting ready for school.*

Me: *How's the bank?*

Dalia: *I can't believe you're asking me that. I'm not working at the bank.*

Me: *Where are you working? WTF.*

Dalia: *I'm freelancing for Tone. Doing social media management and building a website for a band. Mo helped me get the job. I told you that before I left.*

Me: *Fuck, I'm sorry. That last day is a blur. Can I call you?*

Dalia: *Nothing's changed.*

Me: *Let me show you I'm changing.*

Dalia: *I don't know if I want to.*

Me: *Can I see you this week?*

Dalia: *I can't see how that's a good idea.*

Me: *I feel like I can't breathe without you.*

Dalia: *I feel that too. Doesn't change anything.*

Me: *Just let me call you.*

Dalia: *I'll think about it.*

I DIDN'T PUSH. I was pretty desperate to see her, especially being so damn close again, but she needed time, and so did I. For now, I'd take what I could get. If I could get a few words from her every day, then that would have to be enough.

THIRTY-ONE
DALIA

I WAS A PLANNER, and falling for Nick Fletcher hadn't been part of any of my plans. Neither had my job at Tone or my Flamingo. They were all wonderful, glorious surprises.

I could still say that about Nick, even though I ached, even though I missed him with every fiber of my being. No matter what happened, if the ride was well and truly over, I'd never regret my summer with him.

Blue is the Color flew out to England yesterday. I'd been in touch with everyone—Jas, David, Tali, Ian, and I had a group text going. Ian barely talked, though he sometimes sent me pictures of his puzzles, especially if he got stuck, but also when he finished. I basically just shot the shit with the rest of them, like I'd never left.

Nick texted me daily, and if I wasn't buried under anxiety and sadness, I texted him back. I refused to let a few sweet texts soften my heart.

Today had been what I could only hope was my last first day of school ever. By seven, my brain was shot from all the reading and the computer work I'd done. I picked up my phone just to see if I had any messages, and surprisingly, there were none. Even more surprisingly, I sent one to Nick.

Me: *Have you seen Harry Potter?*
Nick: *Can't say I have. Harry Potter doesn't just walk around England.*
Me: *Have you ever been to Hogwarts?*
Nick: *No, but I'd go if you wanted to.*
Nick: *How are you?*
Me: *It was my first day of school. Brain=toast.*
Nick: *Did you take one of those adorable first day of school pics?*
Me: *Sorry to disappoint, but I didn't. Did you take any pics of England for me?*

Instead of texting, he sent me a picture of himself in front of a red telephone booth flipping off the camera.

Nick: *That middle finger was directed at David, btw.*
Nick: *Send me a picture.*

I scrolled through my camera roll and selected a picture of Flamingo dressed as a flamingo last Halloween. I knew it wasn't what he wanted, but it felt safer.

Nick: *LOL...hope I get to meet him one day soon. Can you send me a pic of you? I'll take anything, even your middle finger.*

I snapped a picture of my feet, ensconced in the knitted socks Bea had given me on the airplane that felt like a lifetime ago.

Nick: *Let's make a deal. You send me a pic every day, and I'll send you a line of your song.*

My heart hammered in my chest. I'd let myself forget about the song. It was easier to pretend I didn't mean enough for him to have written about me. But still, through the ache, I yearned to hear it. To claim those words.

Me: *Deal.*
Nick: *Small lips, big mouth*
Me: *Yep, that's definitely about me. Goodnight, Nick.*
Nick: *Night, Dal.*

THEY DID three shows in England and a stop in Ireland. Nick sent me pictures every day, taking me on tours of their locations, and I would have given almost anything to be with him. *Maybe someday*, my mind whispered.

I'd sent him a picture of my shoulder, hand, and knee. He'd sent me three more lines of my song.

Small lips, big mouth
Keeping quiet
When you should shout
Secrets come

Tonight, I sent him a picture of my chin and neck, and he told me how much he loved my "pointy little chin." I felt myself crumbling. The longer we were apart, the more I realized I wasn't just falling for Nick, but I'd already fallen. I loved him, and it was a big love.

Nick: *and then they go*
Me: *I wish I knew the melody so I could sing it to myself.*
Nick: *Want me to call you and hum it?*

Me: *Just hum? No talking?*
Nick: *If that's what you want...*
Me: *Okay.*

I didn't know what the hell I was doing, I was just desperate for more of a connection, even if it was akin to scooping out my heart with a dull spoon.

When I picked up his call, neither of us said anything. The air between us, oceans apart, was silent except for pained breathing. Then he started to hum my song. I closed my eyes, trying to absorb the melody. But I was kidding myself to think it would take any effort. As soon as the first note hit my ears, it was branded on my heart.

When he was quiet again, I didn't rush to hang up. It would have been wise, but I couldn't. I was a Brenner, and we loved with our whole hearts. Sometimes we loved so much, we spent months by candlelight, but we couldn't help ourselves. It was who we were.

After a long minute of breathing, he said my name. Rasped it.

My heart stuttered. I loved him enough to know I didn't trust him.

"Goodnight, Nick."

HE CALLED ME FROM FRANCE, and when I didn't answer, he texted instead. I sent him a picture of my eyebrow, and he sent me another line of my song.

I worked and went to school and played with Flamingo and hung out with Melly. But every single moment in between was spent either thinking about Nick or texting with him. Two more days in France, two more lines, one picture of my ear, and another of my ankle.

and then they blow
Dragging me down
we ebb we flow

In Madrid, Nick sent me a picture of him at a table with a giant dish of paella.

Me: *Tell me you had sangria.*
Nick: *I had sangria. Too much. Can I call you?*
Me: *Why? What's changed? I don't think I'm ready to talk about us.*
Nick: *Let's talk about sangria and Spanish cuss words.*

I stared at my phone for a long time. Probably ten minutes. And then I said fuck it. I wanted to talk to Nick, and if it was at the expense of myself, so be it.

He picked up immediately. "Dalia?"

"Hey." *Jesus, how am I shy talking to the man who spent hours buried between my legs a couple weeks ago?*

"Fuck." There was some rustling and breathing. "I didn't think you'd call."

"What are you doing?"

"Laying in my hotel room, watching Spanish TV. I've gotta warn you, I'm half-drunk."

I let out a mix of a laugh and sob. "You *did* say you had a lot of sangria. I didn't realize you meant so recently."

"Yeah...it's late here, but people eat dinner at midnight. We went out after the show, but I would've come back to the room if I'd known you'd call. Shit, I hate that my brain is fuzzy right now."

"Nick...this doesn't have to be the last time we speak. Just tell me about Madrid, okay?"

I laid in my bed, on the other side of the world, listening to him tell me about how beautiful Madrid was. He said it was hot as hell there, but they were going to Barcelona next, so he hoped the sea breeze would make it cooler. He promised to take a picture at the beach, and I was overcome with wistfulness, both for him and a place I'd never been.

I sent him a picture of my thigh, and he sent me another line.

Daydreaming coffins

The picture of Nick on the beach in Barcelona was of the entire band and Tali. Their arms were wrapped around each other and everyone was smiling. I hadn't realized how lucky I was to be a part of them, the way they'd pulled me into the fold, until it was all over.

That night, I sent him a picture of my lips, and he sent me two lines. He said my lips were worth two.

Breath like chocolate
Dip in the middle

The picture he sent me from Berlin was in front of a section of the wall that still stood. I called him because I knew he wouldn't call me first.

"Dalia. Hi. How are you?"

"Hey, I'm good." I was quiet for a beat, chewing my lip and working up the nerve to ask what I'd been wanting to. "Um...a few weeks ago you said you had a big talk with the band. Can you tell me what it was about?"

I heard him exhale slowly. "We're taking a year off."

I gasped. "What? Are you okay?"

"No, no, I'm fine. I mean, I'm fucking heartbroken, but that has nothing to do with the band."

"You're heartbroken?" I asked weakly.

"Dalia, come on. I'm wrecked. You're the love of my life and I don't know if you'll ever forgive me. So yeah, my heart's pretty much in pieces over here."

I wasn't quite ready to touch Nick's broken heart. Mine was more than enough to handle. So I asked about the band instead, and he told me about their big talk. I *never* would have thought he'd admit he needed time off, or ask for it.

"I need to know who I am outside of my band. I hadn't even realized how resentful I'd started to get until we made the break official. I just thought I had to keep going and going because it was what they all wanted, you know? And I wanted it too, for a while."

"What are you going to do for an entire year off?" I asked.

He chuckled. "I don't even fucking know, and I'm kinda excited about it. Maybe I'll start a hobby."

"Cross stitching?"

"You laugh, but watch, I'll try it and be a total boss at it."

I smiled to myself, picturing big, tattooed Nick sewing delicate flowers. He probably *would* be amazing at it.

"I tried crocheting once and ended up with a wad of yarn. I couldn't even make a scarf."

"Maybe we can try again together."

"Maybe," I said.

He inhaled sharply. "I miss you like madness, baby."

I rubbed my forehead aggressively. "I miss you too. Of course I do. I'm wary, though. I can't stop thinking about the way you looked at me that day. Like I was nothing."

"I know you don't want to hear my 'I'm sorrys.' It won't wipe it away. But if you'd let me see you again, I'd show you you're *everything*. Absolutely everything, Dalia. I have a million fucking doubts, but not about you."

I blinked back the tears burning my eyes. "You don't know how hard it is for me to hear that."

"But *why*? Why were you constantly ready to bolt?"

"Because! You're this huge deal, and I'm just me. The only way I could even accept you wanted to be with me was to pretend you were just this regular guy."

"I am! I am. You know I am," he argued. "Is that why you never came to our shows?"

I threw my hand up. "No! Yes! Maybe..." I sighed, then decided to be completely, vulnerably honest. "Yes, the answer is yes. Sometimes I felt like I was in the middle of this massive practical joke everyone was in on except me. Famous rock star slums it with poor college student, you know?"

He growled. "I never wanna hear you call yourself 'slumming it.' I came from less than nothing. What I have now...that's luck. I met a woman in Indiana, Melanie, who's probably twice as talented as some of the most successful singers. But she's in this little town, singing in a tribute band, because she didn't have the same luck I did. I'm not saying there wasn't hard work and grit involved, but I'm just a man—a man who got lucky a time or two."

"Luck and a gorgeous voice, genius brain, and an amazing band. I don't like your music and even I can see that," I said.

He let out a short laugh. "Still don't like my music? Even your song?"

"I think I love my song, but I'm reserving judgement. And I do like your music." And then I added, muttering, "Some of it."

"You saw my show that last night, right?"

"Yeah, I did."

"Do you believe I love you, Dalia?"

I nodded for a moment, my lips pinched, before I was able to speak. "I do believe it."

He slowly breathed in and out, in and out. "Then I'll just

have to show you none of the rest of it matters. I'm not the 'I'm sorry' guy. Not anymore."

We didn't talk for much longer after that. I heard the fatigue in his voice—it was the middle of the night in Germany—and I was tired from the raw emotion I'd expelled.

Before I went to sleep, I sent Nick a picture of my hip. He replied with five more lines.

Hands on me like riddles
And lately, I can't
solve you. I can't
stop the dissolve
of crumbling walls

Through Germany and Italy, we talked every day. He told me things about his mom he'd never told anyone. Her indifference, her abandonment, and then showing up again, looking for money when he got famous. He told me more about Reinece too —the resentment he'd carried from her hiding her diagnosis for so long. Feeling abandoned by her too.

He sent me pictures and my song, I sent him body parts. I had most of my song—my tits got ten lines—and it was beautiful. *He* was beautiful. I loved him in a way that left our tour love in the dust.

We weren't perfect. I didn't know if we'd get there over the phone. But we'd found our way back to each other over hushed conversations, bridging the ocean between us. I believed Nick had filled his own cracks—or at least he was working on them. With each phone call, the tether between us was repaired, and the hurt we'd cause each other seeped away. Another month of phone calls wasn't going to be enough—not for me anyway.

So, I did what I do. I made a plan.

THIRTY-TWO

I FORGOT WHERE WE WERE. Prague or Budapest maybe. One of those countries I could never quite master "please" or "thank you" in their native language. Wherever we were, I was ticking off the days in my mental calendar. Another month until I was back home. Another month until I had a shot at seeing Dalia.

And yeah, I thought I did have a shot. Sometimes we just talked for a few minutes, some days it was for an hour. She called me as much as I called her. It was clear we were both wary. Neither of us wanted to fuck up the potential of a second chance.

We still had a month before that could happen, though, and it felt more like a year. I needed to see her. To confirm we were gonna be okay. To look in her eyes and see she had both feet in this time.

"Ready for tonight?" Jas asked.

I nodded. "Yep. No sweat." I took a sip of my tea and swept the room with my eyes. I wondered if it would feel brand new when I was back here a year or two from now. Because right now, this dressing room looked like a thousand others. Hell, I coulda been beamed to an entirely different country, set down in another dressing room, and I'd never know the difference.

Tali handed me the set list, which never changed, but she always made sure we had it before each show. "We're switching it up a little tonight. Czech audience likes things a bit slower," she said.

I studied the list, and a lot of it was the same, but there were more ballads than usual, and more of our older stuff. We hadn't talked about this in soundcheck, but it wouldn't be a problem. These songs were in our blood.

"Everyone good with the change?" I asked.

Jas nodded, David yelled, "Hell yeah!," and Ian spun his sticks between his fingers, grinning broadly. That was the biggest reaction I'd seen from him in a while. Guess we were all looking for a change.

On stage, I settled into my role like an old sweater. David and I did our normal banter—I confirmed we were in Prague before we went out—and the crowd loved it. Felt like it was going to be a great show.

I prowled to the front of the stage, my eyes sweeping the crowd. "You know who we are. You know what you came for." Red caught my eye—and I stopped. Squinted. Tried to go on with my lines while my brain rationalized what I saw. "Hard and rough, then slow and easy. And you're gonna take it all. 'Cause we're Blue is the Color—" My Dalia was standing in the VIP area in front, smiling up at me. I shook my head and smiled back, " —and you fucking love us!"

My girl had flown over the Atlantic to be here, and I'd never loved another person the way I loved her right then. I had a show to get through before I could haul her ass outta there, but I'd give her the best damn show of her life.

I turned to Jas, and he laughed. On my other side, David

gave me a devious smirk, and behind me, Ian smugly tapped his drums. These fuckers *knew* and didn't tell me.

How I got through the songs, I'd never know. Mostly, I tried to keep my focus *off* Dalia, because thousands of people who could give two shits about my personal life were there to see us rock. And rock we fuckin' did. I was wired with adrenaline, wailing out the lyrics, pacing the stage, giving them my insides. I gave them all of it, and every so often, I'd see flashes of red, and I wanted to give it all to her too.

I approached Jas and David toward the back of the stage as we paused to take a drink of water. "I've got to sing her song tonight."

Jas pointed to the side of the stage where a roadie held a wooden stool. "We figured you'd want to. You ready?"

I took a deep breath and let it out slowly. "Yeah. I am."

Jas gave the nod, and the lights went low, leaving a spotlight where the stool had been set up. I changed out guitars and took my place, finding Dalia's eyes.

Holding the mic close to my mouth, I said, "Hey," and the crowd went nuts. I laughed, letting them get it out of their systems. "We're gonna slow it down for just a minute. I've got something new I want to play. Something different, but fucking amazing. Will you indulge me?"

They went wild again, and I took the moment to drink Dalia in. She hadn't changed, but I saw her differently. She wasn't mine. Not a thing to cling to. She was a beautiful, whole woman, and I loved every part of her. She wasn't just my island, she was my home.

"This one's called 'Settling In.'" My eyes never left hers as I sang to her. I gave her the slow and soulful she liked, but not without an edge.

Small lips, big mouth

Keeping quiet
When you should shout
Secrets come
and then they blow
Dragging me down
we ebb we flow

Daydreaming coffins
Breath like chocolate
Dip in the middle
Hands on me like riddles
And lately, I can't solve you. I can't
stop the dissolve of crumbling walls.

And I'm screaming
The only one who understands
Takes it all and offers her hand
The only one who drives me mad
Takes it all, takes it all

Wide hips, my house
settling in
and you're crying out
Holding on
this has to last
Circling around
forget the past

Round eyes, deep well
Seeing inside
the heavy pail
Carrying loads in
the smallest hands

spilling over
the wet sand

Daydreaming coffins
Breath like chocolate
Dip in the middle
Hands on me like riddles
And lately, I can't solve you. I can't
stop the dissolve of crumbling walls.

One step, high ledge
shaking hands
skating the edge
spice on your lips
heating my all
and living dreams
of toys and dolls.

And I'm screaming
The only one who understands
Takes it all and offers her hand
The only one who drives me mad
Takes it all, takes it all

She wiped tears from her eyes as I sang, one hand clutching her chest. She might as well have been clutching mine. I felt her all over my heart. She owned it.

AT THE END of our set, Dalia had disappeared, and I hoped like hell she was waiting for me backstage. After our final encore, I stormed through the halls and threw open our dressing room, only to find it occupied by Tali and some suit.

"Where is she?" I snarled.

Tali stood. "She's at your hotel, Nick. She's waiting there." She put an arm over my shoulder. "There's a car waiting for you. I'll walk you."

"Thanks. And thanks for bringing her here. Just...yeah."

She laughed. "She brought herself here, Nick. The guys and I just handled some logistics, but this was entirely on her." She patted my back as I climbed in the back of the limo. "Be good to her. And remember, tomorrow's an off day. I don't want to see your face for at least thirty-six hours."

The ride, the walk through the lobby, the elevator, was all a blur. My vision cleared as I swiped the key card to my suite and stepped inside. I didn't have to hunt for her, because she was waiting for me in the living room, standing by the couch in all her fucking glory.

THIRTY-THREE
NICK

I DIDN'T HAVE to haul her anywhere. She came to me with open arms, a smile blossoming on her face.

I swept her up, breathing her in, the softness of her almost buckling my knees. Her mouth was on mine in a searching kiss, and I was found. I tangled my hand in her curls, tipping her head back. Her mouth was open to me, and I went deep, but it wasn't enough. It never was with her, but I was becoming unhinged by my need for her.

I started to push her shirt up, but she stilled my hands. I jerked my head back to see where I'd misread her, and she said, "I need to look at you for a second."

She ran her hands up my abs to my chest, stopping at my heart, our eyes remaining locked the entire time. "Nicky," she whispered.

I leaned my forehead on hers, cupping her jaw. "Can't believe you're here."

"Here I am." She lifted her shirt over her head, dropped it on the floor, then unhooked her bra and let it fall off her shoulders. "I'm here."

My mouth and hands were all over her. How was it possible

I'd let myself forget how good she felt? The way her tits fit in my hands and the silk of her skin against my tongue? My cock ached to sink inside her, but at the same time, I needed to hold her for hours.

Dalia pushed my shirt up, her fingers gliding over my chest and down my back. I was sweaty, and if I really was a real gentleman, I'd shower before I touched her, but I couldn't deny myself any longer. I ripped my soaked shirt over my head and pulled her against me, but it wasn't enough. With my hands on her ass, I lifted her, and her legs instantly wrapped around my waist. I carried her to the closest wall, my mouth fused to hers, lapping at her tongue. Pressed against the wall, my cock aligned with her pussy, the heat seeping through her leggings.

"I need you," I said.

She scratched down my shoulders, her eyes burning into mine. "Have me then."

I set her down, kneeling in front of her to yank her leggings and panties off, then I slung her leg over my shoulder and ate her like I was starving. And I was. I was hungry for her taste. Ravenous for her sounds. Greedy for the thrust of her hips and squeeze of her legs around my ears.

I pulled her clit between my teeth, and she was done for. Her hands yanked at my hair, and her legs went stiff as she cried out my name and how much she loved me. I'd had a lot of people say they loved me over the years, but I'd never believed someone more than right now. I heard the thickness of it spilling from her lips, like the feeling had been choking her and releasing it was the only way she'd survive.

Standing, I rid myself of my jeans and had Dalia up in my arms, legs around my waist again in a heartbeat. My cock slid between her folds, needing in, but holding out.

"Look at me, Dalia."

Her eyes locked with mine. "I'm looking."

"Do you believe I love you?"

Heat flickered behind her eyes as she ran her hands up my shoulders to my cheeks. "I *know* you do."

Slowly, I pushed inside her, and her head fell back against the wall, but her eyes never left mine. "It doesn't matter what city or country I'm in, *this* is where I want to be," I said.

"Nick, Nick, have me."

She clenched around me, and I couldn't go slow. It'd been six weeks since I'd touched her. Six weeks since my cock found its home inside her. Six weeks of aching for this exact moment.

I drove in and out of her, fast and hard. Later, we'd take it slow and easy, but that wasn't what either of us needed. We needed this physical connection after weeks of connecting emotionally. I needed to look in her eyes and watch her as I slid home again and again.

Her legs gripped my sides, and her nails dug into my shoulders, marking me. Her breath was hot on my lips, but I didn't kiss her. I held her eyes with mine while I fucked her with abandon. Wild, but not reckless abandon. I'd never again be reckless with her.

But it still wasn't enough. I carried her to the bed and sat on the edge with Dalia straddling me. With my hands on her ass, I pushed her down on my cock over and over. She swirled her hips, grinding onto me wildly.

I couldn't stop looking at her. Her wild hair, curls everywhere. Her freckled nose and cheeks—the only constellations I'd ever let guide me. Her little heart mouth, parted and panting. Gorgeous tits bouncing as she rode me. She was a dream. A pin-up. A retro centerfold. The most beautiful woman in the world. I'd never, ever have enough.

Flipping us around, I lay on top of her, cradled in her thighs, plunging into her pussy. She arched, pressing her chest to mine, and I swore I could feel her heartbeat thumping in time with the rhythm of mine.

Running my hand up her chest, I cupped her throat, holding her there. Her eyes were pinned to me as I used my other hand to reach between us and rub circles around her clit. She shuddered and writhed, her pussy clenching so tight, I got lightheaded. I'd have to pass out before I'd stop fucking her—and from the stars behind my eyelids, that was a real possibility. She took everything out of me and filled me back up again. My brain had nothing but Dalia pumping through it. *She* was the stars I saw.

I brought her over the edge, coming with a sigh, then used my hands to push her legs all the way up to her chest so I could get as deep as possible. My balls slapped against her, but it still wasn't enough. It was never enough. She raised her head up to kiss me and murmur the sweetest words against my lips. She told me she loved me. To let go. That she'd never leave.

And that's what did it. Her promise to never leave sent barreling me over. I roared, spilling inside her until I could barely breathe.

Before either of us caught our breath, I hauled Dalia to the shower, washing my show stink off and fucking her hard against the tiles. And even then, I eyed her just as hungrily as she toweled off.

"We have two days. Can we take a break for a couple minutes?" she asked.

I tugged at my wet hair. "Two days, huh?"

She leaned into my chest. "I have to go back to school. I'd stay if I could..."

I hugged her and buried my face in her curls. "I'll take it. Whatever you have to give, I'll take it. Two days, ten years, a lifetime, I want it."

"I'll give it to you, Nicky."

She wanted to order ice cream, so we ordered ice cream. Which meant we had to put on clothing temporarily. The blue of Dalia's shirt caught my eye, and when she saw me looking, she pulled it taut so I could read the words.

In Twitter format, her T-shirt read, "I went to a Blue is the Color show and all I got was the love of my life. @NickFletcher #BlueIsMyColor."

"Melly made it," she explained.

I shook my head in disbelief, my eyes darting from her face to the words on her chest. "Shit, baby, I love you."

She laughed. "I love you too. I took a really long plane ride to tell you that."

"Can't believe you got on a plane for me."

"I'd do a lot more than that for you. Although, Tali secretly upgraded the ticket I bought to first class. I'm not sure I'll ever be able to go back to coach."

I pulled her down to sit next to me on the couch, her legs tangled with mine. "Spoiled, huh? I like that."

She held my hand, her fingers toying with mine. "I guess so. I'm ready for the finer things in life."

A wave of seriousness washed over me. "You know I'll give that to you, right?"

Her mouth quirked, and her eyes were soft. "I know you'll want to. And I'll try my damnedest to accept it. That's something I'm still working on, accepting the good. Not just things, but you. The way you love me. I was scared before of being swept up and tossed aside."

I traced a finger along her jaw to her chin. "You're not now?"

"No," she said adamantly. "I watched you perform tonight and realized how ridiculous I'd been. You were always the rock star with me. Because that's just a part of who you are. Not the whole of it, but a part. I probably would have loved you if you were a plumber, but that's not how either of our lives played out."

I gripped the point of her chin gently. "Did you like your song?"

Her eyes closed for a beat. "Nick," she breathed. "It was gorgeous."

"I started writing it the day you walked on my bus."

Her eyes flew open and she squeezed my hand. "Did you have to heavily edit it?"

I laughed. "There were definitely some earlier drafts."

Our ice cream came, and mine melted while I watched Dalia devour hers. When she was finished, she climbed into my lap, kissing me with cold lips.

"I love you fiercely," she said.

"Stupidly fierce?"

"No. I love you with my eyes wide open. There's nothing stupid about it."

"Nah, I think it's the wisest decision either of us has ever made."

Together, we were our own island. Yeah, there were huge fucking peaks and there would be valleys—wouldn't be an island paradise without them—but no matter what kind of job Dalia took or how far I traveled, I'd always walk on ledges for her and she'd fly over oceans for me.

I took her to bed then, and we were a raucous, wild, and untamed island in a never-ending sea.

EPILOGUE

Seven Months Later
Dalia

I TAPPED out my final Tweet of the day, then clicked my laptop shut.

"All work and no play makes Dalia a dull girl," Nick said.

I pushed back from my desk, grinning. "Are you calling me, Dalia fucking Brenner, dull?"

He leaned over, his hands on the arms of my chair, caging me in. "Never. I think I just need some attention."

I pulled his mouth down to mine, giving him a long, hard kiss. "Should we go for a hike?"

He rubbed his thumb over my bottom lip. "I think that is an excellent idea. Finished work?"

I waved at my laptop. "I've got some stuff to do, but it'll be okay. I'd rather spend my time outside with you."

May was early in the tourist season for Maine, especially Acadia, so when Nick suggested we spend a week here, we'd had no trouble finding a cabin to rent. I never thought of myself as a cabin in the woods kinda girl, but then, I'd never had the chance to test that theory.

Maine was gorgeous, and I loved being secluded with Nick, but I could say pretty definitively I was more of a beach person.

Once I graduated college, I was at loose ends. I still had my job—the label offered me something more permanent, but I kind of dug the freedom of freelancing.

Nick's ends were slightly less loose. The guys and he had decided to start an indie record label—Rein Records—but surprisingly, David and Jasper had taken the lead, finding talent and producing music. Nick was involved, but his was more of a supporting role, which he didn't mind at all.

So, we traveled. We spent time in Florida, and I finally got to go to Disney World. Nick wore his hat and only signed a dozen autographs the entire time. We went to the Grand Canyon and San Francisco. We took trips to Hilton Head, and my favorite—we went back to Chicago.

Since I moved in with Nick, Melly and I shared joint custody of Flamingo. He was still my boy, but he was pretty crazy for her too.

I would have felt guilty about leaving Melly, but Malka moved in with her, and the two of them became instant besties. Sometimes, I got a little jealous, but then Nick would lick my neck and call me his little intruder, and I'd remember my situation was pretty damn peachy.

There'd been no more "I'm sorry, I love yous." Of course we fought at times, but we didn't fight dirty. I'd shown him I wasn't going anywhere, and he'd shown me he could be the solid man I needed to let me fly free.

I'd never say Nick was a *nice guy*. He had plenty of rough edges, but then, so did I. So, while he wasn't necessarily a nice guy, but he *was* a good guy.

Truly the best guy.

I strapped on my boots and tied a bandana over my hair—no one wants to fish ticks out of this mop—and we set off. Our path was probably more of a walk than a hike, trailing the edges of a crystal-clear lake.

"We'll have to come back here when it's warm enough to swim," I said.

Nick stared off at the water. "Yeah. Not sure I'm a nature guy, but I dig this place."

I linked my hand with his. "Where should we go next?"

He turned back to me, smiling softly. "How about we stay home for a while? I think Mingo misses you."

I nudged him with my shoulder. "I'm picking up what you're putting down. *You* miss him."

"I do. He's weird, but he grew on me."

"Kinda like me?"

He pulled me close, his hands on my ass. "Yep. Just like you."

I grinned. "I'm not even offended."

"I gotta ask you something, baby."

I rubbed his chest, feeling his pounding heart. "Anything."

He leaned his forehead on mine, our eyes connected. "What do you think about becoming Dalia fucking Brenner-Fletcher?"

A choked laugh bubbled out of me. "Are you proposing to me with my ass in your hands?"

"Yeah, I think I fucking am."

"The answer is yes. Absolutely, uncategorically yes!"

He lifted me in his arms, kissing me all over, then hauled me back to the cabin where he had a simple platinum and sapphire ring waiting for me. He got down on one knee and asked me again in a more official, we-can-tell-our-kids-about-this-someday way.

"Dalia Brenner, I'm never going to have enough of you. Not enough time, enough closeness, enough adventures, but I'd really like to try. Will you do the honor of being my wife and chase 'enough' with me?"

I kneeled with him, cupping his scruffy cheeks. "I want nothing more than to spend my life with you."

He slipped the ring on my finger and wrapped me in his arms. Against my hair, he asked, "Still hate my music?"

"Only a little."

He chuckled. "I love you fiercely, little intruder."

"I love you the fiercest, Nicky."

He was my whirling, swirling dervish, but instead of tossing me around, he held me close in the calm center of him, taking me on a ride I'd never, ever got off of.

PLAYLIST

Playlist Spotify Link

- "Kiss With a Fist" -Florence + The Machine
- "Learn to Fly" -Foo Fighters
- "High Hopes" -Panic! At the Disco
- "Good Old Days" -Macklemore, Kesha
- "Holocene" -Bon Iver
- "Skinny Love" -Bon Iver
- "Above the Cloud of Pompeii" -Bear's Den
- "Broken" -lovelytheband
- "By Your Side" -Sade
- "Chasing Cars" -Snow Patrol
- "Island in the Sun" -Weezer
- "Stay" -Thirty Seconds to Mars
- "Agape" -Bear's Den
- "Blame It On Me" -Post Malone
- "Sweetest Thing" -Alman Brown
- "Walk on the Ocean" -Toad The Wet Sprocket
- "Times Like These" -Foo Fighters

ACKNOWLEDGMENTS

Times Like These was scary for me to write. When I first typed out c-u-n-t, I wondered if my readers would ever forgive both me and Nick! Do you forgive us?

I have to thank my beta readers who told me it was okay to use the c-word. Sarah, who said it was so unlike me, but it made the story more real. Tonya, who said Nick and Dalia almost surpassed her favorite couple of mine Laurel and Avi (which I take as high praise). Ellie who said this story was still on her mind weeks later. Jennifer who was the first person to call Times Like These "gritty", but not the last! Danielle who sent me the sweetest feedback.

And Janet, my personal, beta reading rock star. What would I do without your notes?

Thank you to Monica, my editor and proofreader. I love getting your edit notes, which are all very serious and technical, interspersed with a random "YAAASSS"! They do my fragile artist heart so much good!

To my Amy Queau, you made my vision of Nick and Dalia come to life. I'm so lucky I found you a year ago, and that you continue to put up with my indecisiveness seven covers later!

I have to make a big, huge, smoochie shout out to my RomCom/HNY author friends. You are the best of the best and knowing all of you has certainly made me a better author and happier person.

Thank you to the bloggers and bookstagrammers who've been with me since Cut Short, especially Red Hatters Book Blog, Sea Reads, Brittany Elliser, and JBookCorner (there are so many more, but these are the OG's!). You took a chance on a newbie and your support meant and still means everything!

ABOUT THE AUTHOR

Julia Wolf is a lover of all things romance. From steamy, to sweet, to funny, to so dirty you'll be blushing for days, she loves it all.

Formerly a hair stylist, she spent years collecting stories her clients couldn't wait to spill. And now that she's writing full time, she's putting those stories to use, although all identifying characteristics have been changed to protect the not-so-innocent!

Julia lives in Maryland with her three crazy, beautiful kids and her patient husband who she's slowly converting to a romance reader, one book at a time.

Visit my website: www.juliawolfwrites.com

STAY IN TOUCH

Sign up for my newsletter: www.subscribepage.com/t7m4u4

Join my reader group:

www.facebook.com/groups/JuliaWolf Readers

Made in the USA
Lexington, KY
03 November 2019

56508846R00171